GRIMM DEATH

GRIMM DEATH

Dorothy Foster Brown

COACHWHIP PUBLICATIONS
Greenville, Ohio

Author's Note

The characters and situations in this story are all entirely imaginary. If the name of any actual person, living or dead, has been used, it has been used accidentally and without intention. For the sake of verisimilitude, certain larger cities and towns are referred to by their proper names, but their locations are not accurately given.

Grimm Death, by Dorothy Foster Brown
© 2021 Coachwhip Publications edition

First published 1946
Dorothy Foster Brown, 1901-2011
CoachwhipBooks.com

ISBN 1-61646-514-x
ISBN-13 978-1-61646-514-8

Settings and Character

Place: Highbrook Ridge, in New England
Time: November

Characters

LEONARD GRIMM. The Deacon. Alive or Dead, He Made Trouble.

RUTH CUMMINGS. His Widowed Sister.

EMERY CUMMINGS. Her Son. Mrs. Cummings and Emery do not appear in person, as they are in California when the action of the story takes place.

ARCHER BRETT. A Sergeant in the State Police. He did all the Wrong Things, but got the Right Results.

FRANK PATTERSON. A Farmer, with Six Hundred Acres and a Level Head.

LUCY PATTERSON. His Wife, who was an Incurable Optimist.

ANN BARBOUR. Her Cousin. She was Beset by Difficulties.

FORREST MARTIN. A Man who didn't Believe in Worrying.

THOMAS (TAD) PATTERSON. A Boy in a Thousand.

WARNER BUCKLEY. A Retired Business Man. He Raised Hens for Fun.

RHODA BUCKLEY. His Wife. She Married Him for his Money.

GUS LAFOND. An Ex-Bootlegger who Turned Dishonest Pennies.

CLARABEL LAFOND. His Wife. Her Profession was an Old One.

DANNY CHEEVER. Her Brother. He wasn't Quite Bright.

ROSE NORTON. The Highbrook Telephony Operator. Her Silence was Golden.

DR. FINLEY PARTRIDGE. The Medical Examiner. He didn't Claim to be an Expert.

FELIX GOLDING. The State's Attorney, who had a Very High Opinion of Himself.

CAPTAIN NORMAN RANDALL. Commandant of the State Police. He Insisted on Taking a Vacation.

HENRY BURKE. A State Police Trooper, who didn't Believe in Going Hungry.

ALFRED HALEY. Another State Police Trooper. He Hated to Hurry.

LUKE PRINDLE. A Simple Soul.

EMILY CROSSE. Sergeant Brett's Housekeeper.

EDWARD MUNSELL. A Lawyer of No Importance.

BELLA. The Pattersons' Dog. She Knew More than Some People.

NEWSPAPERMEN, TOWNSPEOPLE, POLICEMEN, etc., etc.

1

Saturday—*Corpus Delicti*

It was a cold, raw, rainy night, early in November. Archer Brett gave a sigh of satisfaction as he stepped inside his warm kitchen, and draped his wet raincoat over the back of a chair. The clock on the kitchen shelf told him that it was twenty-five minutes of eleven, and he had been out on patrol since eight o'clock that morning. Between week-end football traffic and slippery roads, he had had a busy day. There had been three minor motor accidents to untangle, besides a chase after a stolen car, and an informal wrestling match with a drunken man who was trying to beat up his wife. (At least, she said she was his wife!) Oh well, Archer reflected, it was all part of a State cop's job. He was a sergeant, to be sure, and most of the work was routine stuff that could have been handled by the troopers. But there weren't any too many troopers; two were sick and another off on leave, couldn't grudge 'em leave once in a while, they certainly earned it. Archer was an accommodating person, who took things more or less as they came; he wasn't too jealous of his dignity, and he liked his job. But for once he did feel like calling it a day. He yawned, and started to take off his boots. But when he had one off, the telephone rang. "Damn!" Archer said, and hoped it was a wrong number. He crossed to the hall and lifted the receiver: "Hello?"

The voice that answered was a woman's, clear and businesslike: "Is this Sergeant Brett of the State Police?"

Archer admitted that it was.

"This is the telephone operator at Highbrook," explained the voice. "There's been a . . ." she hesitated for an instant, "an accident at Highbrook Ridge, about five miles from here. The town constables don't amount to much, and we thought it would be best to notify the State Police at once, so they could send somebody right over. I remembered that you'd been here before, so I thought I'd call you direct and ask you to come."

"Well, what's the trouble?" Archer asked, as she paused. "A smashup?" He recalled that some months before he had investigated a hit-and-run case at Highbrook Village, which was a small country town about twenty miles from the city of Rumford, where he was stationed.

The operator hesitated again. "No," she said, "a man in town here, Deacon Grimm, has been found dead—it looks as if he might have been murdered. He's just been discovered, and nobody knows anything about it yet, except the people who found him. They thought you'd want it kept quiet until you got here."

"All right," Archer said, with a sigh. "I'll be out and look into it. Whereabouts was the man found? How do I get there?"

"He's at the Patterson Farm. If you come straight to the Village, and stop here at the Exchange, I'll tell you how to go. It's rather complicated getting there. I haven't called a doctor yet," she added. "Will you bring one, or do you want me to get hold of a local one?"

"I'll see about the doctor," Archer told her. "We'll be there as soon as possible. And don't talk to anyone, please." He hung up. "Just my luck," he thought disgustedly, as he pulled his boot on again. "Some darned hysterical fool of a woman sees a man lying asleep or drunk or something, and thinks he's been murdered, and does me out of a night's rest. Damn!"

He determined that if he had got to lose his sleep, somebody should keep him company. So he called the Medical Examiner, Dr. Partridge, and explained what he wanted. "Sorry to get you out such a rotten night, Doc, but I'd be much obliged if you'd go out there with me. I'll take one of our cars so you won't have to drive. Can I pick you up in ten minutes? Okay." He scribbled a hasty note for the benefit of his elderly housekeeper, and left it on the kitchen table. Archer had learned that it pays to be considerate of people, even elderly housekeepers.

It was still raining, he found, and growing colder—a nasty night. He had considered telling his superiors of the call to Highbrook, but decided he'd better investigate first. The Rumford Commandant, Captain Randall, was away, and it was probably only a false alarm anyway. Felix Golding, the State's Attorney, might be available, but Golding was a politician, and a notorious credit grabber. "And if it should turn out to be a real case," thought Archer, "I might as well get the credit as anybody— I'll have to do most of the work! Maybe if I got famous as a sleuth, I could go into politics and make some money, like Golding— I don't think!"

He stopped for Dr. Partridge at the latter's house, and they set out for Highbrook. It had snowed earlier in the evening, but now a cold rain was freezing as it fell, coating trees and roads and fields with glittering ice.

"Swell night for a ride," Archer observed, as they skidded around a corner. "Probably nothing in it, either."

"I don't mind," Dr. Partridge said. He was a stoutish, middle-aged man, with a cheerful manner and shrewd, observant eyes. He seldom let the unpleasant aspects of his job interfere with a naturally easygoing disposition; but he was a sufficiently able doctor, and not lacking in common sense. As a matter of fact," he went on, "I was glad when you called up. I was playing contract with my wife and a couple of her expert friends . . ." he made a face. "Anything's preferable to that, even hunting for a murder in an ice storm."

"And which probably isn't a murder at all," Archer said. "But it's got to be looked into, of course."

Dr. Partridge nodded, and they hummed along through the storm in silence; the driving claimed most of Archer's attention, and the doctor decided to take a nap while he had the chance.

Twenty miles can seem like a long distance at night, over winding, hilly, unfamiliar roads, treacherous with ice. But at last scattered houses grew more plentiful, and became a small village, clustered around its church, library, and General Store. There were no signs of life anywhere except in a house opposite the church, where light streamed through an uncurtained window.

Here they slid to a stop, and Archer went up on the porch. Before he had time to knock, the door opened, and he found himself blinking in the glare from a powerful flashlight. Apparently reassured by the sight of his uniform cap, the wielder of this weapon turned it off and invited him in.

The room that housed the Highbrook "Central" was warm and homelike, though crowded with well-worn furniture and enough potted plants to start a greenhouse. A solemn-faced clock ticked on the mantle between brass candlesticks, and a fluffy cat lay asleep in a battered Morris chair. Behind the latter, in one corner, a miniature switchboard upheld the dignity of the New England Tel. & Tel.

Archer took a good look at his now visible informant, and felt encouraged. This was no hysterical female, but a pretty and sensible young woman who seemed wide awake, in spite of the fact that she wore bedroom slippers and a bathrobe, and had her blond hair arranged for the night on elaborate metal wavers. Serenely unconcerned about her looks, she seated herself at the switchboard and motioned the sergeant to chair.

"I'm Rose Norton, the operator," she began. "Just before I called you, I had a call from a friend of mine at the Ridge—Lucy Patterson her name is. They'd found the body of a man in their barn. It was Deacon Grimm, and he was dead."

"Were they sure of that?" Archer demanded.

"They seemed pretty sure. Lucy thought he'd been stabbed with something. I'm afraid there isn't much doubt he's dead, from what she said. Her husband is away, and she's upset, naturally, and didn't know what to do. Our constable doesn't amount to Hannah Cook, and I expect he's drunk tonight, anyway—he usually is on Saturday night—so I thought the best thing was to call you. I knew you had handled that case last summer, and you'd see that everything was done properly. It was half-past ten when Lucy called me—I noted it. I called the Rumford Headquarters first, but they said you'd gone home, so the operator got your house. I hope I did the right thing."

Archer was favorably impressed, both by Miss Norton's competent manner and by her obvious confidence in Sergeant Brett's ability to look after things in general. "You did fine," he said, getting up. "Now I'll get over there, if you'll tell me how to find the place. I've got the doctor with me. You say nobody knows anything about this business?"

"Not as far as I know. Lucy said she and Ann—that's her cousin, Ann Barbour, who lives with them—she said they hadn't told anybody but me, and wouldn't. And the Deacon's people are in California, so we couldn't notify them." She added, with the first hint of excitement she had shown, "This'll make a sensation in town when it gets known—if he really is dead, that is."

"Big man in the town, is he?"

Miss Norton nodded. "Oh yes, one of our leading citizens." Was there a faint overtone of sarcasm in that remark, Archer wondered?

"Well, don't tell anyone about it yet," he ordered, "And you better stay on duty for a while. If it's serious, I'll have some calls to put through. Now, how do I go?"

Rose Norton went with him to the door, and pointed with her flashlight. "Straight up that hill beyond the store, and where the road forks, keep to the left. About a mile farther along there's a four-corners, and you take the right. Then take the next left again, and about two miles along that road there's a brick schoolhouse on the left, and the Pattersons' is the second house beyond it, on the same side; a square, white house, with a big barn. You can't miss it."

Archer hoped she was right. "Okay, then," he said. "I'll see you later if I have more questions to ask."

"I'm always here," Miss Norton assured him, and closed the door.

"Seems to be something," Archer told the waiting doctor, as once more they headed into the storm. "Well, we'll soon know whether we're on a wild goose chase, or whether it's the real thing."

But certain people whose acquaintance they had yet to make knew all too well that it was the real thing.

Three people and a dog kept each other company in the Pattersons' comfortable sitting room, and looked with uneasy eyes from the clock to the door, to the windows, to each other, and back again.

"They ought to be here pretty soon," Lucy Patterson said, looking at the clock for the eighth time in five minutes. "It's been three-quarters of an hour since Rose called them."

Lucy was an attractive, capable-looking woman in her early thirties, with fluffy brown hair, bright eyes behind her rimless glasses, and a determined chin. She was plump in the right places without being in the least fat; and, though pale and slightly rumpled at present, she had lost only a little of her natural self-possession and ability to take things as they came—qualities which twelve years as a farmer's wife had, if anything, intensified. But this present happening was a good deal beyond anything she had ever had to cope with, and she couldn't help being upset and frightened.

Ann Barbour lighted a cigarette with hands that were surprisingly steady, considering what she had just been through.

"The roads are probably pretty bad," she said. "They can't make very good time when it's so slippery, you know. They'll be here before long."

Ann was younger than Lucy, more slender and less settled-looking. She certainly never thought of herself as beautiful, and tonight her face looked strained and tired. But there was something curiously appealing about her,—a remote, unobtrusive charm; and her gray eyes, under dark, level brows, belonged to a woman with humor and character, under a pose—or perhaps it wasn't wholly a pose—of weariness or tragedy. Her brown hair was worn long, and done up behind her ears; this rather severe style, together with the plain black dress she wore, gave her an appearance of being in mourning for something or somebody. The cousins resembled each other in some ways, but Ann was imaginative where Lucy was practical; she was less tolerant than Lucy, and harder to get along with, for her life had been difficult, at times, and she had failed to achieve the kind of happiness that had made Lucy cheerful and contented.

"I wish they'd hurry up," Lucy repeated. She moved uneasily. "I wish Frank was here." Frank was her husband, and it was about the sixtieth time she had wished it during the last hour. Lucy thought a good deal of her husband at most times, but she had seldom desired his presence much more ardently than she did tonight, when he was a hundred or more miles away at an Odd Fellows' Convention.

"You could phone Frank at the hotel at Winchester," Ann suggested. "But it might be better to wait until the police get here. I suppose we must be careful not to seem to be doing anything behind their backs."

"Yes," Lucy agreed, "we'd probably better wait."

So they waited. The clock ticked, and, outside, the wind howled dismally; and, in the pauses between gusts, the telephone wires hummed with loud, persistent monotony. The minutes dragged, and the house was full of unusual and inexplicable noises. The hired man had gone home long before they made their discovery, and the two women had no desire to do any searching or investigating by themselves. So they locked the doors, and waited. And talked, and speculated, and waited. And *waited*.

Tad Patterson, aged ten, who had been allowed to stay up because of the unusual circumstances, was amusing himself by holding an automobile show on the sitting room floor. He was a self-contained child, not easily excited, and older than his years, owing to his family's habit of treating him as an equal. People seldom "talked down" to Tad, for some reason. Missing a favorite truck, he went to the kitchen after it. His mother called him back. "Don't go wandering around out there, Tad."

Tad said there was nobody out there.

"I know that," Lucy said, "but do stay in here, where it's light."

Ann followed Tad to the kitchen, and Bella rose and trailed after her. Bella was part police dog and part collie—

a combination that had made for intelligence if not for good nature. Lucy said that Bella was smarter than lots of people. The dog undoubtedly realized that something uncommon was up, and that her companions were worried. She was almost as restless as they were.

Ann put a stick of wood in the kitchen stove. A sudden gust of wind blew the sleet against the windows and roared in the chimney. Ann shivered with a cold that was more than physical. This horrible, incredible night seemed to her like a culmination of all her troubles; she fought against a sense of helplessness and suspense and growing panic. What was going to happen? Yet she remembered so many nights just like this when she had been untroubled and contented; had loved the uproar of wind and rain outside, knowing that they were powerless to hurt her. She had been safe, then, and happy. But not now . . . not any more. . . .

Bella refreshed herself from the pan of water under the sink. Then she raised her cold nose and thrust it against Ann's hand; it was the only comfort she could offer. Ann patted the dog, reflecting with a kind of wonder that things were almost the same as usual, on the surface. Almost the same, only there was that gnawing awareness of what had happened, of what was lying out in the barn—Deacon Grimm. "The Deacon" most people called him. And he was dead. Not naturally dead, but killed. Killed by violence. And in their barn. It didn't seem possible. The whole thing was a nightmare, it must be! But she knew that it wasn't.

She went back into the sitting room, back to Lucy's comforting presence. The temptation to talk about the Deacon was almost irresistible, yet Ann knew that there was no sense in repeatedly going over it all, they'd have enough of that when the police came, more than enough. She wondered what the police would do—if they would believe what she and Lucy had to tell. Would it sound reasonable? Would it? But it didn't do a bit of good to keep talking about it, and it only confused her thoughts, instead of making them clearer.

Lucy reached for the telephone: "I'm going to ask Rose if she's seen anything of them." But while she spoke they heard the sound of a car; there was a squeal of brakes in the yard, the bang of a door, a stamping of feet on the piazza. Lucy gave an exclamation that was half apprehension, half relief. But Ann grew a little paler, and the line of her jaw hardened, as if she braced herself to meet something—something dangerous. Then she grabbed Bella by the collar as Lucy opened the outside door. Bella disliked strangers, and was likely to show it.

The women regarded Archer and the doctor with an anxiety which they did their best to hide, but the two representatives. of the law seemed definitely reassuring. The sergeant was a tall, straight man of thirty-five, who knew how to wear his uniform, and who had that air which all good policemen have: an almost visible aura of competence and responsibility. Although his tanned face looked a little hard in repose, it crinkled pleasantly when he smiled; and his bright brown eyes, though sharp, were not unfriendly nor accusing. He looked able, but at the same time considerate, as if he could exercise good judgment as well as excellent muscles. Dr. Partridge was even more comforting: such an agreeable, everyday sort of man that Lucy and Ann took to him at once. They were immediately thankful that they had men like these to deal with, in this highly unpleasant and dangerous situation. Even Bella eyed the intruders with less distrust, and decided she might not have to bite them after all.

Archer introduced himself and the doctor, adding, "I understand you need our help here."

"Yes, we do," Lucy assured him earnestly. "I'm Mrs. Patterson, and this is my cousin, Miss Barbour, And my boy, Tad. What shall I . . . do you want to see the—him—first thing?"

His quick eyes took rapid stock of both women—of their faces, clothes, general appearance, and manner. He sensed the excitement and nervousness that lay under their surface calm; well, that was natural, and he was thankful not to find them in hysterics. They were trying to be sensible without acting hard-boiled, and the sergeant appreciated the effort. Nor did they look dumb or cheap—words that Archer used to cover a number of undesirable characteristics. He saw plenty of cheap women in the course of his duty, and got very tired of them. They had their points, of course, but—! On the whole, he liked the looks of these two, and Mrs. Patterson reminded him faintly of his sister, who was also a farmer's wife, out in Iowa. The other girl was less easy to place, he thought. She looked attractive, but a little high-hat, the kind that might be hard to manage, under some conditions. He noticed that she had nice legs, but didn't seem aware of the fact—something very unusual, in his experience!

Mrs. Patterson had put on a sweater, and was lighting a lantern. "Do you want us to show you the way? It—he's out in the barn."

"Perhaps you'd better, if you feel able to," Archer agreed. "Then you can tell me whether everything is the same as it was when you found him." He still half expected to be shown nothing more serious than a bad case of alcoholism. People just didn't get murdered in a place like this!

Archer and the doctor both had flashlights, and Ann had provided herself with a second lantern. Keeping close together, they crossed a big shed (which seemed to Archer to contain all the discarded farm machinery in the world), and went single file through a narrow passage into the barn itself. Archer didn't know, then, that this barn was called the second largest in the county, but he wouldn't have questioned the claim for a second! It was a huge, draughty place, where their footsteps echoed hollowly, and the weak light from the lanterns flickered in the cold air. The wind whistled and howled up among the great rafters, the sleet beat against the roof, and out of the black shadows all around them came rattles and thumps and rustlings—sounds always present in barns, no doubt, but now unpleasantly suggestive, as of unseen watchers, lying in wait. . . .

As they huddled together, their lights made a pool of brightness on the rough floor; in it, indifferent now to light or darkness, lay the body of a man.

Lucy made a motion with her lantern, "There . . ."

Thus were they introduced to Leonard Grimm, who could no longer acknowledge introductions.

He looked to be fifty-two or -three years old; a strongly built man, dressed as most active New England farmers dress in winter, in corduroy breeches, high laced boots over woolen stockings, and a windbreaker jacket, with sheepskin lining and collar. He lay partly tumbled on one side, and behind him the rear bumper and fender of an automobile supported his half-reclining position, as if he had fallen against it. His head hung forward on his breast, his arms were limp at his sides; he looked for all the world like a well-dressed scarecrow, dumped unceremoniously there. But his jacket was open, and the dark, ominous stain that had soaked through his flannel shirt could not have come from any stuffing of straw. The stain was small, comparatively; yet they all knew, somehow, that the man was dead, that he had died swiftly, and had been dead some time. More than that, the instrument of his death lay on the floor beside him—a long-handled, three-tined pitchfork. And its wicked points gleamed darkly, and were faintly, nauseatingly sticky.

One of the women gave a gasp; but, although he turned quickly, Archer could not tell which one it was, for they stood close together, holding each others' hands. Tad, large-eyed and silent, gripped his mother's arm.

The sergeant looked around. "Does everything seem to be the same as when you found him?"

They nodded.

"You didn't touch anything?"

Ann Barbour said, "I touched his hand, to see if it was—cold. We didn't touch anything else at all." She was very pale, and so was Lucy; their faces looked ghostly in the uncertain light, and they swallowed convulsively.

Dr. Partridge said quickly, "We don't need to keep them here any longer, do we?"

"No," Archer returned, "they can go back now. Can you manage all right by yourselves?" he asked them.

Ann said, "We'll be all right."

"Take it easy," Archer advised, "but please don't go to bed yet, for I'll have questions to ask."

He turned to the doctor, and they set to work.

Back in the sitting room, Ann said, with a desperate calm that fought down hysteria, "They seem harmless."

"Yes," Lucy agreed. "They're quite human." She, too, was deliberately matter-of-fact; it was the only way to avoid downright panic. Lucy took a good, firm grasp on everyday things; she said thoughtfully, "I wonder if they'd like something to eat? Called out late like this, they must be hungry."

Ann made a sound between exasperation and laughter. "Don't, Lucy! I believe if you were waiting to be hanged, you'd ask the—the executioner if he didn't want a little something to eat! I don't feel now as if I even wanted to think about eating—not after that!"

Lucy confessed to a similar feeling. "But men are different. And, of course, they're used to such things. It doesn't affect them the way it does us." She sat down, feeling suddenly shaky. "O dear, I do wish Frank was here."

"The sergeant said you could phone him, didn't he?"

"Yes, and I'm going to, right away. He said I mustn't tell Frank what's happened, but to have him come home as soon as he can."

But the operator was unable to reach the hotel at Winchester. "It's on account of the storm," she said. "The wires are down, somewhere. But I'll keep trying, and will ring you as soon as I get them."

"Thanks, Rose." Lucy hung up, and suddenly remembered her son, who had a genius for effacing himself when he didn't want to be noticed. "Tad, you ought to be in bed." But she said it half-heartedly.

Tad protested. Ann said, "Let him stay until we go, Lucy. I don't blame him for not wanting to go alone." She paused. "There's one thing about Tad, even if he is a kid; he knows how to keep still. Don't you, Tad?"

Tad nodded.

A look passed between the two women—a curious look, indefinable, but almost as if they realized something subconsciously that they were unable, or unwilling, to understand.

"I guess it's murder all right," Archer said. In their brief examination, they had disturbed the dead man as little as possible, for Archer wanted pictures taken before the body was moved.

"I don't see how it could be suicide, certainly," Dr. Partridge agreed, getting to his feet. They looked down rather dubiously at the mortal remains of Deacon Grimm, silently speculating about his life and the reasons for his death. He was, to them, a problem to be solved, a job to be done. But what might he have been to other people? To one other person in particular?

"It's pretty hard to tell how long he's been dead," the doctor went on. "What with the nature of the wounds, and this ungodly cold place, he may have been dead anywhere from an hour to four or five hours. He'd get cold quick here, and rigor seems to be setting in already; but rigor depends on so many things it don't help us much. I'd hate to swear to the time of death at all, myself, though some of these young know-it-alls would pretend they could tell you to the minute. But call it he's been dead not more than four hours nor less than two." He looked at his watch. "It's five minutes of twelve now. I'd say, very roughly, that he died around half-past nine. Call it between eight and ten, if you want a broad time to check alibis. But I don't swear to that, mind you."

Archer nodded. "There's no doubt what killed him?"

"No, I should say it was the pitchfork, without any question. They're just the kinds of wounds it would make, and not much blood. The internal bleeding killed him, unless one of those points pierced the heart. Have to find that out at the autopsy. I can't see to make a very accurate examination here. Did you notice . . ." He checked himself.

"What?"

"Nothing, perhaps. Wait till I do the autopsy, then I can be sure. My gosh, this is a cold place!"

"I'll send for the ambulance," Archer said, "and a couple men, and get the pictures and fingerprints and so on. Then they can take him, and you can do your autopsy as soon as convenient." He regarded the body thoughtfully. "He wasn't a very pleasant-looking customer, was he?"

He wasn't. The clean-shaven face looked thin and unnaturally pallid now, with hollow cheeks, a predatory nose, and a full-lipped mouth that was twisted into a dreadful, involuntary grin of pain or astonishment. The partly closed eyes were red-rimmed under jutting black eyebrows; and the thick, curling black hair, only slightly peppered with gray, grew to a point on the forehead. The Deacon's cap lay on the floor near him, a cloth cap with ear-lappets and a green sateen lining.

"I don't suppose any of us 'ud look very prepossessing under the circumstances," the doctor replied, brushing hay and chaff from his trousers. "He might have been quite a dashing fellow when he was alive, a type the ladies admire. But I don't think I'd trust him far, especially if I were a lady. Did you say he was a big shot in the town, a Deacon or something?"

Archer nodded. "Funny kind of an end for a Deacon to come to," he observed. "And it's not going to be any cinch, discovering who killed him." He held a lantern over his head, but its feeble light only made the barn seem bigger and darker. "No use trying to do any more out here until I get more light. I'd only mess up what clues there are—*if* there are any. When the others get here we can look around inside and out, but right now we may as well get back where it's warm, and see what those girls have to say. What did you think of them?"

"They seem all right," Dr. Partridge replied cautiously. "They aren't fools, by any means, and they're good-looking enough. But I reserve judgment until I've seen a little more of them."

They inspected the automobile against whose bumper the body still rested.

"Nineteen-thirty-eight Plymouth," the doctor announced. "And it's still wet in spots, so it must have been out today, after it commenced to storm." He glanced inside—a woman's coat, a robe, an umbrella, and a quantity of dog hairs. He would have opened the door, but Archer stopped him.

"Wait until it's been fingerprinted."

They went back to the house, and removed their damp outer garments in the kitchen. The sergeant looked younger without his cap, and his dark hair, like his smile, had a crinkle in it. The doctor rubbed his bald brow, and looked around with reminiscent interest; he had been born and brought up on a farm. The gaunt pump standing sentinel at one end of the sink, the glass lamps on swinging brackets, the painted chairs and braided mats might have come out of his own mother's kitchen. Evidently, "rural electrification" had not yet reached Highbrook. But the crisp cottage curtains and bright china were wholly up-to-date.

They entered the sitting room, and Archer said briskly, "While we're waiting for the ambulance, you folks can tell me all you know about this." His pleasant, unofficial manner, and the doctor's friendliness had gone a long way toward putting Lucy and Ann at their ease (and off their guard, too, if they had only realized it.) They had nerved themselves for an ordeal, but were finding it less frightening than they had expected.

Archer put his call through to Rumford, and gave his brief orders without any explanatory details. Dr. Partridge, who had been trying to make friends with Bella, thought better of it. Dogs usually liked him, he told Lucy in an aggrieved tone.

"Bella's got a mean disposition," Lucy admitted. "But she knows a lot."

Archer inquired, "Did you reach your husband, Mrs. Patterson?"

Lucy explained about the wires being down, and said that the operator was doing her best.

"Then we'll get going," the sergeant said. He produced a pad and pencil, preparatory to taking notes if necessary, and began:

"Which of you made the actual discovery?"

Ann Barbour said, "I did."

"Just tell me about it in your own way," Archer said, "and I'll try not to interrupt with questions until you get through. Wait a minute, though, what's the full name?"

"Ann DeLacey Barbour."

"Miss?"

"Yes"

"Age?"

"Twenty-seven."

"And you live . . .?"

"Here, mostly, but I have a room in Boston where I store some things, and where I work, sometimes, in the winter. Twelve-fifteen West Mayfair St., Allston," she added, and wondered whether she would have to divulge her religion, politics, and how she made her living, such as it was. Apparently not, for Archer said, "Okay, go ahead."

"I went to Rumford early this afternoon," Ann began carefully, "to buy some things. The weather wasn't so bad then, though it was threatening. I hurried to get home early, because I knew Frank—Mr. Patterson—was away, and Lucy doesn't like to stay alone after dark. I didn't notice what time I got home, especially, because of course I didn't know this was going to happen; but I should think it was about half-past five. It must have been half an hour before supper, and we had that by six, I should say."

Lucy nodded.

"I drove the car into the barn," Ann went on, "and left it, and came right in here. And there wasn't anybody in the barn then. I drove right over where he—where the body is now, and there was a little hay on the floor but nothing else. I didn't see a soul."

Ann was still pale, Archer noticed, but not at all confused. "She doesn't look like the jittery kind," he thought to himself.

"Then we had supper," Ann continued, "and after we'd done the dishes we came in here. We talked, and then I read for a while, and Lucy talked with Rose over the line. Then we talked some more, and decided to go to bed. I don't know what time it was, exactly, but sometime between half-past nine and ten, Lucy got the milk and cookies that we usually have before we go to bed. Just as we were eating, I happened to wonder whether I'd turned off the switch in the car. Sometimes it stalls when I drive in, and I forget to turn it off. I knew Frank would be disgusted if I ran the battery down; it's happened once or twice, and it's his car. I couldn't remember for sure, so I took a flashlight and went out to see. You probably noticed how that narrow passage comes into the barn, right behind where we leave the car, beside the horse stalls. I came out there, and sort of swung my light around, toward the car, and I saw—" She stopped for the first time, and drew a long breath, "I saw a man lying there, all kind of doubled up, and partly leaning against the back of the car." She stopped again.

"She's not quite as cool as I thought," Archer discovered, "but she's got good control of herself." Aloud, he said, "Take your time, Miss Barbour. You're making everything very clear. What did you do when you saw the man? Did you think he was dead? Try to remember every little detail."

"I didn't know he was dead, of course. When I saw his—his feet, I thought at first it was Luke—he's the hired man—and that he was drunk. He does get drunk once in a great while. Then I saw his head, black hair, you know, and I knew it couldn't be Luke, for he's bald. Then," she shivered slightly, "I don't know; I guess I got afraid all at once. I felt funny, as if I might be going to faint, but I didn't. I went back into the shed and sat down on a box

for a few minutes, until I felt better. Then I ran back here
and told Lucy. We got Bella and another light, and went
back to see who it was, and what was the matter with him.
Do you mind if I have a drink of water?"

The doctor jumped up, but Lucy was already getting a
glass from the kitchen.

"Thanks," Ann said. "That's about all. We looked at
him and saw it was Deacon Grimm, and he was dead. Then
we saw the blood," she shivered again, "and the—the pitchfork. I—we were afraid we'd be sick, so we came back here
as fast as we could, and Lucy called Rose, and asked her to
get you. We didn't disturb the—him—any, I'm sure, and
we didn't touch or upset anything out there that I know
of." She smiled faintly. "We both read mystery stories, so
we know the proper things to do under circumstances like
these."

"That's fine, so far," Archer said. He turned to Lucy.
"Can you add anything, before I ask questions?"

Lucy shook her head. "It's exactly what happened, as
far as I can remember."

The doctor put in a query: "How did you know the man
was dead?"

Lucy swallowed. "He—he looked dead. Ann touched
his hand, and held her flashlight up to his mouth, but
there wasn't any breath showing on the glass. There wasn't
any sound of breathing, and the blood . . ." Lucy picked
up the glass and drank what was left of the water.

"I think he was dead by ten o'clock, in all probability,"
Dr. Partridge said. "That was about the time you exam-
ined him, wasn't it?"

Ann shook her head. "I don't know. It could have been
earlier."

"I looked at the clock when I called Rose," Lucy said,
"and it was twenty of eleven. But that clock's fast. And

then it took us a few minutes to get—to get straightened 'round."

Archer knew how hard it is to estimate time when you are excited or upset, especially after the event. It seemed better to leave the time element a little vague than to invite inaccuracy by insisting on a definite hour and minute. Besides, in his experience, women seldom keep track of time unless they have some special reason for doing so. As soon as they realized its importance, Lucy and Ann had conscientiously noted the time; before then they could only guess at it, and they might guess wrong. He said, "You say this man is a Deacon Grimm; I take it that you know him?"

He looked from Ann, who nodded, to Lucy, who also nodded and went on to explain: "Leonard Grimm. He lives—lived almost across the road from us. We've known him for years, ever since we've been here. His sister and her son live with him; she's a widow, Ruth Cummings."

Archer asked whether it was true that the Deacon's family was away?

"Yes," Lucy said, "they went to California about a month ago. Los Angeles, I think."

"We'll notify them," Archer said. "Was that all the family he had?"

Lucy said it was.

"Was he living all alone?" Archer persisted.

Lucy and Ann exchanged glances. Lucy said, "He had a—housekeeper, who looked after things while his folks were away."

Archer saw the glances, but pretended he hadn't. "I'll want to see her. Know who she is?"

"Yes, Clarabel Lafond. She lives near, down on the Old Road. But I don't think she was at the Deacon's this afternoon. She and Gus—that's her husband—always go into

Rumford Saturdays, to do their trading. At least, they usually do."

"They did today," Ann interposed. "I saw them parked in front of the Palace, just as I was leaving."

"I'll get hold of her," Archer said. "And I'll also have to see that hired man of yours. Where does he live?"

"Luke lives about two miles away, on the Preston road," Lucy answered. "But he left early this afternoon, before Ann got back. His brother came for him, and I saw them drive off; they were going to the movies. He couldn't know anything about it."

"Not unless he came back," Archer said drily. "I have to suspect everybody, you know. They may all look innocent, but somebody's guilty."

At this point the telephone rang. Archer took the brief message and relayed it: "The operator says she finally got the hotel in Winchester, but Mr. Patterson isn't there. His party hasn't arrived, at all."

Lucy looked disturbed. "I don't understand that. I don't see what can have happened to them."

The sergeant was beginning to wonder what had happened to the ambulance. He hoped it hadn't got lost in the wilds of Highbrook. "When did Mr. Patterson leave home?" he asked.

"About eleven this morning, and they planned to get to Winchester sometime late in the afternoon."

"He was with a party?"

"Yes, he and Bob Gillis and Ray Summer all went from Town in Ray's car, but they were going to join a lot of others in Rumford. They'd chartered a bus."

Ann offered a suggestion. "Maybe they went to another hotel, or direct to the Convention Hall?"

"Perhaps," Lucy said doubtfully. "But they had reservations at the Clinton, I know."

Archer said, "Probably the storm delayed them. We'd have been notified if there'd been an accident."

They heard the hum of an approaching vehicle; it slowed down, and crunched heavily to a stop in the yard—the ambulance at last. Archer went out to take charge of operations, leaving the doctor to keep on with the questions if he wanted to. Dr. Partridge didn't much fancy himself as a detective, but he was always interested in people, just as people. So he kept the conversation going, and was ready to pick up any unconsidered trifles of information that might be dropped.

Ann asked a question: "Do you think Sergeant Brett will be left in charge of things, Doctor?"

"I couldn't say, but I think likely he will be. He's a sensible fellow, and as good as anybody they've got, outside of Captain Randall. And *he's* away at present."

"I hope Sergeant Brett is left in charge," Lucy said. "He seems very capable, but he's kind, too, and that means a lot, from our point of view." The doctor doubted whether kindness was one of the first requirements of a successful man-hunter, but he agreed that Archer was a good scout. "The only thing is," he said, "sometimes Golding likes to take a hand in things himself. In that case . . ." he shrugged.

Ann crushed out her cigarette on the ash tray. She had smoked so much that her tongue felt funny. She asked, "Is that Felix Golding, the State's Attorney?"

"That's the man. Do you know him?"

"No, but I've heard of him." Ann's tone implied that she did not want to know the gentleman in question.

"Mr. Golding," the doctor said drily, "is a great man— in his own estimation. He and his kind are part of the price we pay for democratic government, and I admit that sometimes the price seems a little high. He . . ."

The telephone rang, and Lucy seized it. "Yes?" She listened. "Well, for heaven's sake! Where do you suppose he is?" She listened further, and after various exclamations, indicative of surprise and concern, she hung up, looking more disturbed than before. "That was Ray Summer," she explained. "He and the others have just got to the Hotel Clinton, at Winchester. The storm delayed them. But he says Frank missed the bus at Pinkney, and got left behind. They stopped there about five o'clock to get some lunch, and so on; and then they got started again in a kind of a hurry, and nobody noticed Frank was missing until they'd gone quite a ways. Then they figured he'd hire a car and drive to Winchester, so they didn't go back. I hope he'll be all right. Ray says he'll have Frank call me the instant he gets there." She frowned, and added, "I didn't want him to go to the old Convention anyway, but he insisted on it."

It was nearly one o'clock. Tad had gone to sleep on the couch, a little disappointed at the unexciting actions of the police; they hadn't arrested anybody! Lucy wondered if she and Ann would ever get to bed. The sergeant was still out in the barn, and he would probably have a lot more questions to ask when he came in. Still, she wouldn't feel like going to bed until she knew that Frank was safe and sound somewhere. How had he managed to miss that bus?

At Ann's request, Dr. Partridge started to describe the usual police procedure in cases of violent deaths. Then he remembered that he was supposed to ask questions, not answer them, and he brought the conversation back to Deacon Grimm, and his place in Highbrook's scheme of things. "Was he a real deacon?" he asked.

Lucy explained Leonard Grimm's connection with the Highbrook Consolidated Church, as far as she knew it. "But I hardly ever go," she confessed, "so I don't know as much as I might. Rose could tell you more about church affairs than I can."

"Was he a well-to-do man?"

Lucy, nodded. "I've heard Frank say he must be worth between eighty and a hundred thousand dollars. That's well-to-do for Highbrook, I can tell you!"

The doctor was a good listener; before long, he found himself getting an excellent picture of small-town affairs in general, and of Highbrook's affairs in particular. He learned what the current tax rate was, and who was "on relief" and why. He learned that the Road Agent was feathering his own nest, that the Selectmen were not overburdened with brains, and that the storekeeper charged too much for beefsteak. But as soon as he approached matters that were even remotely personal to Ann or Lucy, they either shied away or stopped talking altogether. During one of these pauses Archer and his assistants came into the kitchen, with much foot-stamping and low-voiced discussion. Bella made a leap for the door, and had to be forcibly restrained.

"She seems to be a mighty good watchdog," the doctor remarked. "Isn't it funny she didn't notice any strangers around?"

This thought had already occurred to Ann and Lucy, but they had carefully refrained from mentioning it. Now Lucy said, "Not necessarily. Bella's getting old, and she doesn't hear as well as she used to."

Dr. Partridge let it go at that, but filed the point for future reference. He hadn't noticed anything wrong with Bella's hearing, and she didn't seem like a dog who would allow any stranger the run of the premises without doing something about it. But, if the murderer were not a stranger?

The sergeant appeared with two companions, one a trooper, the other in plain clothes. He indicated the former. "Burke's going to stay here with me. Willoughby's going back with the body, and you better go with him,

Doctor. We've done all we can out there, for the present. Did you get hold of your husband, Mrs. Patterson?"

Lucy described her husband's predicament, conscious that her explanation didn't sound too convincing. But Archer made no comment beyond a nod. He turned to the doctor, who was putting on his overcoat, and they went out, talking in undertones. Then Dr. Partridge called back a hasty "Good night," doors slammed, and the ambulance drove crunchingly away.

Deacon Grimm was gone—physically. But he was not gone from their thoughts, nor from their lives. He still had power over them; more now, perhaps, than when he had been alive. That would please him, wherever he was, Ann Barbour thought, wryly. Leonard Grimm had always liked to make people feel that they were in his power. His perverse spirit, wherever it might be, would rejoice at this posthumous mastery, this domination that Death had not ended. Even Lucy, less imaginative than Ann, remembered vaguely something she had read about "the evil that men do" living after them. . . . She wished Frank would call up. Surely, he must have reached Winchester by this time. It was such a rotten night, and the roads were so slippery . . . Lucy resolutely turned her thoughts away from such possibilities.

Then Archer Brett returned, followed by the trooper, whom he introduced as Henry Burke. Trooper Burke was a large young man, with a face which was by nature round and placid, but upon which he was trying to impose an expression of severity more in keeping with his profession. When he forgot himself, which was fairly often, he looked amiable if unimpressive. He was a sound and practical young man, if not a brilliant one; and he both admired and liked the sergeant, with whom he had worked before.

Archer himself, while more noticeably watchful than he had been at first, was still considerate. "I'll try not to keep you up much longer," he said, "but there are still a few things I want to ask about tonight." He glanced at his notes. "Was the barn door fastened on the inside when you found the body, Miss Barbour?"

Ann said, "I couldn't say. But afterwards, when Lucy and I looked, it was fastened. But there are other ways of getting in and out of the barn, if you know about them."

Archer had already discovered this fact during the hasty search that he and Henry Burke had just made of the barn and its adjacent buildings. That the big barn doors were securely fastened on the inside was no sign that the murderer hadn't left the barn. He might have left by some other exit (of which there were at least four), or through the house, even. Or he might still be hiding in that great ark of a place; it was big enough to conceal a hundred murderers, and was honeycombed with rooms and passages. Archer wondered why under the sun the early New Englanders had built such enormous barns; lumber and labor, he reflected, must have been cheaper then than now. So perhaps the murderer was still there, hidden in some dark corner; or perhaps he had a confederate, who had fastened the doors behind him; or perhaps the girls were lying—he mustn't overlook that possibility; or perhaps the Deacon had been killed elsewhere, and planted in the barn, pitchfork and all, although that idea did seem pretty farfetched. Lucy said she thought the pitchfork was theirs, but all pitchforks look a good deal alike; she couldn't be sure. Or perhaps, oh, half a hundred things. Why did deacons get murdered, anyway?

This unprofitable speculation was interrupted by the telephone. Lucy, who was the nearest, answered it before the sergeant had a chance to. It became evident, from her half of the ensuing conversation, and from her relieved expression, that the caller was her husband. But she followed Archer's instructions; she didn't tell Frank what had happened, but only that "something" made it imperative for him to come home at once. "We're all right," she repeated, "but come along as soon as you can . . . no, nobody's sick . . . no, I'm all right, I tell you . . . yes, I will. . . . Yes. Well, you be careful, too. . . . All right . . . yes, yes . . . good-bye."

"He's got to the hotel at last," she told them. Archer looked at his watch; it was a quarter of two. "He hired a car in Pinkney," Lucy went on, "but it broke down between there and Winchester, and he had an awful job getting it going. And then he had to drive so slow it took him until now to get there. He says he'll get the next train back to Rumford; it gets in around eight in the morning. But somebody'll have to bring him over from Rumford."

Archer promised to provide transportation. Then he resumed his questions: "Have you any idea why the Deacon was in your barn?"

They hadn't.

"You hadn't asked him to come over for any reason?"

Certainly not.

"Could he have come over to borrow anything?"

Lucy didn't think so, "If he'd wanted anything," she said, "he would have come and asked me about it, not gone out there to help himself. We weren't friendly enough for that."

"You mean, you weren't on friendly terms?"

Lucy hesitated. "N—no, it wasn't that. But we weren't— we didn't neighbor much. Besides, the Deacon must have known Frank was away."

Archer, who had never lived in the country, wanted to know how he would have known.

Ann smiled faintly. She said, "Everybody knows everybody else's business here; you'll soon find that out. And what they don't know, they suspect."

Lucy concurred. "And everybody knew Frank was going to the Convention; he's been talking about it for a month."

"I see." Archer was thoughtful. He said slowly, "I don't suppose either of you knows of anyone who wanted—er— Deacon Grimm out of the way, who might have done this?"

Silence.

Lucy started to speak, but thought better of it. She felt happier, now that she knew Frank's whereabouts; but she didn't intend to do much talking until she had seen him.

Ann smoothed her hair back over her ears. They were pretty ears, Archer observed, and she wore earrings of dull silver.

"Do you?" he asked sharply.

The silence continued. Then Ann said, not looking at him, "There are quite a number of people, I believe, who didn't like the Deacon much. But what we could tell you would be only gossip or hearsay, at the best. I think we'd rather not name any names just now."

Archer was annoyed, but he couldn't help smiling at the careful phrasing of that reply. Would it do any good to insist? He thought not, at present. "Never mind, then," he said. "You must both be tired, and I won't keep you up any longer. Burke and I will have to be here for a while— we've got a lot to do. But we won't make any more extra work than we can help." He rose and smothered a yawn. "Come on, Henry, I want to take another look around out-side. Good night." He and the trooper went out. It was ten minutes past two.

Lucy and Ann slept in the same room, behind a locked and bolted door. Tad occupied a cot there, too, and Bella lay at the foot of the bed. The girls were tired and ner-vously exhausted, but they found it hard to sleep. Ann was saying, "I thought it was wisest not to say anything about anybody at all unless we were asked outright, and couldn't avoid answering. I thought it would be best to wait until we had advice, perhaps. But now . . . I don't know. Maybe we should have told the sergeant all the gossip and every-thing. Somebody's sure to, if we don't, and it might have been a good plan to get our version of things in first. I wish I had, now that it's too late. What do you think?"

Lucy was equally uncertain. "But I'd say it was safer to say too little than too much," she said. "Let's wait and see what Frank thinks. Perhaps we ought to see a lawyer."

Ann had a low opinion of lawyers. "Besides, won't that look as if we expected to be suspected, or had something to hide? But I don't know. The sergeant seems to believe us, though he has only our word for what we told him. We might be lying our heads off, for all he can tell. He'd be a fool not to suspect us a little."

Lucy asked quickly, "Do you think he does?"

"I don't know."

There was a long pause. Then Lucy said, "It's a good thing he questioned us together, instead of separately."

With which cryptic remark Ann agreed.

At four o'clock Archer Brett and Trooper Henry Burke returned to the Pattersons' kitchen, where a lamp burned dimly. The driving sleet had changed to snow again, but the wind had gone down, and the house was quiet.

"I'm all in," Archer said. "I'm going to lie down on that couch in the sitting room for a couple of hours, and rest my brains. You stay awake and look after things."

"Okay," said Henry Burke. He looked around the room and gave an exclamation. Archer followed his glance; then he laughed. On the kitchen table stood a large pitcher of milk and two glasses, a plate of sandwiches, a plate of doughnuts, and three-quarters of an apple pie. A piece of paper propped against the pie plate directed them, "Help yourselves."

"Say," said Henry Burke, "I don't believe either of those girls had anything to do with bumping the old feller off, do you?"

Archer cut a piece of pie and sampled it. It was good. "You never can tell," he said, "but I'd hate to think so!"

2
Sunday—*No Day of Rest*

Henry Burke woke Archer up when the latter had slept two hours. It was half-past six o'clock, but still dark and still snowing, although not very fast. Archer got up and stretched, and relinquished the couch to Burke. "Your turn, now," he said. "I feel almost as good as new."

"It's the pie," said Henry Burke, with a grin.

Whatever it was, the sergeant felt better. The data he had gleaned so far was too scanty for any theorizing, but he felt that given time, he could sort it into a fairly coherent pattern. Archer was a man who liked to have things set out clearly in black and white. He sat down at the not-quite-antique secretary, commandeered a pad of paper that was handy, and put down a few ideas that had occurred to him, under the heading,

Remarks:
1) I got the impression Mrs. P. and Miss B. didn't care much for Grimm. I think they know of others, or possibly only one other, who had it in for him, but they weren't giving anything away. Thought best not to press them yet. They alibi each other, but could be in cahoots, I suppose. Ask Dr. P. if a woman could have done it?

2) Must see Grimm's housekeeper and her husband. Something there? Also the hired man.

3) Check alibis of everybody even remotely connected with Grimm for time between 7:30 and 10:30 Saturday night. Especially, any persons with known or possible motives. Check Patterson's movements.

4) Listen to neighborhood gossip to get a line on Grimm, who hated him, and why. Gossip has to be discounted some, but there's usually something in it.

5) Question Mrs. P. and Miss B. again. Separately! Question the boy?

6) Why didn't the dog make a fuss? Or did she?

Then he made a list of the things he had found on the dead man's person. The articles themselves had been taken to Rumford, along with the body and the pitchfork, for expert examination. Archer knew the "expert examiner," and was positive that he wouldn't discover anything new. But that was the rule. Anyway, the Deacon's pockets hadn't yielded anything very significant or enlightening.

Pants pockets:

1 Howard watch, gold case, new. Nothing in back. Stopped at 11:37, apparently run down.

1 large jackknife, nothing unusual about it.

1 key ring, holding seven keys: two Yales, one Corbin, and four ordinary house or door keys.

1 receipted feed bill from Clinton County Farmers' Exchange.

1 pencil stub, very dull. Looks as if it had
   been chewed, in fact,
1 pigskin change purse, containing thirty-two
   cents.

Inside coat pockets:
1 black leather wallet, fairly new, containing:
Fifty-seven dollars in bills.
Automobile driver's license, made out to de-
   ceased.
Insurance Co.'s Identification Card, ditto.
4 three-cent stamps.
1 small piece white paper, folded once across,
   on which was written in pencil, "Tell M.
   about—?"

Outside coat pockets:
1 handkerchief, soiled.
1 pair woolen gloves.
1 package Lucky Strikes, containing nine cigarettes.

That was all. Barring the brief penciled query, there
was nothing a bit suggestive or out of the ordinary. The
fifty-seven dollars and thirty-two cents did seem to indi-
cate that Deacon Grimm hadn't been killed for the sake of
robbery; that was one motive out of the way, at least.

As for the question scrawled in pencil—it was interesting but vague. After all, there are a good many "M"s in the
world. Archer wondered if the writing could be identified
as the Deacon's. If the writer had considerately set down
what (or whom) "M" was to be told about, it would have
been a help. Still, it was a clue, of a sort.

Archer had not yet found any other objects which he
could recognize as clues—no odd buttons, cuff-links or

lipsticks, dropped by an accommodating murderer. There were no mysterious symbols of any secret society, no monogrammed cigarette cases, torn scraps of cloth, unexplained doo-dads of any description. Not even any vagrant cigarette ends or ashes, to be carefully collected and analyzed! He had already collected the three ash trays in the Pattersons' sitting room, on the off chance that they might reveal traces of Luckies, or even Deacon Grimm's fingerprints, if by any chance the Deacon had been in the house. Ann, he recalled, had been smoking Camels.

The actual scene of this crime was a particularly bad hunting-ground for clues, anyway. There were so many queer things in that barn! Some of them the city-bred sergeant didn't even know the use of, and most of them seemed to have no legitimate reason for being where they were. How was he to tell whether or not they had any connection with the Deacon's death? There might be dozens of clues lying right under his nose, but if they weren't recognizable as such, what good were they?

If Archer had been a devotee of detective fiction, (which he wasn't), he would have instantly recognized his shortcomings as an investigator. He would have compared himself with Philo Vance, Fleming Stone, or Lieutenant Valcour (among others), and, faced with their almost superhuman knowledge and deductive power as opposed to his own modest mental equipment, might have committed suicide on the spot. But luckily he was unacquainted with these gentlemen and their marvelous achievements, so that his inability to rise to their heights didn't trouble him as much as it might have done.

All the same, he was uncomfortably aware that this case was entirely different from any he had worked on before. The only murders he had dealt with, prior to this one, were comparatively ordinary, as murders go: one was a gang killing, involving some known Boston bad men; one was a shooting fatality, the probably unintentional result of an attempted holdup; the third was a drunken fight over a woman between two of her admirers, one of whom had finally succeeded in throttling the other. These cases Archer had been able to handle in a more or less routine way, and they had been concluded satisfactorily. But this affair was different. He had little to go on except the Deacon himself, his relationships with other people, the commonplace articles found on his body, and the pitchfork that had killed him. And of these, it seemed to Archer, the most was to be learned from the people involved, whoever they turned out to be. He believed that the behavior of human beings is more enlightening, as a rule, than the evidence of inanimate objects, although he knew well enough that human reactions are doubtful propositions, especially where crime is concerned. And he realized that the motives of men and women are harder to trace than rifled bullets or deadly poisons or conveniently located fingerprints. Their causes are obscure and their workings devious, and their results, in many cases, deplorable. But they are more fascinating than anything else in the world. Archer didn't know whether he could get to the bottom of this business or not, but he certainly meant to try.

He stopped his reflections long enough to damn the snow, which was still falling. A break for the murderer, that snow was. If he'd left any traces outside anywhere, they were gone now.

About two-thirty, before it began to snow, he and Burke had looked around outside as well as they could, and he had made rough notes and a rougher diagram of the vague tire and foot marks near the house and barn. The tire marks were recognizable as having been made by the Patterson car. But, owing to the condition of the ground, the footprints were so indefinite as to be practically worthless. Most of them were large and shapeless; they might have been made by one person or by several people. Only one set seemed smaller, faintly resembling in places the marks made by a woman's high-heeled shoe. Possibly (but this was pure conjecture), one set had been made by the Deacon; one by the hired man; one by Ann Barbour, who wore high heels; and one by the unknown murderer, provided he was not one of those already mentioned. But it was all guesswork, and now the snow had covered them. It was only because he was determined not to overlook anything that Archer had taken note of them. So, for what it was worth, he added the diagram to his collection of facts; it wasn't evidence, but it might help, somehow.

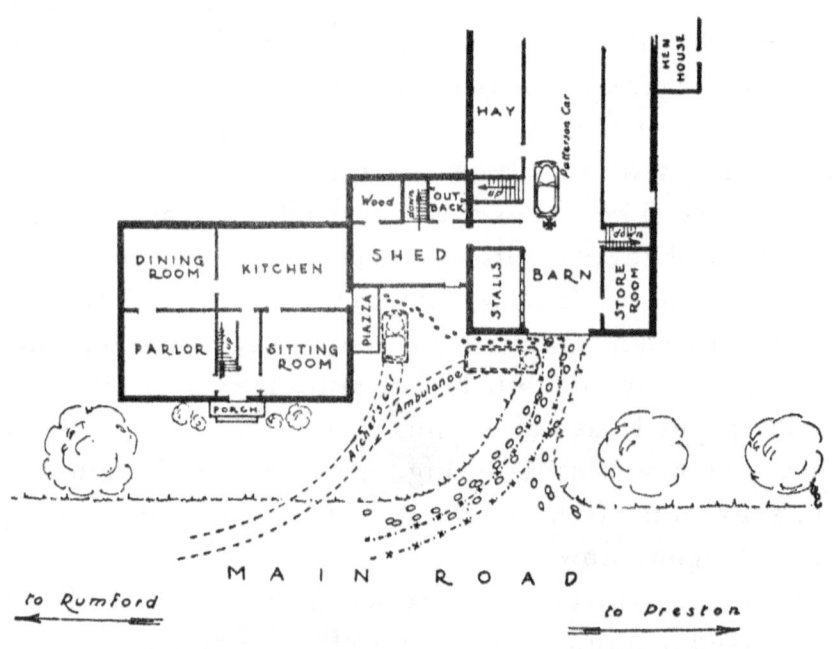

The sergeant heard a sudden thump overhead, and a murmur of voices. Evidently, his hostesses were getting up. He wondered if he would be able to screw any further information out of them today; it would require tact and patience.

Archer hoped that he wouldn't have to hand the case over to anyone else, to State's Attorney Golding, for example. He thought that if he showed average common sense in carrying on the inquiry, and made even a moderate amount of progress in a reasonable time, that Captain Randall would see that he was left in charge. There was no love lost between the Captain and Golding, and while the latter usually got his own way in routine matters, the Captain sometimes saw fit to oppose him, and when that happened, it was Golding who backed down. Archer had learned from Mrs. Randall that the Captain was hunting in New Brunswick; she was trying to get in touch with him, and would notify the sergeant when she succeeded.

"So it's up to me," Archer reflected, "to show the Captain when he gets here that I'm the man to keep on the job." For some reason he wanted to keep on, although the case didn't look as if it was going to be easy. The type of crime and the kind of people concerned in it were both new to him, but they were interesting. Yes, although it meant hard work, with probably no thanks at the end of it, he wanted to solve this crime himself, and according to his own ideas. "I wish I were a Northwest Mounted Policeman," he thought enviously. "They just use their own judgment, and the government backs 'em up." He sighed at the mere thought of such a heavenly arrangement. "Mounties" weren't pestered by newspaper reporters, either. Archer was thankful that Dr. Partridge shared his own dislike for the gentlemen of the press, and wouldn't notify them of what had happened until the State's Attorney made it necessary. Damn nuisances, the reporters would be, and so would the State's Attorney and his henchmen. "If they'd leave us alone, we could accomplish ten times as much as we do! Ten? A hundred!" Well, he was at liberty to use his own judgment for a while, anyway; and by the time the inquest was over, he ought to be able to unearth some kind of a lead. "Good thing I don't need much sleep!" he reflected.

Feet clicked on the stairs; and the door opened to admit Lucy Patterson. In a blue-checked dress and ruffled apron she reminded the sergeant still more strongly of his distant sister. "Well," she said, "you've kept it nice and warm down here. Did you manage to get some sleep? I could have put you in one of the spare rooms, but I never thought."

"The couch was very comfortable," Archer said, smiling. "And much obliged for the lunch. Burke and I appreciated it."

Lucy laughed. "I thought you would. Now I'll see about some breakfast."

Archer followed her into the kitchen. "It's mighty nice of you to treat us so well, Mrs. Patterson, when we're here on such unpleasant business."

"The business isn't your fault," Lucy returned, as she produced eggs and a frying pan from a cupboard. "Besides, Ann and I appreciate your kindness. Some policemen would have given us the third degree, whatever it is."

Archer doubted whether any policemen would have gone that far. "But I find it pays to treat people as if they had feelings and were decent," he said. "At any rate, until I'm sure they aren't."

Lucy agreed with him, at some length. "I tell Ann," she concluded, "that most people have some good in them, no matter how much we may dislike them personally. She thinks I'm too charitable. But I say, treat people as you'd want them to treat you."

Archer applauded this sentiment, and thought it was a good opportunity to stress an aspect of it which Mrs. Patterson and her cousin seemed to have overlooked. "It's always a good idea," he said, "in a case like this, to tell the police everything you know, or even only suspect. It's a mistake to keep things back, for any reason at all. So if you or Miss Barbour know anything you haven't told me, I hope you'll reconsider and let me have it. It's always wisest, in the long run."

But Lucy was silent. She intended to consult Frank before voicing any further knowledge or suspicions.

Archer changed the subject. "What does your cousin do?"

"She writes. Verses and things, and then she does book reviews for a Boston paper. Hack work, she calls it. She'd like to write real books and poetry, but she doesn't ever seem able to get started, somehow."

Archer said he had heard of cases like that before.

Lucy continued, "Ann's clever; she could do something worth-while, if she'd keep at it. But she lacks gumption, and she's lazy, in a way, though I hadn't ought to say that." She beat the eggs violently, as if indignant with Ann for being lazy, or with Providence for creating her so. She added, "I think a lot of Ann, but I do wish she had more stick-to-it. She gives up too easily."

"Hasn't she any folks?"

Lucy explained that Ann's parents had died when she was small, leaving her in the care of an aunt until she grew up.

"After Aunt Amy died, Ann visited us quite a lot, and we always got along first-rate. So now this is really home to her, especially since . . ." Lucy realized that she was talking more than she had intended to, and stopped abruptly.

Before Archer could get her started again, Tad and Ann had appeared on the scene, the latter remarking that she had shut Bella in the bedroom, for safety's sake.

"Yes," Lucy said, "it would never do for Bella to bite a policeman, of all people!"

Ann was wearing a flowered-print dress with short sleeves instead of the black of the night before, and both she and Lucy looked so fresh and unrumpled that it was hard for Archer to remember that they were mixed up in

a murder, and hadn't gotten to bed until after two o'clock
that morning. He marveled at the recuperative powers of
women, but reflected unkindly that probably make-up had
a good deal to do with it!

By this time the eggs were scrambled and the coffee
and bacon ready. While they ate, Archer noted that both
women acted as if he were an ordinary casual acquaintance
instead of a policeman. He tried not to feel as if he were
taking advantage of their attitude, but knew he would have
to do just that, little as he might enjoy it.

Ann asked suddenly, "How about reporters, Sergeant
Brett? Will we have to talk to them, and have our affairs
spread all over the papers?" Her dislike for the prospect
was evident.

"Not unless you want to," Archer told her. "They'll be
here, all right, as soon as they hear the news, but we'll try
to keep them from bothering you. They can go to Golding
for information—he loves to spread himself for the Press.
You may get photographed if you go outside, but you don't
have to let reporters in the house, or talk to them unless
you want to; in fact, I hope you won't. But I don't expect
they'll show up until tomorrow."

Ann and Lucy looked relieved. "We can stand having
our pictures taken if we have to," Lucy declared, "but
we don't want newspapermen overrunning the place, and
printing all sorts of stories about us. Frank's people over
in Westhaven will have fits as it is, without reading a lot
of sensational stuff in the papers."

"I'll do my best to discourage 'em," Archer promised.
He hoped that gratitude might make Lucy and Ann tell
him things when nothing else would. He finished his coffee. "I must get busy now. Your husband will be along
pretty soon, Mrs. Patterson; I arranged for Trooper Haley
to meet his train and bring him over. I want to go and see

the Deacon's housekeeper now, and your hired man. Or will he be along here, anyway?"

Lucy said that Luke was due any minute.

Archer hesitated. Then he said, "I'm going to ask you both, and Mr. Patterson, too, when he comes to stay around the house today, and not to talk to anyone outside about the case until I say the word. No one knows what's happened yet, except the police and you folks and the operator."

"And the murderer," Tad put in unexpectedly. The word, apparently, caused him no misgivings.

"And the murderer, of course," Archer agreed hastily. "By the way, is the operator dependable? Miss Morton?"

"Yes indeed," Lucy said warmly. "You can rely on Rose absolutely. Telephone operators aren't supposed to gossip, but Rose really never does."

"Good. Then do I have your promise to stay here today, and not to talk?"

Ann was looking out the window at the snow, her thoughts apparently miles away. She wore white pearl earrings this morning, Archer noticed, instead of the silver ones. He kept wondering what it was about this girl that interested him. He'd seen dozens of women prettier and more provocative. But there was some elusive quality about her that was different, that was the only way he could put it, and he knew how silly that sounded.

With an effort, Ann brought herself back into the present, and said, "We're in your hands, Sergeant Brett. I'm quite willing to do what you ask."

"So am I, of course," Lucy said. "That is, if Frank thinks it's all right, when he gets here."

Archer smiled. He was becoming more and more curious to see what kind of a man Frank was, that his wife held such a high opinion of him. A regular superman, evidently.

Lucy prepared generous breakfasts for Bella and the household cats. There were three of the latter, "coon cats," long-haired and dignified, who would have been no discredit to a cat show, although they claimed no fancy pedigrees. Two were tigers and the third was yellow, and they answered (at mealtime) to the highly unoriginal names of "Lady," "Teddy," and "Buffy." They ate their breakfasts daintily, and watched Bella out of the corners of their eyes.

Archer waked Trooper Burke, whose breakfast was waiting for him in the warming oven, and gave him some low-voiced instructions. "Stay here until I get back," he finished, "and keep your eyes open. I don't want the girls to put anything over while I'm gone."

"No girl," Henry Burke said indignantly, "can put anything over on me!"

"Well, they probably won't try," Archer put on his coat and cap, and went out. He needed a shave, but it would have to wait.

About six inches of snow had fallen. It lay like a soft, fluffy blanket over everything, and looked so smooth and white that it seemed a shame to walk in it. There was still snow in the air, so fine that it was almost a mist, and the unbroken clouds were dull and lead-colored.

Archer made a circuit of the Patterson buildings, and was thankful to find that his were the only tracks in evidence. The snow was unbroken, except for the partly obliterated marks that he and Burke had made in the night. (There were a few of Bella's near the piazza, but they didn't count.) So the murderer had either left before it began to snow, or else was still somewhere on the premises, a highly improbable contingency. No, unless he was a fool, he had beat it while the beating was good, and while he could escape without leaving any telltale traces behind him.

Archer walked out to the main road, where overlapping tire marks showed that a few cars had passed. But they hadn't stopped, or taken any interest in the Patterson place, to all appearances. He stood in the middle of the road, and surveyed the general outlook. Lucy had already described the neighborhood for him, in considerable detail, so that he could tell who lived where. Almost opposite the Pattersons' stood Leonard Grimm's farm, which had belonged to his father before him, Lucy said. It looked neat and prosperous,—a rambling white house, with a large red barn on its farther side. Beyond the barn, appeared the upper part of another good-sized house, painted yellow, and with smoke rising from its big, square chimney. That, Lucy had informed him, belonged to a man named Buckley, a retired business man, who bred fancy fowls for a hobby. On the same side of the road as the Pattersons', but almost opposite the Buckleys', Archer could see the chimneys of still another house; but it sat back from the road, and was so surrounded by evergreen trees that little of it was visible from where he was standing. That must be the old Wayland place, which Mrs. Patterson had said was empty.

The Lafonds', where he wanted to go next, was in the opposite direction. For purposes of timing, he decided to walk there, and set off down the hill, turning up his coat collar against the biting, wind driven snow.

He looked away at the distant hills, their white fields and purple woods standing out against the gray sky. Solitary farmhouses clung to some of them, and in a dip between two hills he could see a church steeple; that would be Preston, probably. Although he had been stationed in Rumford for six years now, Archer came originally from a hustling industrial city; after its crowded dinginess the restful hills and wide valleys of New England appealed to him greatly. The hills weren't high enough to be forbidding, like those out West, but they offered contrasts and an ever-changing variety not found anywhere else in the country. A pleasant place, New England; a place that avoided extremes, like its people.

At the foot of the hill, a small bridge crossed a partly frozen, but still turbulent brook. Before reaching the bridge, however, the sergeant saw a narrow road leading off to the right—the "Old Road." It had not been broken out, but stretched smoothly white between irregular, snow-piled stone walls. The first house, Mrs. Patterson had said. When he reached it Archer looked at his watch; it had taken him nine and a half minutes to walk there. Without the snow it wouldn't have taken more than five or six, he reckoned, if one were in a hurry.

The Lafond house was a story and a half affair, badly in need of paint and shingles. An icicle-fringed Chevrolet sedan stood in an open shed nearby, and a grimy washing hung limply across one end of the sagging porch. The whole place looked neglected, but a radio aerial rose from one gable, and from within came the raucous sounds which too many present-day orchestras produce instead of music. Archer stamped the snow from his boots, and rapped on the door. Then he rapped again, louder. The raucous sounds ceased, and after an interval heavy footsteps approached, and the door opened eight or nine inches. In the opening appeared a sullen, unshaven, and very unprepossessing countenance, with a cigarette drooping from one corner of its mouth. "Here," said the countenance, "what d'you want, making such a row?" The bloodshot eyes took in Archer's uniform and changed expression, becoming wary. "A cop!" exclaimed their owner. "What d'*you* want? What's up?"

"I want to see Mrs. Lafond," Archer informed him. "She lives here, doesn't she?"

"Yeh, she lives here, but she ain't up. What d'you want to see her for?"

"I'll come in and tell her that," Archer replied, and did so. The door opener retreated, and Archer entered a small, cluttered, dirty room, which smelled of stale whiskey, staler grease, and, stalest of all, cigarette smoke. Its furnishings were expensive but gaudy—that is, they had been gaudy before dirt and abuse had toned them down. Archer couldn't help thinking what a contrast this room was to the Pattersons' plain but cheerful kitchen. His host backed across the room to a partially opened door, and stuck his head inside. "Get up, Clarabel."

He shut the door, and sat down at the untidy table, regarding the sergeant morosely. "What's she been up to?" he demanded.

Archer thought to himself, "If I'm looking for a murderer, here's one made to order!"

The man certainly looked the part. He was heavily built, although short. His greasy black hair and week's growth of black stubble, together with the bloodshot black eyes, and a thick, ugly nose, made him look exactly like most people's idea of a gangster. He wore a dirty pinkish shirt and wrinkled brown trousers, thrust into unlaced boots. All in all, an unattractive specimen. But not necessarily a murderer, of course.

"Are you Gus Lafond?" Archer inquired, sitting down on the edge of a soiled armchair.

"Yeh, that's me. You ain't told me yet what you want of Clarabel."

"I came to see her on Deacon Grimm's account," Archer said, watching Mr. Lafond closely for any possible reaction. None was noticeable.

"Yeh? What's he want?"

Before the sergeant could reply, the bedroom door opened and he got a surprise. He hadn't expected to see a girl like the one who stood in the doorway, regarding them nonchalantly. The Deacon's housekeeper was young, not more than nineteen or twenty, and startlingly pretty, from her bare ankles to her permanently waved, golden-brown hair, which was becomingly tousled. She wore a tight, dark dress, which showed all the good points of a figure nearly as perfect as her complexion, and her eyes were large, blue, and heavily mascaraed. "Boy, what a charmer!" Archer thought. "Why isn't she in the movies?" But her voice, when she spoke, was coarse and common—a giveaway: "You want to see me?"

"If you please, Mrs. Lafond."

Clarabel Lafond seated herself on a corner of the table, exposing long and shapely legs. Taking a cigarette from an opened package, (Luckies, Archer noted), she placed it between her full, reddened lips. "Well, here I am, Big Boy. Why not get what's troubling you off your mind?" she struck a match.

Archer decided that there were very few brains behind that movie-magazine-cover face; very few brains, and even fewer scruples. She was a perfect example of a type his profession had made him all too familiar with—at thirty she would be a hard-faced harpy, and at fifty, if she lived that long, a sodden drab. But now, what a looker! He said, "I'd like to ask you a few questions. When did you see Deacon Grimm last, Mrs. Lafond? I understand you kept house for him."

If Clarabel noticed his use of the past tense, she gave no sign of it. "The Deacon? After supper last night, of course. Why?"

"Suppose you tell me about it. I have good reasons for asking."

Clarabel looked at her husband, who said suspiciously, "I don't see what business it is of his, but go ahead and tell him. We ain't got no secrets."

"Well," Clarabel said, "We got home from Rumford late, so I was late getting up to the house to fix the Deacon's supper. 'Bout seven, I guess it was, or half-past six."

She seemed hazy about time. "Anyway, I got his supper and ate with him, and washed the dishes after. Then I came back here, and pretty soon me and Gus went to bed."

"What time was it when you left the Deacon's house; do you remember?"

"Oh, I don't know. Around quarter to eight."

"Was he in the house when you left?"

"Sure. He was reading the paper in the kitchen."

"Did he say anything to you about going anywhere?" Archer prodded her.

She shook her head. "I don't remember anything. He said something about he wouldn't need me any more that night, and I better get home before the storm got any worse." She gave her husband a sidelong look. "So I did."

"Was that the last you saw of him."

"Sure it was. I don't go up Sundays unless he wants me for something special. But why—"

Lafond broke in. "Yes, what's the idea, asking Clarabel all them questions? She ain't the Deacon's keeper."

Quite the reverse, Archer was inclined to think, but kept that to himself. He considered rapidly what would be the best line to take with this pair, and decided on the truth, since they would have to know it before long, in any case.

"Deacon Grimm has been murdered," he said baldly, "and I advise you to tell me all you know now, and save yourselves possible future trouble."

If he had hoped for fireworks, he was disappointed. The man's pasty face grew a little pastier, and Clarabel dropped her cigarette, but that was all. A cool couple, evidently. Lafond said with a sneer, "We don't have to talk until we see a lawyer, and you know it!"

Archer shrugged. "Maybe you don't, but I'd advise it, just the same. If you haven't done anything out of the way, you can't do yourselves any harm by talking, can you?"

Mr. Lafond considered. "It's like Clarabel said," he replied at last. "She come back here before eight o'clock, and we listened to the radio a while, and then went to bed. And you can't prove anything different," he added, with a disagreeable smile.

Damn! Another mutual alibi! Archer said, "Have you any other witnesses to that? You may have to give evidence later, remember."

"Yes, we have," Lafond snapped. "Danny Cheever was here all the time, and can swear we're telling the truth."

"Who's Danny Cheever?"

"My brother," Clarabel explained. "He lives with us. He'll tell you we never went out at all last night. He—"

She closed her lovely mouth with an effort when her husband looked at her.

Archer demanded, "Is he here now?"

"No, he ain't," Lafond retorted, "but you can get him easy enough. He works up to Buckleys'." He jerked his head toward the wall telephone.

The sergeant went across to the instrument and turned the crank, watching his companions while he did it. "Number, please?" came Rose Norton's clear voice.

"Miss Norton, this is Sergeant Brett. Will you get me the Buckleys' house, please?"

"Just a minute." A bell rang several times; then there was a click, and a new voice said, "Hello-o?" It was a woman's voice, and was curiously slow and rich, like thick syrup.

"Is this Mrs. Buckley?"

"Ye-es," said the rich voice. "Who—what is it?"

"If Danny Cheever is there, will you please have him come to his sister's at once? There's been an accident."

Lafond got angrily to his feet: "Say—"

"Oh, sit down," Archer told him. Then to Mrs. Buckley, "Thanks very much. Tell him to hurry, will you?" He hung up, and turned to Lafond. "Don't try any of that tough guy stuff with me," he ordered. "It may work with some people, but I know your kind. Also your record," he added untruthfully.

Gus mumbled something, but made no further protests. Clarabel looked as if she wanted to ask questions, but didn't dare with her husband's eye on her. She sauntered across the room to a somewhat dilapidated couch, and draped herself gracefully on one end of it, where the sergeant couldn't fail to notice her undoubted physical attractions.

But Archer's mind was taken up with other things. It was filled with conflicting ideas and conjectures. He wanted to get back and talk with Frank Patterson and his hired man; they must have both arrived by this time. But he also wanted to see Danny Cheever, and to question the Lafonds some more. There was so much to do, and he could be in only one place at one time. He shook himself mentally; no sense in getting flustered. The thing to do was to go along in a systematic way and collect all the facts, or as many of them as he could find. Then they could be compared and weighed and considered afterwards. But get the facts first, and don't get confused. Still, he wished he were twins.

He continued to question the Lafonds, as skillfully as he knew how, but learned little more. They had told their story and they stuck to it. Archer decided he would get better results if he tackled them separately; perhaps after he had acquired more information from other sources. He turned the conversation to other people, and had no trouble learning what Gus and Clarabel thought of the Deacon, the Buckleys, and the members of the Patterson household. Although Gus had probably never heard of "de mortuis nil nisi bonum," he played safe by applying it to Deacon Grimm. But he was outspoken enough in his opinion of the others: Warner Buckley, he said, was a

hen-pecked old fool, and his wife was a meddler; while as
for the Pattersons and that stuck-up Barbour girl—Gus's
thick lips curled in a sneer. "Thinks he's all Hell, Patterson does," he complained. "Just because his old man left
him a good farm and money enough to run it, he makes
out he's better'n ordinary people. His wife and that Ann
Barbour don't hardly speak to Clarabel, who's just as good
as they are, and a lot better looking. Just because their
people have been around here for a long time, and left 'em
a little money, they think they're better than us, and look
down their noses at us. But there's a time coming," said
Mr. Lafond darkly, "when they'll get theirs. You wait and
see!" Clarabel endorsed her husband's views as far as her
limited vocabulary (and gray matter) allowed her to. Her
unflattering opinion of Mrs. Buckley was interrupted by
the arrival of Danny Cheever, who stumbled breathlessly
in, and shook snow all over the floor. "What's-matter?" he
gasped. "Mrs. Buckley said-accident!"

Clarabel's brother was about seventeen, and looked like
a caricature of Clarabel. He had the same golden-brown
hair, an untidy mop of it, and the same large blue eyes
stared from his vacant, pink-cheeked face. He was tall and
awkward; and it was plain, even at first glance, that Danny
was not quite "all there," His face twitched, and his hands
and feet moved with nervous jerkiness. But he was by no
means a fool. Archer calmed him down by explaining that
Clarabel was unharmed, that the "accident" had happened
to Deacon Grimm, and that he, Archer, merely wanted to
ask Danny a few questions. The boy grew less jittery and
seemed to understand, although he still looked frightened.
And his answers, to Archer's disgust, only confirmed Gus
Lafond's story. Danny had returned from the Buckleys'
about half-past six the night before, and had eaten supper with his brother-in-law. Clarabel had arrived before a
quarter of eight (he thought), and they had all listened to

the radio—it was Silly Billy and his Oxtail Orchestra, on
Station WHY. Yes, Gus and Clarabel had been right there
until he went to bed. No, they hadn't gone out at all. No,
he hadn't seen Deacon Grimm since early Saturday morning, when he saw him doing his chores. How was he sure
that Gus and Clarabel had been home all night? Why, they
said they had! Archer gave up. It was no use questioning
Danny with the Lafonds present; he was too much under
their influence. But the sergeant concealed his opinions,
pretended to accept their alibis, and smoothed them down
as well as he could. They would be notified, he said, when
and where their evidence would be required; in the meantime, they were not to talk. He dexterously avoided answering their questions, and left, with three more suspects
to add to his list.

Frank Patterson arrived home about nine-thirty. His
state of mind was far from serene, for he had been unable to pry any information out of Trooper Haley during
the drive from Rumford, and he was still in the dark as
to what had happened. When the police car stopped in
his yard, Frank was out of it, up the steps, and through
the kitchen door before Haley, a leisurely person, had slid
from behind the wheel. Lucy rushed into her husband's
arms, and the kitchen was filled with excited explanations
and reassurances. Ann, Tad, and Henry Burke hovered on
the outskirts; the latter, when the noise had died down,
took his fellow trooper aside and asked for the latest developments from Rumford. Haley produced the pictures
and fingerprint reports that Archer had requested, and
handed them over. Dr. Partridge, he said, was already per-
forming the autopsy, and would ring the sergeant about
one o'clock. The fact of the murder had not yet leaked out
to the newspapers, and State's Attorney Golding was away
somewhere—in Timbuktu, everybody hoped. Mrs. Randall

had contacted the Captain, who would try to get to Rumford on Monday, or in time for the inquest on Tuesday, anyway. And he, Haley, was supposed to go right back to Rumford, too.

"Too bad you can't stay," Burke said commiseratingly. "Mrs. Patterson is some swell cook. You ought to see the dinner she's getting ready now! Oh, boy, I hope the Sergeant don't solve this case too quick!"

Haley sighed and left, to dine on cold corned beef and soggy potatoes in his Rumford boardinghouse.

When Archer got back from the Lafonds', he found Burke helping Tad with a jigsaw puzzle. Lucy was getting dinner and Ann was helping, while they told Frank about the Deacon, and he told them about his various misfortunes between Rumford and Winchester. "When I finally got the damn car started," he was saying, "the road was so damn slippery I couldn't go more than ten miles an hour— just like glass it was—and I thought I'd never get there—"

Archer was introduced to Frank, whom he had expected to find a cross between Solomon and Clark Gable. He was a little disappointed when Lucy's husband turned out to be an ordinary-looking man of about forty, slightly built and of average height, although lean and wiry. He had a pleasant face, with humor in it, long-lashed bright blue eyes, and reddish hair, now standing on end where he had run his hands through it. He looked shrewd, but didn't seem to justify Lucy's abnormally high opinion of his ability and wisdom.

As a matter of fact, though, Frank Patterson was extremely able, as well as being one of those men who always seem to have good luck in their ventures. He needed to be able, as well as fortunate, to make more than a bare living on a New England farm!

The hired man, Luke Prindle, was also on hand, having arrived at his usual time or a little later. Luke was middle-aged and bald, with a mild, sheep-like face. A few words with him convinced Archer that, unless he was the world's finest actor, he knew nothing about Deacon Grimm's death. In fact, he appeared to know very little about anything, outside his regular farm work, although he was an enthusiastic movie fan, and well acquainted with the private lives and loves of his favorite stars. But as a potential murderer or even a useful witness, he seemed to be a total loss. He had not been alone for more than five minutes since he left the farm with his brother on the previous afternoon; he had been in the bosom of his brother's family all the evening; and, furthermore, he had been sick in the night, from about nine o'clock on, and was able and willing to produce seven or eight relatives, "in-laws," and neighbors to bear witness to the fact. Thankful to dismiss one suspect, Archer warned him not to talk and let him go back to his work.

The sergeant's talk with Frank Patterson wasn't wholly satisfactory, either. Frank went over his adventures in detail; but his narrative was entirely uncorroborated, as yet, and a good deal of it would be difficult, if not impossible, to check. If Frank was telling the truth, (that was the great trouble, everybody's story had to be prefaced with that if), but *if* Frank was, he had been seventy-odd miles away when the crime took place, tinkering with the engine of a hireling Chevrolet, somewhere on the road between the village of Pinkney and the city of Winchester. He explained further that a delayed visit to the "rest room" during the stop at Pinkney had resulted in his missing the bus. "I didn't think they were going to leave in such an all-fired hurry," he said sheepishly. "It takes some of the conceit put of a fellow when his friends drive off without him, and don't even miss him for five miles!"

Frank was friendly, cordial, and ready to help; anything he could do, he said, he would be glad to do. He even went

so far as to invite Archer to make his headquarters there at
the house, instead of going back and forth to Rumford, or
seeking the dubious hospitality of a certain Mrs. Winckler, who took "summer boarders," and would (presumably)
take winter ones also, if pressed. After consideration, Archer decided to accept this invitation. In some ways, he
would have preferred the Winckler ménage, but the opportunity to live on the spot, among some of the people
closely involved in the case, seemed to him too good to
pass up. Also, time might be saved by the arrangement;
and the sergeant may not have been wholly uninfluenced
by the comfortable room put at his disposal, and Mrs.
Patterson's excellent cooking, as well as other things. Various personal belongings which Haley had brought out for
his colleagues were therefore taken upstairs to one of the
spare rooms.

The prints and reports that Haley had brought Archer
put away for later study. There was time before dinner to
visit the Deacon's empty house, so he took the Deacon's
keys, which he had retained for the purpose, and set out
again, hoping that the house where the dead man had lived
could contribute some information about him.

Henry Burke was left to keep unobtrusive watch over
the others, and to enjoy the tantalizing smells that escaped
from the oven.

Lucy and Ann discussed their situation with Frank,
whose voice was likely to rise when he was excited. "But
why did the Deacon come over here?" he demanded. "After
what I told him last month—"

Lucy pinched him, and looked warningly toward the
sitting room where Burke was ensconced.

Frank lowered his voice. "Anyway," he continued, "I
think we better do about as this fellow Brett wants us to,
as long as he's reasonable. If we don't agree to what he asks
as a request, he might repeat it as an order. I guess likely

he could. He seems a decent sort, and I don't think it would pay to antagonize him, the way we're fixed."

"Do you think we ought to consult a lawyer?" Ann asked.

He looked at her quizzically. "I don't know. We didn't kill the Deacon, just because he was found in our barn. At least, I know damn well I didn't, and I don't s'pose either of you did?"

"Of course not," Lucy said. "But will he believe us? Ann thought it might be wise to see a lawyer, just on general principles."

"Lord knows I don't like lawyers," Ann said. "It's only this: if Sergeant Brett keeps on the case I wouldn't worry much. He seems intelligent and conscientious, and fair, too. But if he should have to hand it over to Golding, well, you know what a rotten, crooked grafter Golding is! He'd probably arrest one of us as being the easiest and handiest, me, for choice. And then he'd never look any farther, but would push a conviction through, just to bolster up his reputation. You know that would be just like him!"

Frank admitted that her fears were not unfounded. "Leave it this way," he suggested. "As long as Brett's in charge, we'll do as he says, and help him along, within reason. If Golding takes over, we'll have a lawyer right off, the best one we can get. And Golding wouldn't necessarily pick on you, Ann; he doesn't love me any too well; I worked against his nomination, and he hasn't forgotten it."

That course of action settled, they returned to speculations concerning Deacon Grimm, and certain persons who would have been happier without him. But they refrained from mentioning names, so Henry Burke learned little from the words and phrases he overheard. When Archer returned, dinner was on the table. It came up to even Henry Burke's expectations!

The Deacon's house had been a disappointment, Archer said. In a rapid but fairly thorough inspection of it, he had found nothing suspicious or even significant. Clarabel had evidently done a better job of housekeeping there than in her own home, for everything had been orderly and clean. But the papers in the Deacon's desk were ordinary, and nowhere were there any indications of the fate that had been in store for Leonard Grimm. It seemed as if he had simply put on his outer garments, that stormy Saturday night, and walked out of the house, locking the doors behind him. Everything looked as if he had intended and expected to return. But he hadn't.

Halfway through dinner, Dr. Partridge called up. He had finished the autopsy, and would have the official report ready that night. "The actual facts," he said, "are about as I told you. Grimm died as a result of internal hemorrhages caused by the sharp points of the pitchfork. It's all down in technical language. The time of death I gave you was approximately right; a chemical analysis of the stomach content showed that death took place around nine-thirty o'clock. I don't take much stock in that stomach content business," he added parenthetically, "but they swear by it nowadays. Anyway, the time of death stands, about as I told you." He stopped.

"Is that all?" Archer inquired.

"No," Dr. Partridge admitted, "there's something else. I suspected it when I looked him over, but I wanted to make sure before I said anything. He was full of dope."

"What?" Archer cried.

"I thought that'd make you sit up," the doctor said, with satisfaction in his voice. "Yes, Deacon or not, he took cocaine, and was, I should judge, a regular addict over quite a long period; his general condition indicated that. Better find out who was selling the Deacon snow,

Archer—our Federal friends will want to know. Just another little chore for you!"

Archer said something uncomplimentary. "Anything else?"

"No, not now," Dr. Partridge said sweetly. "Isn't that enough?"

Archer agreed that it was. He rang off, after arranging for a meeting the next day with the doctor, Golding, and Captain Randall, if the latter arrived home. "I'll hope to have a lead by that time," he said. But to himself he thought, "Hope is the word!"

After dinner Archer sent Henry Burke off on a gossip hunt, as he called it. "Collect, all the dirt you can," he told Henry. "Make whatever excuses you want to, but get people talking about the Deacon, and find out all you can about him. Learn what you can about the people here, too, and about Lafond and his wife. You can take the car. Don't let out any more about the murder itself than you have to, but you won't be able to avoid spilling the actual fact; they'll have to know about it pretty soon anyway." He added, "I know you're good at this kind of thing, Henry; that's one reason I wanted you to work with me."

Gratified, Henry Burke departed.

Haley had brought out a compact but complete fingerprint kit; Archer now took everybody's prints, including Tad's. No one made any objection, and Tad showed great interest in the process. He had already decided, in his own mind, to be a detective like Sergeant Brett, when he was old enough.

Frank took an after-dinner nap on the sitting room couch—he was behind on his sleep. So were Lucy and Ann, but apparently they didn't feel the loss; they were absorbed in the Sunday papers that Trooper Haley had considerately brought from Rumford. Tad returned to his beloved jigsaw puzzle. Archer envied him. That puzzle, he surmised, would be fitted together long before his was solved. He set to work comparing fingerprints, a job he hated. Outside, intermittent snowflakes drifted down, and the leaden sky remained unchanged.

At the end of an hour, the sergeant was convinced that the fingerprints were a frost. There were plenty of them, but they all belonged to members of the household, and were in places where no suspicion could attach to them. No prints corresponding to the Deacon's had been found anywhere in the house or barn (not even on the ash trays), which Archer took to mean that Lucy and Ann had told the truth up to a point, anyway. Archer felt that it was a waste of time to pore over those miserable whorls and lines any longer. It might be far more profitable to pay a visit to the Buckleys, who were an unknown quantity so far. Also, he might catch Danny Cheever there, away from Gus and Clarabel's influence.

Archer was a little dubious about leaving Ann and the Pattersons alone, but decided that if they wanted to hatch any schemes they had had ample chance to do it already, and it wouldn't do any harm to leave them now. The snow would insure their staying in the house, and he put into effect a simple trick that would make the telephone useless while he was gone.

He had tried to extract some useful information from Tad, but learned only that; (1) Tad's father was going to run the town differently when *he* got to be Selectman; (2) Ann had given him (Tad) a stamp album, and he could already tell Chinese stamps from Japanese; and (3) his mother had as good as promised him a bicycle next spring if he got promoted in school. Those were the only subjects on which Tad grew conversational; all others failed to interest him, and the sergeant's questions met with silence or a mumbled, "I dunno." Archer gave Tad up as a bad job. He hoped the Buckleys would prove more communicative.

It had finally stopped snowing, but the sky was still lowering, as if prepared to start in again any minute. As Archer walked past the Grimm barn, Luke Prindle appeared in the doorway; he was caring for the Deacon's stock temporarily.

The Buckleys' place, seen close to, looked attractive and well cared for—a Colonial-type farmhouse, restored and modernized. It was surrounded by a neat picket fence with a gate in it, and altogether was more pretentious and luxurious than either the Grimm or Patterson farms.

The front door was opened by Mrs. Buckley—as soon as she spoke Archer recognized that rich, voluptuous voice. He thought that when she had been younger that voice hadn't been the only voluptuous thing about Rhoda Buckley. She must be forty-nine or fifty now; but before her tall figure grew too heavy and her black hair turned iron-gray, she must have been a handsome woman. Her dark eyes were effective still, and her voice; but her other charms had gone the way of all flesh, and he had an impression that she resented this fact out of all proportion.

She smiled in a friendly fashion, and invited him into a modem, well-furnished living room. He must take off his coat. Her husband was away, down to the Village, but would be home before long. What could she do for him? Of course she had heard about poor Leonard—she was the first person who had called the Deacon by his Christian name—but she didn't know anything about what had happened. Danny, who told her the news, had known only the bare fact. She talked smoothly along, in that creamy, melodious voice, and Archer discovered that he didn't need to ask questions at all; Mrs. Buckley seemed to anticipate them. She had a persuasive way of talking, and the sergeant suddenly caught himself answering her casually put questions. That would never do. He steered her back to a general discussion of Deacon Grimm's relations with his neighbors, and found her ready to talk about them at length, with seeming intelligence and insight. Archer began to think he had come to the right place, if it was information he wanted; Mrs. Buckley showed none of the misguided reticence which had prevented Lucy and Ann from telling all they knew. But he realized that he must be careful not to swallow whole everything that Mrs. Buckley told him. There was danger of it, for she was a convincing talker. He broke in, referring to her last remark:

"Then you think perhaps Miss Barbour had some grudge against Deacon Grimm?"

"Oh no." Mrs. Buckley smilingly denied such an implication. "I wouldn't say that. But, naturally, she resented what he did in connection with Forrest Martin, when they were going together. Of course, if Forrest had amounted to anything, he would have stayed to face things, instead of running away, but—"

"Wait a minute," Archer interrupted, "Who's Forrest Martin?"

"Oh!" She seemed surprised. "Hasn't Ann told you about him? No, I suppose she wouldn't, under the, circumstances. Well, he owned the old Wayland place, across the road from us; and he and Ann were, well, everyone expected them to get married; they'd gone together long enough. Leonard held a mortgage on the place, and when Forrest couldn't keep up his payments, Leonard foreclosed, naturally. Forrest, who had an insane temper, took it very badly, and made all kinds of threats against Leonard. Leonard was really in fear of his life, for Forrest was a big man, and younger than Leonard, and, as I said, had this terrible temper. But when Leonard took steps to protect himself, and swore out a warrant for Forrest's arrest, Forrest disappeared; and nobody seems to know where he went, or where he is now. Unless Ann does," she added, with a movement of her plump shoulders.

This was all news to Archer. He would have a few more questions to ask Miss Ann DeLacey Barbour. He suspected, although she had not said so, that Mrs. Buckley was not overfond of Ann; that fact might color her story, of course. But she did not strike him as being a spiteful woman, and the whole tone of her conversation seemed tolerant and reasonable. Archer inquired about the Lafonds and Danny Cheever.

"Yes, poor Danny," Rhoda Buckley said. "He doesn't have a very good home life, I'm afraid. I wouldn't say a word against Clarabel to him, for she's his sister, and he thinks the world of her; but, after all, she's not the proper person to look after a delicate boy like Danny. And while I don't like to talk against anyone, I do think that Gus Lafond is a very bad influence over any young person. He drinks, and I've even heard that he takes drugs. I do what I can to help Danny, but it's very difficult."

Archer let her talk. If he had known that such a ready source of information was so close at hand, he might not have sent Burke all the way to Highbrook Village after gossip. But it was a good plan to get various viewpoints; there was always the danger that one person might be prejudiced or misinformed. Mrs. Buckley seemed to have a pretty comprehensive knowledge of all the Highbrook inhabitants add their doings, and she liked to discuss them. But she had comparatively little to say about Leonard Grimm himself; only that his death came as a shock to her, and that she would miss him, although he had not always been an ideal neighbor. But she refused to enlarge on his faults, if any, merely remarking charitably that they were just "his way."

At five o'clock, as Mr. Buckley had not returned, Archer felt that he had absorbed all he could, for the time being, and took his departure. Rhoda assured him that she and her husband were at his service, and would be delighted to help him in any way they could. Archer thanked her; then, seeing Danny Cheever's tall figure half-walking, half-running down the road, he hurried after him. But the boy's awkward gait was surprisingly fast, and the sergeant decided he would save his breath and interview Danny later. He returned to the Pattersons'.

Rhoda Buckley watched him out of sight. Her dark eyes were bright, and faint color showed in her olive cheeks. "An attractive young man," she thought, "and not a fool, either. I shall be glad to help him whenever I can. It will be a real pleasure!"

Archer restored the telephone to normal, and asked Tad, who was still working over his puzzle, if he would fetch Ann Barbour, wherever she was. Tad obliged, and presently Ann came in, dressed in black again, but minus her silver earrings. Archer thought he could succeed better as an inquisitor without Tad for an audience, so Ann persuaded her young cousin to retire to the kitchen temporarily. Frank and Lucy were upstairs.

Ann closed the door after Tad, and looked at Archer inquiringly.

He said bluntly, "Where is Forrest Martin now, Miss Barbour?"

Ann was badly startled, but she recovered quickly. "I don't know."

"Why didn't you tell me about him—" he emphasized "him" "when I asked what people might have reasons for hating Deacon Grimm?"

Ann replied promptly, "Because Forrest has been away from Highbrook for more than a year. I didn't see that it had anything to do with him. I don't now."

"Don't you?" Archer thought, but he only said, "Is it true that you were engaged to marry Forrest Martin?"

Ann raised her chin, and looked at him as if he were something definitely malodorous. "You've been listening

to Rhoda Buckley, haven't you? Yes, I was engaged to Forrest. I still am." She was quite calm.

"If I could only make her mad," the sergeant thought,
"I might learn something." He said, and tried to make it
sound insulting, "You're engaged to a man, but you don't
know where he is?"

"I don't."

"Have you seen him since he left Highbrook?"

"No."

"Have you heard from him?"

Ann said, "I shan't tell you anything more. I don't consider it's any of your business."

"Hell," thought Archer, "this won't get me anywhere.
I'll be the one to get mad, if this keeps up!" He counted ten to himself, and held back the reply he wanted to
make. Instead, he said, "Please remember I have to ask
these questions, Miss Barbour. I don't want to. I did listen
to what Mrs. Buckley had to say, naturally; but I'll gladly
listen to whatever you have to say, if you'll only say it!"

Ann lighted a cigarette. "What did Rhoda tell you?"

Archer gave her an abridged resume of Mrs. Buckley's
remarks about Forrest Martin. "Is that the truth?" he
wanted to know.

"It's a malicious distortion of the truth," Ann declared
angrily, "with half the facts left out. Forrest hasn't got
an insane temper. Any threats he may have made against
the Deacon were only threats to protect his own interests.
The Deacon deliberately broke an agreement they had; he
had no right, moral or legal, to foreclose that mortgage,
but when he did, Forrest didn't have the money or the influence to fight him. Forrest did talk too much, I admit,
but he had plenty of reason, and Deacon Grimm talked
far worse against Forrest, and made worse threats than he
did, too. Rhoda didn't tell you that, did she? I don't know
where Forrest is, but he didn't have anything to do with
the Deacon's death, I know that!"

"I wish you'd be more frank with me, Miss Barbour."

"That's all I can tell you. If you want to believe what Rhoda Buckley says, go ahead and believe it. She hates me, and she'll probably tell you all kinds of things, if she hasn't already. It's quite immaterial to me."

Archer began to realize that he had been right when he thought this girl looked as if she might be hard to manage. He prayed for patience, but was inspired to say just the wrong thing. He said, "She showed a much more reasonable attitude than you've done, Miss Barbour."

Ann said frigidly, "No doubt. If Rhoda's reasonable, I'm thankful to say I'm not like her. I don't go throwing hints and accusations around, in a swarmy kind of way, the way she does. If I did, I'd say that she's as capable of killing the Deacon as anybody, and I know she hated him, too, for some reason. But I'm not going to say another word. If you don't believe what I've told you, ask Lucy and Frank."

"I intend to," Archer said grimly. He was almost ready to say that he would enjoy seeing Golding taking a crack at this aggravating girl. The State's Attorney wouldn't stand for any back talk. Maybe, when Golding was browbeating her, as he knew how to do, she'd realize how indulgent and forbearing he, Archer Brett, had been. Maybe she'd understand— "Stop it, you fool!" he told himself.

Ann said suddenly, "I'm sorry. I'm tired, and it's been pretty upsetting. And it makes me so mad to have people talk that way about Forrest, when he can't defend himself. He always got blamed for things, whether he did them or not. And now to try and lay this on him, when he isn't anywhere around. . . ." she sighed, "But, honestly, I can't tell you anything more about him. Please believe me."

"Very well, Miss Barbour," Archer said stiffly. "That's all for the present. Will you ask Mrs. Patterson to come in for a few minutes now? Perhaps she'll be more helpful than you've been." He half expected a retort, but Ann left the room without answering.

Lucy, unlike Ann, was willing enough to talk; but, like her cousin, had nothing that was new to impart. For all her frank planner, Archer thought that she was keeping something back, too; not an actual fact, perhaps, but some idea or suspicion or hunch that might be useful to him if he could discover it. But he couldn't. He asked about the trouble between the Deacon and Forrest Martin, and got what might be termed a neutral reply. It was true that Forrest had talked unwisely about the Deacon. But Lucy thought that there was probably something to be said on Forrest's side. She didn't understand about mortgages and things, but she didn't doubt the Deacon had been unreasonable and grasping. Yes, she knew that Ann and Forrest had been engaged, but was quite sure Ann didn't know Forrest's present whereabouts. Ann hadn't wanted him to leave Highbrook, Lucy knew; but Forrest had his own way of doing things, and was as stubborn as forty mules. He hadn't liked the idea of being told what to do by any woman, not even Ann. So he had suited himself and disappeared. And Ann felt it.

"Did they have a quarrel?" Archer inquired.

Lucy didn't know, but thought not.

Archer asked more questions, about the Lafonds, the Buckleys, the church people; but Lucy was tactfully unhelpful. She didn't think much of Gus Lafond, and considered Clarabel a morally irresponsible moron, but that was as far as she would go. Mrs. Buckley she had always liked, and Mr. Buckley was a harmless old thing who wouldn't hurt a fly. Archer became immediately suspicious of Mr. Buckley. These harmless old things who wouldn't hurt flies sometimes went haywire and did unbelievable things. But the person he was most interested in was the missing

Forrest Martin. They would have to broadcast for him, and send out a general police flyer, with description, and so on. Probably Martin would then show up in Miami or South Bend with a perfect alibi. But he'd have to be found, that was sure.

Lucy thought that the church people were all unlikely suspects. "I can't see the minister doing it," she said, "though I heard they had some trouble over a girl in the congregation. But I don't know a thing about it, and it was probably just talk."

Archer questioned her again about the discovery of the Deacon's body, but she couldn't (or wouldn't) tell him anything he didn't already know. He asked if Ann had seemed upset when she came in after finding the Deacon.

Lucy gave him the kind of a look usually reserved for half-wits. "Well, naturally!" she said indignantly.

"How badly upset?"

"Why, I can't tell. She seemed kind of pale and shaky—who wouldn't be? It's a wonder she didn't faint, I know I would have, if I'd been the one to find him!"

"Was she gone very long? Ten minutes? Five minutes? Fifteen minutes?"

But Lucy couldn't tell. It hadn't seemed long; that was all she knew.

Not much help there.

Archer asked, without much hope, "Did your husband ever have any unpleasantness with the Deacon?"

For the first time, Lucy was slow to answer, and seemed unready with a reply. At last she said, "They didn't agree about politics. Frank's going to run for Selectman next spring, and the Deacon wanted a friend of his to have it."

"They never had any other trouble?"

"No," Lucy replied, but her tones lacked conviction.

"Aha," thought the sergeant, "something there?" But if there was, he failed again to find it. Lucy stuck to it that, while not particularly fond of each other, Frank and the Deacon had had no definite trouble that she knew of.

Seeing that his persistence was making her more set, Archer dropped the subject, and by the time Lucy left to see about lunch, she was her usual self, to all appearances. Archer asked her to send her husband in to answer a few questions, and she did so. But he thought she gave Frank a warning look, as she left him at the door. Or was that his imagination?

Frank was not difficult, like Ann, nor helpfully noncommittal, like Lucy. He gave his opinions freely, but didn't seem deeply concerned whether the sergeant believed him or not. Archer asked him the same questions that he had asked Lucy, about Ann and the missing Forrest, and got much the same replies, except that Frank volunteered the opinion that Forrest was too pigheaded for his own good. "Sometimes you've got to give in to the other fellow," Frank went on sagely. "Or pretend to, anyway, even if you're right and he's wrong. I've found that out." Asked if he had any idea where Forrest was, Frank said he hadn't. "But I wouldn't believe he had anything to do with killing the Deacon," he added, "even if he was somewhere around here. And he isn't, so far as I know."

The Lafonds Frank considered not very desirable citizens. "Clarabel's a damned pretty little bitch," he declared, with more frankness than delicacy, "but she's a bad actor. I guess Gus is a kind of a bad egg, too, but he seems to mind his own business pretty well, though God only knows what it is! He's in with some pretty shady characters over to Rumford, I've heard. And they throw some pretty wild parties down there, sometimes. Still, they don't bother us much, though I admit I wouldn't be sorry if they left town."

Mr. Patterson's opinion of the Buckleys coincided with his wife's, except that he credited Warner Buckley with greater capabilities than Lucy had done. "He's a queer old duck," Frank said, "but not half such a fool as he looks." Asked about Mrs. Buckley, he replied that he guessed she was all right, although inclined to want to run other peoples' affairs.

"She likes her own way, like all women," he went on, "and she's pleasant enough when she gets it, as she 'most always does. She married Buckley for his money—he's got a lot—and he's twenty years older than she is. But I think sometimes that maybe it doesn't do her quite as much good as she expected. Still, she ought to be satisfied. She's got a big car to run around in, and piles of clothes, and a summer place up on the lake. She belongs to a lot of societies and things over to Rumford, too, and has a swell time, from what I hear, bossing the other women and running things generally. If Buckley wasn't quite so old and dried-up, I guess she'd think she was pretty well fixed, as she damn well is, considering how hard up lots of folks are these days! She's always thought, I guess, that she'd have plenty of cash when the old man died, and could maybe take up with something a little livelier; but recently I've heard that he's put a lot of his money into these annuities, so that at least some of it will die with him. But I don't know whether that's true or not." He lighted his pipe, "Don't let on to Lucy that I told you all that. She likes Rhoda, and thinks she has a hard time. Maybe she does, in a way."

Archer, too, thought, that Frank was unjust to Mrs. Buckley, who had impressed him as being well contented with her circumstances. But he realized that he would have to see Buckley before forming a final opinion. He said casually, "I understand you and the Deacon didn't see eye to eye where local politics are concerned? Did you ever have any trouble with him on that account?"

Frank puffed at his pipe. "Had a few arguments, one time and another, Nothing serious."

"Ever do much business with him?"

"No," Frank said. "The Deacon was a bad man to do business with. I told Forrest that, in connection with that mortgage of his. The only way to get along with Leonard Grimm was not to have any dealings with him, really."

Archer nodded. "It's funny," he said reflectively, "that Grimm came over here that night, when he must have known you were away."

Frank removed his pipe and sat forward in his chair. "What do you mean by that?" he demanded.

"Well, your wife says everybody knew you were going to be away this weekend, so the Deacon must have known it. He evidently had some reason for coming over here that wasn't connected with you."

To his astonishment, this innocent-sounding remark had an unexpected effect. Frank Patterson laid down his pipe and glared at the sergeant. "What are you trying to get at, Brett?"

Archer stared at him. He had wondered whether those bright blue eyes and that reddish hair meant that Mr. Patterson possessed a temper, but had seen no signs of it heretofore. He said, "Nothing in particular. I only thought. . . ."

"If you think he came to see my wife," Frank barked angrily, "you've got another think coming! She's not that kind. My wife's straight, and don't you forget it! By God, if I thought. . . ."

Archer interrupted. He said coldly, "I had no idea of reflecting on Mrs. Patterson in any way. I never even thought of such a thing." He looked at Frank steadily. "What makes you think I did?"

Frank cooled down as rapidly as he had flared up. "All right, all right, of course you didn't. My fault for being a fool. But the Deacon was always running after women, and I've an idea he'd bothered Lucy once or twice when I was away, though she never said anything about it to me. When you said what you did, I thought you meant . . .”

“Well, I didn’t,” Archer told him. But to himself, he thought, “If he gets mad so easy with no reason at all, what would he do, given provocation? Or what he might believe was provocation?” He wished these people weren’t all so darned touchy. Mrs. Buckley was the only one of them who had talked freely and without trying to hide something. Pretty soon he would get tired of trying to handle everybody with kid gloves, so’s not to hurt their feelings! What was he supposed to be, anyway, a policeman or a nursemaid?

Frank Patterson broke in on his indignant reflections. “Come along,” he said. “Lucy says lunch is ready.”

Henry Burke came back before the sandwiches were all eaten, and in plenty of time for the gingerbread with whipped cream. Deacon Grimm’s death had made a sensation, all right, he reported. It had leaked out, of course, probably through the Lafonds, and was the universal topic of conversation among the townspeople, old and young, rich and poor—as the newspapers were soon to put it. But Burke waited until the Patterson household had gone to bed—they went early—before going into details.

“We better talk down here,” the sergeant said, seating himself at the desk. “I want to take notes, and this is the only fairly decent light in the house. This kerosene lamp business is one thing I don’t like about the country. Well, you were gone quite a while. Did you get any dirt?”

Henry Burke relaxed in an armchair and ruffled his close-cropped hair. “Did I get any dirt? Say, I got so much I needed a truck to bring it back in, pretty near.”

“Let’s have it then. Or shall I say, dump it?”

“There’s so damn much,” Henry said, “I don’t know where to start. Well, in the first place, there don’t seem to be anybody in town that the Deacon was on real good terms with. He's had some kind of a row, at one time or another, with 'most everybody. Even with the church folks: he scrapped with the other deacons and ordered the minister 'round, and bullied the Ladies' Aid. Though I wouldn't go so far as to say any of the church bunch hated him enough to bump him off; they seemed pretty used to him and his ways. But he was a mean cuss. Did you know he and Patterson had a heck of a row about a month ago?"

"No, where was that?"

"Right down at the store in the Village. The storekeeper told me about it. Seems Patterson wants to run for Selectman, but the Deacon had a crony he wanted to have the job. He told Patterson to lay off, or he'd see he got defeated. Patterson went up in the air and called the Deacon a few things, and said he'd be Selectman or know the reason why. They didn't come to blows quite, but pretty near, I gathered. Anyway, the Deacon said he'd show Patterson it didn't pay to oppose him. Patterson raises apples, and he was all set to sell a lot of them to the buyer for the State. But after the row the Deacon hustled around and pulled strings somehow so that Patterson lost the contract, a pretty juicy one, I guess. He was plenty mad, the storekeeper said, and named a few things he'd like to see happen to the Deacon.

"Then Grimm had a regular feud with his next-door neighbors, the Buckleys. I saw old Buckley. He's a—well, wait till you see him! Their trouble started over a boundary line; it was quite a while ago, and I didn't get all the details. But last spring the Deacon built a pig pen on what *he* said was the line, and it was right close up to the Buckleys' sun parlor, though it was quite a ways from his own house. Old man Buckley was hopping mad over that, and went to law about it, but nothing's settled yet. Then—"

"Hold on a minute," Archer said. He scribbled rapidly. "All right, go on, but talk slower."

"The Deacon's sister and her son," Burke continued, "seem to be nice folks; everybody spoke well of them. By the way, did you get an answer to the telegram you sent them?"

"Yes, they got it, and telegraphed back. They aren't coming home, but have made arrangements for the funeral, and will be back in about a month. The son sent the wire; he said he didn't see what good they could do by coming back right away, and he thought it'd be too hard for his mother. He didn't sound very badly cut-up, I thought."

"That let's them out, though," Henry said. "Unless they hired somebody to do the job while they're away, that is. Where was I? Oh yes, about the Lafond crowd: the man is a tough bird who used to be a bootlegger, back in Prohibition times. Nobody seems to know what he does now, but he always has cash enough, apparently. The girl is a—well, I wouldn't necessarily believe what the women said about her, but most of the men agreed it was about right. The Deacon didn't hire her just for her housekeeping services, that's sure! I don't know whether Lafond knew it, but everybody else did. She's a regular little—" Burke employed a good old Anglo-Saxon word which is still frowned upon in polite society.

"What about the boy, Danny Cheever?"

Henry said that most people had seemed rather sorry for Danny. "Of course, there were one or two who tried to make out he was dangerous and ought to be shut up; but most of 'em thought he was a good boy, even if he isn't quite right in his upper story. They seemed to think Lafond and his wife don't treat him very good, even if she is his sister. But hardly anybody thought he killed the Deacon. That's no sign he didn't, though. I s'pose these goofies are always likely to break out, maybe."

Archer told the trooper he wasn't qualified to act as a psychiatrist. "Did you learn anything new about the people here? Miss Barbour?"

"I was just getting to them. I guess the Barbour girl never had much to do with the Deacon; she's pretty stand-offish. But she may have had it in for him indirectly. Seems she was going with a fellow, Martin his name was, and—"

"I heard all that," Archer said, and related what Rhoda Buckley had told him, with Ann's subsequent corrections. Henry nodded, and said that a majority of the townspeople considered Forrest Martin the most logical candidate for the role of killer; he was known to have threatened the Deacon in the past, and he apparently lacked that background of success or substance which automatically places a man above suspicion, in the average mind. "Then," Henry said thoughtfully, "the Barbour girl may have had it in for the Deacon on her own account. I found out he was in the habit of making passes at all the women who are young or good-looking, and she acts like the sort that wouldn't stand for that kind of thing. Though all women are pretty much alike," Henry added, remembering that he was a hard-boiled policeman, without illusions.

"You better not try to prove that theory," Archer said. "Was there anything about Mrs. Patterson?"

"N—no, not especially. Somebody said she was pretty sore when the Deacon did her husband out of that contract . . ."

(So Lucy had known about that!)

"But she seemed pretty popular, on the whole," Henry concluded.

"Did you learn anything more about this Martin?"

"Not much. You see," Henry explained, "I didn't concentrate on any one suspect, but tried to get a general idea of the lot. I thought that was what you wanted."

"You did okay," Archer told him, trying not to grin. "Well, here's what I found out. I think if we pool our discoveries they may make more sense." He told about his conversations with the Pattersons, Ann, and Mrs. Buckley, and of his failure to learn anything from Tad. "I pumped that kid the best I knew how," he said, "but I didn't get a darn thing out of him. He likes me pretty well, too. He's just naturally close-mouthed."

"He's a regular clam," Henry Burke agreed. "So you think the girls are lying, do you?"

Archer said, "They may be telling the truth, but I'm darned sure it isn't the whole truth. They know (or think they know) something they aren't telling; I'll bet my next month's pay on that."

"Let Golding get after 'em," Henry suggested.

Archer shook his head, "He wouldn't get any more. Even if he arrested 'em, if they stuck to their stories, he wouldn't have a thing on 'em, I'd say. That goes for the Lafond crowd, too. Anyway, I don't like Golding."

"D'you think Patterson's telling the truth?"

Archer shrugged. "I would have said so, but now. . . . hanged if I know. I'll have his story checked, but some of it can't be checked thoroughly, unless somebody that he doesn't know about happened to see him. A story like that's the devil to prove, even if it is true." He frowned.

"Could he have got back here any way, while he says he was stranded there between Pinkney and Winchester, d'you s'pose?"

Archer said, "We'll have to go over that carefully. It doesn't sound very probable, but . . ." The sergeant was thinking of how Frank had flared up at the unintentional implication that Deacon Grimm had been to see his wife. If he were jealous . . . but Archer was ready to swear that Lucy had never given her husband any cause for jealousy.

But some men didn't need any cause. They were just naturally unreasonably jealous—not normal in that respect. He would have to consider Frank and his alibi very carefully indeed. "What was the general opinion on Patterson?" he asked.

"Well," Henry returned, "he seemed pretty well liked. Two or three had it in for him, said he was too almighty sharp at a bargain. Probably he got the better of 'em over something. But the general opinion is that he's a hard worker and a good fellow. And you know what people are," Henry summed up sententiously. "Give 'em a chance to talk about their neighbors and they'll say anything. And gossip ain't evidence, after all."

Archer knew that. If he only had more facts! He had too much suspicion, and not enough proof; too much talk and gossip and insinuation and spite, and not enough honest truth-telling, He supposed that was what you always got when you pried into people's private lives; they all had something to hide, so they tried to distract attention from themselves by talking about the other fellow. Yet people were cruelly eager to uncover their neighbors' secrets, and even to gloat over them, when they proved sufficiently horrific; it was a well-known human failing. But, after all, Archer was not planning to write a treatise on behaviorism. He said, "Did you find out who the Deacon's lawyer is, Henry?"

"Yes, it's Munsell, of Munsell and Peet, in the Taylor Building. I know him by sight. I s'pose we get him to tell us who benefits from the crime, financially?"

Archer said that was the idea. "For instance, if we find the Deacon has left half his property to Mrs. Patterson, say, she looks much better as a suspect."

Henry grinned. "You leave Mrs. Patterson alone. Nobody that can make apple pie like hers could be a murderer. No, sir!"

Archer showed Burke the pictures and fingerprints, and the trooper agreed that they were disappointing. "There were no prints at all on the pitchfork, of course," Archer said. "That proves it was deliberately wiped clean. I didn't expect the fingerprint angle to amount to much—it seldom does—but I was hoping something might show up."

"Well," said Henry Burke, yawning, "what's next?"

Archer looked at the clock, which said twenty-seven minutes of one. "Bed's next," he said. "Tomorrow, I'll see the Captain and Golding; after that, what we do depends on them. Come on, and we'll see if we can sleep on a featherbed."

They could.

3
Monday—*Breathing Spell*

Monday Morning started in uneventfully. A good night's rest had restored the sergeant's optimism, and he was ready to overlook the irritations and annoyances that some of his suspects, if he had to call them that, had caused him. Lucy and Frank were comparatively cheerful during breakfast; but Ann was silent, and ate little. Archer thought she was hiding some strong excitement or emotion, and once he caught Tad looking at her with a curious expression. When he saw her return the boy's glance, the sergeant was sure that there was some understanding between them. But unless he used third-degree methods, he saw no prospect of discovering what it was, especially as Tad left soon after breakfast, boarding the school bus that would take him to Highbrook Village. Lucy had arranged for him to stay there with friends until the current excitement subsided.

Archer made some telephone calls and straightened out his notes. Captain Randall was no stickler for red tape, but he would require reports of some kind; and so would Golding, although *he* was sure to find fault with whatever the police did, or didn't, do. Well, Golding could go jump in the Lake. But to clarify certain facts for his own benefit, Archer decided to set them down, before he forgot any of them. He made a brief timetable of the pertinent events of the day and night of the Deacon's death:

Saturday, Nov. 4, 194–

11:30 a.m.—Frank Patterson leaves home to go to Rumford, in car with one Ray Sumner. (Verify.)

11:35 p.m.—Ann Barbour leaves home to go to Rumford shopping, in Patterson's car. (Confirmed by Mrs. Patterson and Tad.)

4:30 p.m.—Luke Prindle leaves with brother, in brother's car. (Confirmed by Mrs. P. and Luke's relatives.)

5:00 p.m. (about)—Frank P. misses bus, and gets left behind in village of Pinkney. (Verify details.)

5:30-40 p.m.—Ann Barbour returns from Rumford and puts car in barn. Nobody there then, alive or dead. (Only Ann B.'s word for this.) Shuts barn doors, she says, and goes into house. (Confirmed by Mrs. P. and Tad.)

6:30-7:00 p.m.—Clarabel and Gus Lafond return from Rumford. Clarabel goes to Deacon's house to get his supper. (Confirmed by the Lafonds and Danny C.)

7:45 p.m. (about)—Clarabel leaves Deacon Grimm's house, leaving him alive and o.k. she says. (Her return home confirmed by Gus and Danny. Deacon must have been alive then, in order to later reach Patterson's barn, presumably under his own power.)

Sometime between 9:30 and 10:00 p.m.—Ann B. goes to barn to inspect switch of car. Finds body.

10:00-10:15 p.m. (about)—Ann B. and Mrs. P. return to barn and examine body briefly.

(Confirmed by both girls and Tad, who
seems a sensible kid, for his age.)

10:30 p.m.—Mrs. P. calls telephone operator,
who calls police at once.

11:35 p.m.—Police and Dr. Partridge arrive
at Patterson farm.

11:40 p.m.—Police and doctor examine body.
Dr. P. gives his opinion death took place
between eight and ten p.m., roughly.

12:35 a.m.—Ambulance arrives.

12:55 a.m.—Frank Patterson's party, minus
Frank, arrives at Hotel Clinton, in Winchester. (Verify.)

1:25 a.m.—Ambulance leaves.

1:40 a.m.—Frank P. arrives Hotel Clinton,
and calls up from there. (Verify this very
carefully.)

That seemed to be the bare framework of events to date,
a skeleton on which to build up more facts as they were
discovered. Not a very complete skeleton, either, Archer
thought dubiously; several important pieces were missing.
But he left it as it was for the time being.

He told the Pattersons and Ann that they were free
to leave the house, but requested that they go no farther
afield than the Village. He realized that it was unfair to
keep them cooped up while other possible suspects were
allowed to roam more or less at large. But he urged them
not to talk, and promised that if they stayed indoors, Burke
would see to it that the reporters left them alone. Burke
was to stay in Highbrook while Archer went to Rumford,
and was instructed to watch what everybody did (insofar
as was possible) and where they went. The trooper thought
it was rather overestimating one man's abilities to expect
him to watch over the entire population of Highbrook

Ridge, but he said he would do his best. Archer gathered up his notes and drove away.

Frank departed to yard out some wood. Murders may come and murders may go, but farm work has to be done.

Lucy went about her usual housework. After helping her for an hour, Ann announced that she was going to take a short walk, if Burke had no objection. "I want to get some fresh air before those reporters get here," she said, "and before it rains." The clouds were still dark and heavy, but a noticeable rise in the temperature made rain a likely development.

Burke offered his services as escort, but Ann said that Bella was going with her. Poor Bella had spent most of her time since the Deacon's death shut up in bedrooms; she was frantically anxious to get out and race around in the snow.

While Ann was getting into her coat and overshoes, a brown Chevrolet sedan drove by the house, headed toward the Village and Rumford. "Gus and Clarabel," Lucy reported, "going to get in touch with a lawyer, or I miss my guess! I hope they aren't running away."

"Don't worry," Burke said, "the cops in Rumford and around will look after them."

Ann walked up the road in the wake of the Chevrolet, Bella floundering ahead of her with snow on her nose, in a transport of canine emancipation.

Burke stayed talking with Lucy for half an hour, until he had seen a large and succulent roast of pork into the oven. Then he went out and followed a rough track that led from the back of the barn to the wood lot where Frank and the hired man were working. Having made himself useful there for a while, he returned to the main road, walked toward the bridge, and then out the Old Road as far as the Lafond house. He had not yet seen the luscious Clarabel, or her sinister husband, and was half hoping that they had returned; but the brown Chevrolet was still absent. The trooper walked around the house, and behind it discovered a set of footprints in the snow, which led up over a bank and across a meadow, roughly parallel with the main road. Following these, he came out back of the Grimm house; evidently the prints belonged to Danny Cheever, for they continued across to the Buckleys' barn, and Burke saw a gangling form which he took to be Danny's carrying water to some hen houses beyond it.

Burke stopped to look at the controversial pig pen which the Deacon had built, not more than ten feet from the Buckleys' glassed-in sun parlor. That sun parlor must have been pretty malodorous in summer, Henry thought! What a mean devil Deacon Grimm must have been, to do a trick like that. But would anybody be likely to commit a murder on account of a pig pen? Henry Burke doubted it. He suddenly remembered the roast of pork, and headed for home.

When he got back to the Pattersons', he found three carloads of newspapermen cooling their heels (and the rest of their anatomies) on the piazza. They had taken numerous pictures of the house, the barn, and all other external points of interest; but they had not succeeded in getting inside the house to secure any interviews, although they were still hopeful that their patience would be rewarded eventually. Burke told them that there was nothing doing, and to beat it, which they finally did. But he saw all three cars stopping at the Buckleys' gate, a few minutes later.

Lucy unbolted the back door and let him in. "We kept them out," she announced triumphantly, in the tones of a besieged general when his reinforcements arrive. She seemed in good spirits, and Ann, who had returned from her walk, had also cheered up considerably. Archer had called up, to say that he wouldn't be there for dinner, but Henry Burke saw to it that the sergeant's portion wasn't wasted!

Soon after dinner, Archer returned, and, with him, Captain Randall and the State's Attorney. The Captain was a small, chipper, sparrow-like man, with gray hair brushed over a bald spot, and horn-rimmed glasses. He looked deceptively mild, rather like the pictures of Mr. Common Citizen, in Ding's cartoons. But he had been a major in 1917-18, and could swear very efficiently in four languages.

Mr. Felix Golding, on the other hand, looked what he was—a third-rate lawyer jockeyed into public office through politics and pull. He was tall and stocky, with the beginnings of a bay window, although he was barely forty. He had a pale, smooth face, supercilious eyebrows, and unpleasant colorless eyes, of the kind that look like marbles and have about as much expression. His voice was unctuous and his manner, although cordial enough to those whom he judged his equals, was rudely overbearing towards all the unfortunates whom he considered beneath him, either financially or socially. (He placed all policemen in this category.) Still, he was smart enough in his way, being clever at doctoring evidence, intimidating witnesses, and bullying people who were afraid to stand up to him. He was generally disliked outside of his own office, and even Frank Patterson, who was a dyed-in-the-wool member of Golding's party, admitted that the State's Attorney was so crooked you could screw him right into the ground! And that was an admission, coming from Frank, for he was a staunch party man.

Dr. Partridge and two of Golding's "yes men" occupied a second car, and three more cars of newspapermen followed. The threat of rain had been fulfilled; it was coming down in sheets, turning the snow to porous and unsightly mush. The cars were parked in the Pattersons' dooryard, and the official investigation got under way in earnest.

Later, when Lucy and Ann tried to recall the details of that afternoon, all they could remember was an endless

repetition of questions. They answered the Captain's questions and the State's Attorney's questions, and the doctor's
and the sergeant's and the newspapermen's (for several
favored reporters had come in with Golding). Being unable to prevent it, they allowed their pictures to be taken,
figuring that it was better to pose in a dignified way than
to be snapped while unaware. But they refused to smile for
publication. Indeed, Ann was informed later that it was a
wonder the photographer had not dropped dead when she
looked at him, or at least been forced to buy a new camera.

Frank was not interrogated very strongly at this stage.
It was Lucy and Ann, especially Ann, who bore the brunt
of the inquisition. But they stood it well, and were able
to avoid most of the pitfalls spread before them, although
they told their stories over and over. By half-past three
Captain Randall decided that he had heard enough from
them, for the present, and that the Lafonds deserved his
attention. But, before leaving, the whole party made a
farewell tour of the farm buildings, and inspected again
the chalk marks, which, instead of an X, marked the spot
where the body had been found. Mr. Golding held forth
to the reporters, but the Captain chewed on a cigar and
said little. Ann hoped fervently that Golding would catch
pneumonia from standing around in the rain; but she was
quite concerned for Archer, Captain Randall, and the doctor, who had all been as kind as was consistent with their
duty.

Finally, the whole cavalcade left to interview the Lafonds, and quiet descended. But it had been a trying afternoon, and when Archer returned to a very late supper, he
found Ann asleep on the couch and Lucy taking her third
aspirin for a bad headache. Even Frank looked weary,
and the sergeant advised everyone to go to bed early. He
planned to do so himself, for he expected the next day
to be a strenuous one. Henry Burke had gone reluctantly

back to Rumford with the Captain to do necessary routine
work. Among other things, agencies were being set in motion to discover the whereabouts of Forrest Martin, whose
description Archer had secured from sources outside the
Patterson household. Henry was also to look into the Deacon's past history, if any of it was on record in Rumford,
and to find out as much as he could about Gus Lafond.
He was supposed to check Frank Patterson's alibi, too, if
he could. Henry felt, privately, that while Archer might be
in charge of the case, he, Henry, was doing a good share
of the work. But he didn't mind much; the only thing he
grudged his superior was Mrs. Patterson's cooking!

After the others had gone to bed, Archer studied his
notes for awhile, reflecting with unworthy satisfaction that
the Captain and Golding and the reporters among them
had not learned anything more than he had already found
out for himself; perhaps not so much, for their methods
were not always tactful, especially Golding's. They had
gotten even less out of Gus and Clarabel Lafond than the
sergeant himself had done, although the photographers
had struck oil at last, taking enough pictures of Clarabel
to tickle the public taste for weeks to come. But, as far
as new facts went, or any new light cast on facts already
known, they might as well have stayed in Rumford. Archer
blew out the light and went upstairs. The house was dark
and quiet.

Archer Brett was a light sleeper. The slightest noise
would always wake him from the soundest slumber. So,
when he woke suddenly, he knew there must have been
some sound, although he couldn't recall hearing it. He
listened intently, but heard only the drumming of rain on
the tin roof, a depressing sound. His watch said twelve
minutes past three.

Archer slid out of bed, pulled on his raincoat in lieu of a bathrobe, thrust his feet into slippers, and grabbed his flashlight. He tiptoed to the door and opened it; all seemed dark and quiet. He crossed the hall and listened outside the other bedroom doors, but heard nothing. Then a sound came faintly from somewhere below—the gentlest possible closing of a door?

He went softly down the stairs, through the sitting room, and into the kitchen; all dark and still. Hoping earnestly that Bella wasn't loose, he switched on his light and inspected the kitchen. The door leading to the piazza was bolted on the inside, as he had left it. But the door leading to the shed, while still locked, was now unbolted. So what?

It certainly looked as if somebody had gone out, for something. . . . Should he try to follow? No chance of telling what direction they had taken, now. Better to wait for the wanderer's return, and find out who it was. Archer sat down in a rocking chair by the stove, turned off his light, and waited. He dozed, knowing that he would wake instantly at the first sound. . . .

There it was—the click of a key in the lock, the careful opening of a door. Archer put his finger on his light switch, ready to snap it on. The door closed very softly, and the bolt was shot. Now!

He pressed the switch. In the glaring circle of light Ann Barbour stood, one hand still on the doorknob. She wore a dark, fur-trimmed coat, but her hair was loose, held back by a narrow pink ribbon, and beneath the dark coat a foot of pale pink nightgown showed. She looked startled, but said not a word.

Archer set the flashlight upright on the table, so that it illumined the room. He said sternly, "What were you doing outside, Miss Barbour? You know nobody is supposed to go out at night, without permission. Where have you been?"

Ann looked at him coldly. "Really, Sergeant Brett," she replied in a freezing tone, "it is sometimes necessary to go out—out—er—out back, without asking the permission of anyone, even the police!" She turned and swept by him into the sitting room without another word, and he heard her going upstairs. Sergeant Brett felt himself blushing.

He looked at his watch—twenty-four minutes since he had first waked up. "That's one on me," he thought to himself. Then he stopped suddenly. He remembered now that when Ann had stood still and startled in the bright circle of light, he had noticed sparkling drops of moisture on her hair, and on the black fur of her coat. It was raining out-of-doors. But, to reach the place which Ann had modestly designated as "out back," it was not necessary to go out-of-doors at all. "Out back" opened off the shed, and while glacially cold, was quite dry.

"She's clever," Archer thought admiringly. "That was quick thinking!" He went into the shed and turned his light on the floor. Yes, there were faint, damp smudges easily visible. She had been outside, somewhere, and had come in through the barn. Come to think of it, her feet had showed incongruously black and clumsy below the pink nightgown. Overshoes!

Archer relocked the door and went back to bed. Too late to do anything about it tonight. He couldn't drag Ann from behind her locked door and give her the third degree. "But just you wait, my lady," he said to himself. "I'll find out what your game is, yet!" But he couldn't help admiring her nerve.

4
Tuesday—*The Gang's All Here*

The inquest was held at eight o'clock sharp on Tuesday morning, at the State Police headquarters in Rumford. It was purely a formality. In the unavoidable absence of Deacon Grimm's relatives, Clarabel Lafond identified the body, and told, haltingly, of her last visit to the Deacon's house. Nobody had yet been found who admitted to seeing Leonard Grimm alive after a quarter of eight Saturday night, when Clarabel claimed she had left him. Her testimony was kept strictly within limits, so that no interesting, scandalous possibilities were even hinted at.

Then Ann Barbour told her story of finding the body, as she had told it to Archer, and Lucy Patterson briefly corroborated it. (Both felt that they knew that story by heart, and could tell it backwards, almost.)

Dr. Partridge's evidence was short and highly technical (he made no reference to his discovery that Deacon Grimm was a cocaine addict); and Archer's was even shorter, being confined to a mere statement of his summons to Highbrook and his routine activities thereafter. If he entertained any ideas as to who killed Leonard Grimm or why, he gave no indication of them, nor of any future action that was contemplated.

The jurors were then instructed to bring in an open verdict of murder, which they immediately did: Deacon

Grimm, they opined, had been willfully murdered, by a person or persons unknown.

The reporters did their best with that, but were unable to make any very sensational bricks with such a meager amount of straw. The libel laws of the state were moderately strict, and careful papers did not encourage their employees to embroider facts to any great extent. But they had plenty of pictures, which is what counts most with the public nowadays.

The whole of Highbrook seemed to have attended the inquest, and Archer saw several of his possible suspects, although he had not requested their presence. He caught a glimpse of Mrs. Buckley talking earnestly to the *Rumford Eagle's* star reporter and a stranger whom he suspected of being an AP man. He didn't think she could do much harm by talking for publication at this stage of the case, but felt relieved when he saw her leaving with a tall, thin man, whom he took to be her husband. If she insisted on giving interviews later, he might have to do something about it. Clarabel was a danger, too, where the reporters were concerned; but Archer had an idea that her principal contribution to contemporary journalism would consist of those photographs of herself, in numerous delectable poses. Mr. Lafond would keep her pretty mouth shut; like the sergeant, he was not anxious for too much publicity.

Archer saw the Pattersons and Ann getting unobtrusively into their car; they were not talking, at any rate. He was hopeful that the press would soon tire of the Deacon's murder, or forget it altogether, in the rush of more urgent or widespread news. The football season was in full swing, and the "state of the nation" was controversial, as usual. Also, the situation in Europe was daily growing more critical—a fact that kept people's minds off murders, to a great extent. So the sergeant hoped to avoid too much "help" from the press. If Captain Randall could keep the

State's Attorney from interfering, the prospects for solving the case didn't look too bad, at times. At others, they seemed practically nonexistent. "Well, keep at it," Archer told himself, "and do your best." Angels, he recalled, could do no more.

After the inquest, the State's Attorney went out to give a few interviews; he had to think of his public!

"His public!" Captain Randall was disgusted. "As if he was a so-and-so fan dancer, or something!" He snorted.

Archer had told his commanding officer all the facts and, some of the suspicions that he had unearthed, and the Captain agreed with him that there wasn't yet enough evidence against anybody to warrant an arrest. They discussed a tentative program which the Captain thought was the most likely to bring results. "I ought to stay here and tackle the case myself," he declared, "It has some darned interesting possibilities. But this hunting trip is the first real vacation I've had in four years, and I don't mean to give it up if I can help it. Besides, I'm too old for gumshoe work; and it's time some of you younger men got used to a little responsibility. I'm going to leave you in charge of this Deacon Grimm affair. Use your own judgment, and if the newspapers holler, let 'em holler. I've talked to that—that windbag, Golding, and I don't think he'll interfere with you much. My wife will know how to reach me if it's an absolute, matter of life and death; but I'd like to see you finish up the case yourself, and good luck to you! Don't thank me," he warned, as Archer started to do so. "You may wish you'd never heard of Deacon Grimm before you're through!" They shook hands, and Captain Randall left in a hurry; he wanted to catch the 10:25, northbound.

Archer went to see Mr. Munsell, of Munsell and Peet, but the Deacon's lawyer, a precise and desiccated person, was not much help. Yes, he admitted cautiously, he had done some legal work for Mr. Grimm in the past, but he had never drawn up any will. The Deacon had often spoken of the advisability of making a will, but had never reached the point of doing it. "He may have had some other lawyer do it, of course," Mr. Munsell said, "or he may have done it himself. Some people do." His tone expressed his low opinion of such people. He disclaimed any knowledge of Deacon Grimm's private affairs, and if he suspected anyone of having removed his client from this vale of tears, he kept the suspicion to himself. He did not know whether or not he was the "M" referred to in the note found in Deacon Grimm's wallet. He might be the person to whom the Deacon had intended to impart "something," but he had no idea what it could be. He did not think that any of the legal snarls in which Mr. Grimm was currently involved could have resulted in any violence. He did not think that Mr. Grimm had any serious worries. He did not think that Mr. Grimm had carried any heavy insurance. He did not think—had Sergeant Brett looked in Mr. Grimm's safe deposit box?

Sergeant Brett hadn't, but he said "Good morning" to the cautious Mr. Munsell, and proceeded to untangle the red tape incidental to inspecting the Deacon's box in the vaults of the Rumford Fidelity and Trust Co. But he might have saved himself the trouble, for the box yielded no will, nor anything else that looked helpful; only considerable proof of the Deacon's financial stability, in the form of securities, bank books, deeds, mortgages, and so on. There wasn't even an envelope marked "To be opened in the event of my death." No, that was too much to expect!

Archer rather hoped no will would be found; it would be one complication the less, for without one the Deacon's property would presumably go to his sister, whose alibi was above suspicion. There was the very remote possibility that she or her son had hired a third party to dispose of the Deacon in their absence; but, without positive evidence to support it, he thought that possibility could be ignored for the present. There were enough without it!

Henry Burke remained in Rumford under protest. But the sergeant wanted him at headquarters, in case any information came in about Forrest Martin. So Henry sighed, and stayed.

Late in the afternoon, which he had spent in Highbrook, eliciting and checking alibis, Archer remembered with a start that he hadn't yet interviewed Mr. Warner Buckley, whom he had seen in the distance, and for an instant only, at the inquest. Therefore, right after supper, he walked over to the Buckleys', leaving Ann and Frank playing cribbage, while Lucy frowned over the intricacies of a sweater she was knitting. Archer hadn't had the opportunity to talk for more than a minute with any one of them since the inquest. He hadn't even taxed Ann with her deceit of the night before, thinking that perhaps it might be as well to let her believe that she had taken him in completely. But he hadn't forgotten it. When he had finished some of this everlasting running around, and had gotten the routine work well in hand, he hoped to tackle Ann again, and also the Lafonds and Danny Cheever. But unfortunately one man can do only one thing at one time, when it comes to investigating a murder.

Archer found the Buckleys at home, listening to a political harangue on the radio. Rhoda wore a discreetly designed dress of orchid, trimmed with black, and her gray hair had been newly washed and waved. She looked quite striking. Warner Buckley looked striking, too, but in a different way. He was tall and thin and stooping, with a long, bony face and prominent teeth, like an elderly horse. He was entirely bald, except for a modest fringe in back, and had a close-cut, bristling white moustache. But it was his peculiar mincing manner and voice that made

him seem such a queer fish. There was something effemi-
nate and spinsterish about him. If he had shaved his upper
lip and donned an appropriate wig, he could have passed
for a charter member of any Sewing Circle. Looking at
him, Archer was ready to believe that Rhoda had married
him for his money, as gossip said.

Mrs. Buckley received the sergeant with (metaphori-
cal) open arms. She introduced him to her husband, and
made solicitous inquiries concerning the progress of his
investigation. Both she and Mr. Buckley seemed perfectly
willing to explain how they had spent their time between
eight and ten o'clock on the previous Saturday night. "Although," Rhoda said, "I'm afraid our alibis are rather—
what do you call it?—unconfirmed. You'll just have to take
our word for them."

She went on to say that Buckley had gone to the Village
early Saturday afternoon, had met a friend, and gone with
him to a football game, not returning until late. "I got
tired of waiting for him," Rhoda continued, "so I had supper and went to bed early, about half-past eight, I think.
I sleep very soundly, so I didn't hear Mr. Buckley come
in, but he says his friend brought him back about an hour
after that."

Archer looked inquiringly at Buckley.

"Ah—yes," that gentleman agreed. "It was nine-forty; I
looked at the clock in the front hall when I went upstairs.
I saw Mrs. Buckley had—ah—retired, so I went up quietly,
in order not to disturb her. Mrs. Buckley and I occupy—
ah—separate bedrooms."

Archer asked if the bedrooms adjoined.

"Ah—no. They are some distance from each other."

"So they really have no alibis at all," Archer thought
to himself. He said, "Did either of you go out again that
night, for any reason?"

Oh no, certainly not. Why should they?

The sergeant could think of several reasons, but didn't mention them. Instead, he asked them when they remembered seeing Deacon Grimm last. Saturday morning, Mrs. Buckley said, they had seen him around his place as usual. Had they spoken with him? Oh no. Mr. Buckley explained hesitatingly that he had seen Deacon Grimm feeding the pigs, but had not said anything to him, of course. "Deacon Grimm was not on friendly terms with us," he said. "We were not in the habit of exchanging those friendly greetings and little—ah—pleasantries which often make life in the country so delightful. After the way he had—ah—treated us." Mr. Buckley shook his bald head, deeply deploring the Deacon's anti-social tendencies.

Mrs. Buckley gave a sudden start. She had just remembered, she told her husband, that Danny Cheever, before he went home, had mentioned that there seemed to be something wrong with one of the pedigreed Leghorns. Danny thought it had a cold. She had meant to speak of it before, but— Buckley immediately rose and went out, making sounds suggestive of an outsize Leghorn with a very bad cold indeed. As soon as he was out of the room, Rhoda left her chair and sat down beside the sergeant on the davenport.

"I didn't want to say anything before Mr. Buckley," she said, in her low, rich voice, "for he would accuse me of gossiping. But I have some news for you, and real news is never gossip, is it?" Without waiting for a ruling on this point, she went on, "I merely want to suggest that you ask Ann Barbour what she was doing yesterday morning, down at the old Wayland place. I saw her go in there, with the dog, and she was gone all of half an hour, I'm sure. I thought you ought to know about it, in case you didn't." She smiled deprecatingly, and added, "You young men are so chivalrous; you don't like to ask a pretty woman embarrassing questions. Not that Ann is pretty, far from it. But all young women nowadays are so clever and unscrupulous about trying to influence a man, especially a man who is honest and straightforward, and not expecting anything of the kind." She sighed.

Archer said slowly, "That's very interesting, Mrs. Buckley. I'll look into it. Thanks for telling me." He reflected that Ann seemed to be addicted to excursions of a secret nature. He should have told Burke to watch her, even if it meant neglecting the others.

Rhoda moved a little nearer to him on the davenport. She used "Night in Vienna," not too sparingly. Archer suddenly wondered if she had ever been an actress. There was a studied effectiveness about her manner, as well as her voice, that suggested the stage. He was rather surprised that she had married Buckley. But, of course, there was Buckley's money. It wasn't so hard to understand why Buckley had married her.

Rhoda fixed her large dark eyes on him, and continued. "This is such a dreadful business. Do you think you will find out who killed Leonard?"

Archer replied that he hoped to.

Mrs. Buckley went on talking about the Deacon's death, and how deeply she felt it. They had had their differences, but after all, he had been a neighbor, and a fine man, in many ways. He would be a great loss to the town. But she was glad that the investigation into his death was in such good hands. The soothing cadences of her voice rose and fell. She was saying how lonely the country could be without congenial friends, how disappointing life was, in general. She shifted to her husband—a wonderful man, but his interests were so far removed from hers. . . . She moved a little closer to the sergeant. The odor of "Night in Vienna" grew stronger. Archer came to, abruptly. He thought to himself, "Good Lord! Is she going to tell me her husband doesn't understand her? What'll I do then?"

He knew what he wanted to do. He wanted to edge away, in a sufficiently pointed manner. But he was saved from taking any action by the audible closing of the back door. Rhoda instantly rose with leisurely alacrity, and resumed her seat on the other side of the room. "And any help we can give you," she said, raising her voice, "we'll be glad to. Won't we, Warner?"

"Oh—ah—of course." Mr. Buckley lowered his equine length into an armchair. He turned to Archer. "Perhaps you've discovered by this time that Leonard Grimm was not an—ah—easy man to get along with?"

Archer said something indefinite.

Mr. Buckley nodded impressively. "He was a hard man, and vindictive, too. A bad man to deal with, as more than one person here in town has found. His private character was—ah—deplorable, and he was capable of the most—er—despicable actions."

Archer was willing to believe that, although privately he thought that there was something to be said on both sides of most quarrels. But he encouraged Mr. Buckley to talk, and was rewarded by hearing the complete, history of the disputed boundary line and the disgraceful pig pen. Buckley got quite excited by his own recital, so much so that Archer caught Mrs. Buckley looking at him with a slightly anxious expression. It all sounded involved and far-fetched to the sergeant. Still, he knew that people can get murderously angry over even smaller things than an acre of pasture land, or a pig pen built under their noses. Human actions and their causes are motivated by some force outside the present laws of any science. They can't be determined by any hard and fast rules. So he listened attentively until the subject was exhausted. Then, a little fearful of another tête-à-tête with Rhoda, he made a plausible excuse and left. She went with him to the front door.

"You mustn't take what Warner says about Leonard too seriously," she said in a low voice. "He's very—excitable. Leonard did annoy us sometimes, but we didn't hold any grudge against him, really. When any one harms me in any way, or does something they shouldn't, I always try to see their point of view. I always say to myself, 'There, but for the Grace of God, go I,' And when you realize that, you can't *hate* anyone, can you?" Which Archer thought a remark worthy of some study. But he only said "Good night" politely and tore himself away.

It had stopped raining, but was damp and raw. There was a heavy mist in the air, and everything was saturated with water. Clouds were scurrying overhead from east to west, but the sky showed little sign of clearing. Archer stopped for a minute to look at the old Wayland house, huddled among its evergreens. It was very dark in there among the dripping trees, and it looked forlorn and desolate. What reason did Ann Barbour have for snooping around a deserted house, if she did snoop? What reason did Rhoda Buckley have for saying she did, if she didn't? "These damned women!" Archer thought disgustedly. It was a simple matter, comparatively, to get the truth about anything out of a man, but women! Then he remembered Gus Lafond, but decided that Gus wasn't a fair example of his sex as a whole!

When he got back to the Pattersons' everyone had gone to bed, although a lamp had been left burning in the kitchen. Archer saw that the outside doors were locked and bolted on the inside, and made sure that no comfort-loving cats had sneaked into the house with him. Lady, Teddy, and Buffy were not allowed to spend the night in the sitting-room chairs; but they never stopped trying, and frequently had to be chased out the last thing before the family retired. Archer wondered whether Ann was contemplating another trip tonight? She had been out somewhere the night before; he was convinced of that. He supposed he would have to keep watch, and find out what she was up to. And he was dog-tired, and wanted a good night's rest. Damn! He went up to his room, but kept his clothes on, and lay down on the outside of his bed. It had been about three when she went out the night before; he could get some sleep, and would be sure to wake up when anyone went down stairs, no matter how quietly they managed it. He would catch her in the act this time. . . .

There it was, a door closing ever so gently. Archer scrambled into his coat, seized his flashlight, went silently into the hall and down the stairs. Instead of going into the kitchen, he let himself out the front door, to which Lucy had given him a key. This door, used only on state occasions, commanded a view up and down the road. Archer crouched down on the porch, behind a dwarf evergreen, and waited.

It was wet and misty, and water from the porch roof dripped clammily onto his head and shoulders. Hang it all! Whoever had closed that door couldn't have disappeared from sight so soon! It wasn't too dark to see a moving figure, even without a light. The pleasing thought occurred to him that the sound he had heard might have been made by somebody genuinely headed "out back!" But he waited, and, presently, thought he saw a dim shape coming from the general direction of the barn. Or was he imagining . . . no, there was somebody. . . .

As the vague shadow drew abreast of the front porch, Archer made out the uncertain outline of somebody, probably a woman, carrying something—several somethings. He thought it was Ann; Lucy was taller and walked differently. Hard to tell, but he was pretty sure it was Ann. But what was she carrying? There was something big and bulky which she supported with one arm, while something else dangled from her other hand. If she had a light she wasn't using it, but walked slowly up the road, in the direction of the Village. Was she running away? Planning to get a lift, or walk into Rumford? Those bundles looked suspicious, mighty suspicious. Archer followed her, keeping well to one side of the road, in case she looked back. But she didn't. She went on past the Buckleys' house, and disappeared behind a clump of lilacs on the other side of the road, as if heading for the Wayland place. So Rhoda *had* been telling the truth!

By the time Archer reached the lilacs, Ann was vanishing among the trees that surrounded the old house; he caught a gleam from her flashlight. She was going around toward the back of the house, and he made his way cautiously after her. Not daring to use his own light, he crept around a corner of the main building toward a kind of ell at the back, which was completely hidden from the road. Then he heard a faint sound, like a door closing, and saw a pale flicker of light that showed through a window of the ell. Toward this he felt his way, slowly, for fear of running into a tree or falling over something. The windows at the back of the house were not boarded up like those nearer the road; and one of them, fortunately, had an ill-fitting curtain that gaped conveniently at the bottom. Archer found that, by craning his neck, he could see inside without much trouble.

The light he had seen came from a smoky lantern that was sitting on the floor, casting erratic shadows around the dismantled room. Near it stood a small oil stove and several cartons containing canned goods of various kinds. On an upended box Ann Barbour sat, with her feet tucked under her; and, beside her, sitting cross-legged on the floor, was a big, broad-shouldered man, wearing lumberman's boots and a heavy mackinaw, engaged in eating a sandwich. He had strong, rather battered features, a firm mouth, and stubborn jaw, and was in considerable need of a shave. The lantern's rays glinted on gray eyes that showed light in his weather-beaten face, and on thick, sandy hair that curled in spite of its close clip.

Archer took one look at the man, and puckered his lips in a soundless whistle. Well, well. He wouldn't have to search any farther for the missing Forrest Martin, apparently. Here he was, delivered into his hands, as it were, although he had an idea that this large gentleman, with the big hands, and powerful shoulders, might take some delivering! The man finished his sandwich, and took another from the basket Ann had brought. Beside it, Archer now identified the other object she had been carrying; it was a gallon milk can.

To his disappointment, the sergeant was unable to hear a word that was being said—the ell was equipped with double windows—and the speakers were keeping their voices lowered. Ann appeared to be doing most of the talking, while her companion ate sandwiches and depleted the contents of the milk can. He seemed to be in good spirits, and when he smiled, his battered, rather grim face looked younger and less hard-bitten. But when he stood up, he looked formidable enough, being tall in proportion to his breadth, and apparently in first-class condition.

Archer didn't know what to do. The man would have to be apprehended, but should he do it now, or wait until next day, when reinforcements would be handy? Too bad he had left Henry Burke in Rumford. Ann's companion looked like a hefty proposition to tackle single handed, even if he didn't happen to be armed. The sergeant was armed, and was certainly no coward, but he didn't want to start anything that might conceivably end in failure; it might be wiser to wait, though his inclinations were always against delay. He decided to wait until Ann had left, anyway; she seemed to be getting ready to go. Archer

swore at himself for not having guessed what she was up
to. He should have suspected something like this, especially after what Mrs. Buckley told him. But he hadn't,
probably because he couldn't quite believe yet that the
"high-hat" Miss Barbour could have any real interest in
this very doubtful character, Forrest Martin. She must
have some game on, but what was it? He waited, straining
his ears, but could hear only a faint, indistinguishable
murmur. Archer wished Ann would hurry up and go, if she
was going. One of his feet had gone to sleep, and the driz-
zle from the eaves was running down his neck. What a life!
Presently, Ann rose to go, and Archer's doubts as to her
interest in Forrest Martin were reluctantly dispersed. The
big man gathered her in his arms, and they stood so for a
long time. Nor did her companion's need of a shave seem
to trouble Miss Barbour in the least; it was plain she was
not being embraced against her will. The sergeant looked
away, feeling embarrassed and a little disgruntled. He was
still uncertain what action to take; but he moved away
from the house and slid behind a tree, as the door opened
and two figures emerged, to stand talking in whispers on
the doorstep. Archer could catch an occasional word now,
and heard Ann say something about "come down again
tomorrow night." That seemed to mean that Martin wasn't
planning any immediate departure. Should he tackle him
now, or wait? The two on the step were in each other's
arms again, and the unwilling sergeant heard an incau-
tious "Darling. . . ." Other sounds indicative of mutual
affection followed; but finally Ann released herself, and
walked quickly away into the darkness, while Forrest Martin went back into the house and closed the door. Archer
waited until Ann had had plenty of time to get well away
from the vicinity. Then he moved up and looked through
the gap in the curtain again. The man inside was spreading a pair of heavy horse blankets on the floor, with the

evident intention of sleeping on them. The sergeant saw him take something from his pocket, but it was nothing more deadly than a flashlight. Then he blew out the lantern.

Archer went up to the door and knocked.

There was a scrambling sound within, followed by a thump and an exclamation. Then the door opened a crack, and Forrest Martin's voice said, "For God's sake, Ann . . ."

Archer introduced his foot into the aperture at the bottom, and at the same time said calmly, "Sorry, but it isn't Miss Barbour. This is Sergeant Brett, and I'd like to talk with you, Martin." He trained his flashlight on the door, and gripped his pistol with his right hand; but these precautions were unnecessary, for after an instant's silence, Forrest Martin said: "Well, come along in if you want to."

"I'm armed," Archer warned. He stepped inside the door and closed it behind him, just as Martin's flashlight flared into his eyes. They stood, there, staring at each other. Archer half expected a bullet to follow the beam of the other's light, and he kept his pistol ready. It flashed through his mind that if he ever got loose from this case he could qualify without any trouble for a feeble-minded home; he was acting like a born fool now, putting himself into a possible murderer's power this way! But, instead of taking any violent action, the possible murderer merely set his flashlight down on a box top, and said conversationally, "If you'll promise not to shoot me yet, I'll light the lantern, I can't offer you a chair, but there's a fairly comfortable packing-case right behind you."

Archer found the packing-case with his hand, and sat gingerly down on it, keeping his flashlight trained on Mr. Martin's not inconsiderable form. "Okay," he said, "I'm not shooting anybody if I can help it, but don't try any tricks, or I might have to."

A match sputtered, and the smoky lantern sent its flickering light around the room. Forrest Martin removed five cans of Campbell's Soup from the top of another packing-case, and lowered his two hundred pounds onto it. It creaked but held.

"Well," he said, "I suppose you heard Ann go out, and followed her down here; I'm sure she didn't give me away intentionally. We might have known you'd sleep with one ear open and would hear her. We did know it was risky; but I was here, so I thought I might as well stay, as long as the provisions held out. What do you want to do? Arrest me for killing the Deacon?"

Archer was beginning to find Mr. Martin a rather unusual kind of criminal, if he was a criminal. He didn't seem to be making the most of his opportunities. Perhaps he wasn't armed, and was waiting for a chance to overpower the sergeant by taking him unaware. Archer kept his gun ready. "Well, did you kill the Deacon?" he demanded.

Forrest grinned, "Come now," he said. "You wouldn't have me incriminate myself, would you?—even without witnesses. I wasn't around here when the Deacon was killed, in the first place."

"Where were you?"

Forrest considered. "If he was killed around half-past nine or ten o'clock Saturday night, as Ann says, I must have been somewhere between Litchfield and Freyburg, hoofing it along a damned poor road in the dark, and wishing somebody would come along with a car and give me a lift." He took a roll of Life Savers from his pocket, offered it to the sergeant, took one himself, and continued, "But no car came along until I was pretty near into Freyburg. Then a fellow picked me up and took me as far as Foxboro, up on the Lake. But he wasn't coming any farther in this direction, so I walked down from Foxboro and got here—well, it was late Sunday night or early Monday morning. Just in time for the excitement, but too late to have been the cause of it," he concluded.

Archer said, "Can you prove all that?"

The other shrugged. "I might. I doubt it some. The fellow that took me in had a New York car, I remember that. He was some kind of a salesman, and the back of the car was full of sample cases. But I don't know his name or who he worked for, or where he was going. Or where he was from, even. I didn't know I was going to need an alibi, you see. He was a medium-sized fellow with glasses. And he was a Republican, by his talk," he added, as an afterthought.

Archer was afraid the description wasn't uncommon enough to be much help. He said, "I ought to arrest you. You must see there's plenty against you. You had reasons for hating the Deacon, you can't prove an alibi for the time he was killed, and then you're found lurking here near the scene of the crime, secretly, when you must have known we were on the lookout for you."

"I'm not lurking," Forrest protested. "This is still my house, as Grimm would have found out if he'd lived until I scraped up cash enough to hire a lawyer to prove it to him. When I heard what had happened, I didn't try to run away, as I might have done. I thought of coming and telling you the whole story, but I figured you probably wouldn't believe it—no cop would. And Ann was afraid you'd arrest me, because we realized things look pretty black against me. So I decided to mark time for a while, and see if you couldn't find the really guilty party."

"How did Miss Barbour find out you were here, if you only got here late Sunday night?"

"That was a piece of luck. Early Monday morning, Tad Patterson came down by here with the dog; I guess he was giving her a run before you and the trooper got up. I didn't know anything about the Deacon being killed then.

I saw Tad, and thought he could tell me whether Ann was here, or in Boston. I was going up to Pattersons' to find out, if Tad hadn't come along. He told me what had happened, so I thought I'd better keep under cover. I told Tad to tell Ann I was here, and to ask her if she could get down without being seen. So she came down, for a few minutes, later in the morning, and we decided to wait and see what happened. She brought me some milk and grub tonight, and last night, too. We didn't expect the police to be so wide awake. Though I might have known somebody would be sure to see Ann come in here. Who was it, Sister Buckley? That old b— meddler would be sure to suspect something."

Archer said, "It's a damn funny coincidence that you happened to get here just after a man you'd had trouble with was killed."

Forrest shrugged. "Maybe. But that's what it was, a coincidence. I wanted to see—er, I was planning to come back here as soon as I got some money together, anyway. I left the job I was on up north, and worked my way down by easy stages. And it was so late when I got here Sunday night I couldn't go to Pattersons' then. I know it sounds a damn thin story," he broke off. "That's why I didn't tell it before. If I was the murderer you're trying to make me out," he added, "I'd just knock you over the head and beat it, tonight. But I haven't done it, or even tried to—that ought to count in my favor."

"I've got a gun," Archer reminded him, drily.

Forrest seemed to think that the gun wouldn't have deterred a really desperate criminal. And the sergeant had to admit to himself that his companion didn't talk nor act like a murderer, past or present. He was inclined to believe Forrest when the latter said, "If I'd been going to kill the Deacon I'd have done it a year ago. If I didn't kill him then, I sure wouldn't now, when I've earned a little cash to fight him legally. I expect you've heard the whole story—Buckley version. But use your own judgment. While I'm not crazy about being arrested, I've been in tougher places than jails." He went over to the still partly full basket of edibles and selected a banana.

Archer was still in a quandary. "What kind of a policeman am I?" he asked himself, "to be sitting alone with a suspect, at half-past three in the morning, discussing with him whether or not I ought to arrest him!" But his inclination was to believe Forrest Martin. There was something open and aboveboard about the big man that made his story sound reasonable, in its way. If Martin had killed the Deacon, why in heaven's name had he remained in the neighborhood, where he was sure to be found before long? Had he stayed so that the police would think what Archer was thinking, that it was a sign of his innocence not to try to escape? Perhaps. But Martin didn't look like a person whose mental processes would work that way. The sergeant decided that his own efforts at deduction and psychology both were an awful waste of time. The only thing he could do was to follow his hunches, such as they were. He had a hunch that Forrest Martin was telling the truth; very well, he would act on it. He said, "I'm not going to arrest you—now. But you can see that I can't take the risk of leaving you here alone, and having you skip out. Come along up to Pattersons' with me; I guess Mrs. Patterson won't mind one more, and I can keep an eye on you along with, the others. I expect I'm a damn fool," Archer concluded frankly, "but I'll take a chance you're telling the truth."

Forrest grinned again—that disarming, slightly crooked smile that made his battered face boyishly attractive. "That's all right with me," he said, "but Lucy may not like the idea of having me on the premises. She probably thinks I did it, like the rest of the town, state, and country. I gathered from a paper Ann brought down that I'm Public Suspect, Number One!"

"You aren't much more of a suspect than some other people around here," Archer said. "Have I got your promise that you won't try to leave, as suddenly and mysteriously as you came?"

"I give you my word," Forrest returned, "that I won't leave the Ridge without telling you. I don't even want to leave." He gathered up the basket, milk can, and one or two other articles, and blew out the lantern. "Lead on, Sergeant. Or maybe you'd rather I went ahead, in case I had any sinister designs." He did so, and locked the door behind them. "Think how surprised Ann and the Pattersons will be, when I show up for breakfast. By the way, if I'm not under arrest, I suppose I have to pay my own board? Maybe I'd better get you to arrest me, so the state will do it."

"You can pay it yourself, for now," Archer told him. As they walked down the road, he went on, "I'm trying to play fair with you, Martin. I'm counting on you to do the same with me."

Forrest Martin's mouth set in a resolute line. "Don't worry," he said, "I always keep my word, sooner or later."

5

Wednesday—*Private Lives*

Archer's vague fear that he might be doing something risky, even dangerous, by bringing Forrest Martin to the Pattersons' with him faded away when morning came and found the household intact. At Forrest's own request, he had been locked in Archer's room, while the sergeant returned to his old friend, the sitting room couch. (That couch was a useful piece of furniture!) Forrest had not shown any homicidal tendencies, and seemed not much worried by the danger of arrest in which he still stood; he appeared, so far, to be of an equable and easygoing temperament. Archer was relieved, too, to find that Lucy Patterson received the additional boarder with equanimity; he had been afraid that she might be angry or upset, and consider that he had exceeded his authority by bringing Forrest Martin to the house, uninvited. But Lucy and Frank seemed genuinely glad to see Forrest; and Ann, when she found he wasn't under arrest, couldn't conceal her delight at his appearance. In fact, she didn't try to. Even Bella greeted him like a long-lost friend. And Bella, by the way, had not yet come to regard the sergeant with any great amount of cordiality; she tolerated him, but that was all.

Breakfast was quite a cheerful and reminiscent meal, in spite of the slight strain caused by Archer's presence, and the knowledge of why he was there, that was in the air like an invisible but ever present cloud.

Now that her nocturnal journeys were explained, Archer forebore to reprimand Ann for having made them. He saw now that it was the fear that Forrest would be accused of the Deacon's murder that had caused her reticence and disinclination to tell all she knew. Was she merely afraid that Forrest would be wrongfully accused of the crime, or did she have some reason for fearing that he had actually committed it? Archer wished he knew.

After breakfast he outlined the situation frankly. "You're all under suspicion," he told them bluntly. "I hope to find the real criminal and clear everybody who's innocent, but until I do, or somebody does, you'll all have to share the unpleasantness of being suspected, and make the best of it. I'm going to make you responsible for each other's actions, in a way, though I know it's a mean thing to do. But if you're all innocent you should be willing to do it. I don't want any of you to leave the neighborhood without telling me, and I expect you to abide by any orders or restrictions I may give you. I'll be just as reasonable as I can, and we'll hope it won't be for long. If you're all here together, it will enable me to concentrate on some of the other possibilities in the case. So you see how it is." He felt that this was rather an extraordinary speech for a policeman to make, and doubted how it would be received in official quarters. But he was beginning to feel that he was rather an extraordinary policeman! At all events, the speech was received fairly well, although Frank was a little inclined to grumble about constitutional rights, and the fact that an American citizen was supposed to be innocent until proved otherwise. But they all agreed to "stay put" while the sergeant was absent. "I'll help pay for my board by giving Frank a hand with his wood," Forrest said, "and we won't go out of each other's sight."

"That's the idea!" Archer said. "And I'll send Henry Burke out this afternoon, and you can put him to work. See if you can get ten pounds off him!"

He had already talked with Henry over the telephone, and had ordered him to call off the search for Forrest Martin, as that gentleman had been found. "Did you arrest him?" Henry wanted to know, and was surprised at the sergeant's reply in the negative. "I'll tell you all about it when I get there," Archer said. "And see if you can have Dr. Partridge at the office around noon, will you? I want to ask him some questions before I forget them. Okay."

Outside the rain had stopped, and most of the snow had disappeared, leaving the ground wet and soggy. But, overhead, the clouds were clearing before a rising west wind, and a watery sun peered out apologetically. Archer thought it was preparing to turn cold, and hoped that the water would dry up before that happened. He got out his car and drove to the Lafond house.

The unattractive Gus was not at home, but the attractive Clarabel was, seated before a late and sketchy breakfast in the small kitchen, which smelled even stuffier, greasier, and staler than it had done when the sergeant paid his first visit. She greeted him with the professional smile which she kept ready, on tap, for all males, and informed him that she was alone, as Danny was working, and her husband had gone to Rumford.

"He won't get back till late tonight," she said, regarding the well-set-up sergeant with unconcealed approval; she was obviously speculating as to the possibilities of this call. Archer wondered if he would learn anything useful by playing up to her; he wasn't keen on the idea, but felt that he should be willing to make some sacrifices for the sake of possible information. So he followed Clarabel's leads, hoping to gain her confidence and lull her suspicions, if any. If she wanted to think that he had come to see her for personal reasons, knowing Gus to be absent—well, that was all right, if it led to information. So when he thought a sufficient degree of friendliness had been established, he tried a few harmless-sounding questions.

But at the first cautious reference to Deacon Grimm, Clarabel grew instantly uneasy and silent. Archer was sure, then, that she had been ordered to keep her mouth shut on the subject. He wished he had thought to come prepared with a little liquid refreshment; he was willing to bet that a pint of whiskey, judiciously applied, would loosen her tongue. But, anyway, the ice was cracked if not broken, and Clarabel seemed to think they understood each other. Archer crushed out his cigarette and rose, explaining that he had to go to Rumford. "I wanted to see your husband to-day," he said, "but, if he isn't coming home until late . . . ?"

"He won't be home till midnight, probably," Clarabel said, "so I'll be all alone this evening." She gave him a look full of meaning. Archer returned the look with what he hoped was a convincing leer, and left. He heartily disliked using such methods as these, but felt that they were justifiable, under the circumstances. And he must be sure to remember the whiskey.

At the Rumford headquarters, Henry Burke was full of questions and information. Archer answered the first as well as he could, and digested the second, what there was of it. Henry had finished two of his jobs: he had checked Frank Patterson's alibi as far as he could, and he had delved into the murky past of Gus Lafond, or as much of it as had been spent in Rumford.

"Good work," Archer said, seating himself at his desk. "Tell me about it. Let's have Patterson first."

Burke had checked Frank's presence in Pinkney on Saturday afternoon; and had verified the fact that he had there missed the bus. "Seems like it was a genuine accident," the trooper said. "Anyway, he missed it all right. I got hold of the garage-man who rented him a car, and that was all right, too. He recognized Patterson from my description; said Patterson told him about missing the bus, and asked for a car to drive to Winchester. The garage-man let him have a second-hand Chevvie, and he drove off with it about half-past five."

"Did he drive toward Winchester?"

"I asked the man that, but he couldn't tell, from where his place is. Then the hotel people at Winchester checked the fact that Patterson got there about a quarter of two, an hour or so after the rest of his party. They'd got his wife's calls, so they were on the lookout, and as soon as he got there he called her back. That much of his story's o.k. But I can't find anybody who saw him between the time he left Pinkney and the time he got to Winchester. It seems to me, if he really started for Winchester and got stuck, as he says, that it's kind of funny nobody noticed him, or gave him a hand when they saw him stalled and in trouble."

"He says," Archer returned, "that he did try to hail two or three cars, but they just speeded up and beat it. It's a lonely stretch of road along there, and there've been several holdups around Winchester lately, so that's possible. He says it took him over two hours to get his car going after it gave out, and then he had to drive slow on account of the condition of the road."

"Well, maybe," Henry said, unconvinced. "But look here." He spread a large automobile map on the desk. "It's thirty-eight miles from Pinkney to Winchester, and Patterson claims he broke down about fifteen miles south of Pinkney, and then it took him till 'most two o'clock to get to Winchester. But you can see that there are back roads that will take you north from Pinkney to Preston, and then to Highbrook Ridge, and the whole distance is less than fifty miles. And while they ain't State roads, they're in good shape, and on a night like Saturday you could make better time on them than on the State roads, because there wouldn't be any traffic to speak of. If Patterson left Pinkney at five-thirty, he'd have time enough to drive back to Highbrook, kill the Deacon anywhere from eight to nine-thirty, and then get back to the hotel at Winchester and make it look as if he had an alibi."

"What kind of a car did the garage man let him take, did you say?"

"The man said," Henry replied, "that it was a last year's demonstrator, and while the body was banged up some, the engine was okay. And he said he couldn't understand how it had given out the way Patterson says it did. He says it was in good running order, as far as he knew. Anyway," he concluded, "there's between six and seven hours when Patterson hasn't any witnesses or anybody to vouch for

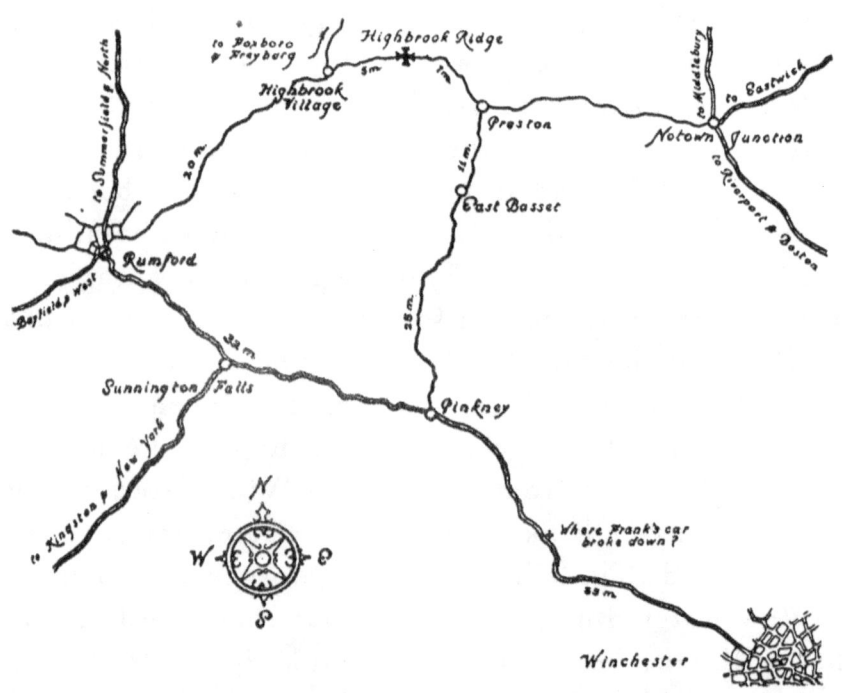

what he was doing. I'm not saying he did kill the Deacon, but he could have."

"The garage man would say that about his car anyway," Archer pointed out. "Did you ever see a garage man yet who would admit there was anything wrong with a car he rented? You did not. And are you trying to make out that Patterson went back home and killed the Deacon there in the barn without the women knowing anything about it?"

"He could have," Henry maintained.

"Seems to me," Archer said, "that you're trying pretty hard to get Mrs. Patterson's husband out of the way. What are you planning to do, marry his widow?"

"That's all right," Henry protested. "You can make fun of the idea if you want to. But I was just trying to show that we can't let Patterson out yet."

"No," Archer admitted. "He'll have to stay on the list, though I can't see him as a murderer, myself. What did you find out about our friend Gus?"

Henry had found out quite a little about our friend Gus; but it was of such an indefinite nature that while it darkened Mr. Lafond's already dingy reputation, it wasn't particularly useful.

"He's got a police record," Henry went on. "Arrested repeatedly for bootlegging, back before repeal, but he always got loose again right away. In nineteen thirty-six he was arrested for running a shady booze and dance joint without a license, and again in nineteen thirty-eight. But, since then, the police haven't had anything on him, and when he went to Highbrook about nine months ago they kind of lost track of him, though they knew he still ran some with his old crowd."

Archer was disappointed. "Nothing that connected him with any dope racket then?"

Henry shook his head. "Not especially. But I talked with one fellow who hangs around the various joints, and he said that some of Gus's friends handled dope, among other things. Said they had a finger in all the rackets—stolen cars, disorderly houses, slot machines, blackmail—you know the kind of thing."

Archer nodded. "So it's still possible Gus was the one who supplied the Deacon with his dope. I guess we'll have to ask the F.B.I. boys to help with that. But even if Gus was selling the Deacon dope it wouldn't give him a motive for killing him; he wouldn't be likely to knock off a paying customer."

"No," Henry said, "unless the Deacon thought he was paying too much, and kicked. Maybe Gus was blackmailing him, threatening to tell the church folks about the dope, and so on."

"Well, in that case," Archer argued, "it would be the Deacon who'd kill Gus, not vice versa."

"Hell, so it would." Henry was disgusted. "Well, *I* don't know. Maybe the Deacon tried to kill Gus, and Gus got hold of the pitchfork and killed him, instead."

"Even that isn't impossible," Archer agreed gloomily. "There are so darned many possibilities in the case! I wish I could name at least one person, and say he (or she) didn't do it! But I can't, not even Mrs. Patterson," he added, as Henry opened his mouth.

The trooper shook his head, stubbornly. "I don't believe it was a woman. This Martin sounds like a pretty good bet to me; but if he didn't do it, or Patterson, then the Lafond guy did. He's the right type."

The sergeant reminded him that Gus had an alibi. "We may not believe in it," he said, "but it's no use trying to pin anything on Gus while that alibi holds. So I'm going to see if I can't find some holes in it." He outlined his plan for the evening's call on Clarabel. Henry stared at him.

"Gosh, Sergeant," he said, "why don't you let me take on that assignment? I haven't had a chance to see her yet.

But, if what the town folks said was true—!" he whistled. "Besides," he added, "that kind of thing isn't in your line."

"I suppose that's meant for a compliment," Archer said. "No, Henry, I've got to tackle the fair Clarabel myself, though I just as soon tell you I'm not looking forward to it. You'll have to stay at the Pattersons'. But I heard Mrs. Patterson say this morning that she was going to make a chocolate layer cake today, and a date pie."

"You're welcome to Clarabel," Henry said.

Dr. Partridge arrived then, and the trooper left to get his lunch. "Bring me back something potent," Archer called after him. "I don't care what brand, so long as it's the goods."

"Hello, Archer," the doctor said, cheerfully. "Is the case driving you to drink already?"

"Pretty near," the sergeant admitted. "I know I need some kind of help! First, I want to know whether you think a woman could have killed Grimm?"

The doctor scratched his head. "I've given that quite a lot of thought," he said at last, "and all I can say is that a woman could have done it; but I don't believe one did. It's not physically impossible, but it's not like a woman to kill anybody that way, in my opinion. Why? Have you any new reason for thinking a woman did?"

"No," Archer told him, "I just wanted your opinion. And another thing: what's your verdict on the boy, Danny Cheever? You saw him Monday, didn't you?"

"I saw him," the doctor admitted, "and talked to him a bit, but that's a different matter from examining him, you know. And I don't claim to be an alienist anyway, so my say-so wouldn't go far in court. But, as a plain police doctor, and on general principles, I'd say the boy was harmless. Not exactly bright, but definitely not dangerous. But any psychiatrist would laugh at my qualifications to say even that."

"I'd take your say-so," Archer said, "a darn sight sooner than I would the drivel handed out by those conceited nit-wits who call themselves psychiatrists. I call them—well, never mind." By which it may be seen that Sergeant Brett's attitude toward the self-appointed pioneers of modern mental research was old-fashioned, not to say prejudiced. "Still," he continued, "I suppose I can't count Danny out entirely, any more than I can Frank Patterson. Burke has been trying to show me how Patterson could have done it."

"I don't believe he did," Dr. Partridge said, "but how about this Martin? I understand you found him right on the spot, practically."

Archer explained, as well as he could, how he felt about Forrest Martin. "But my feeling is only a hunch," he confessed. "As far as opportunity goes, and motive, and all, he could have done it, and his alibi isn't as good as Patterson's. But he doesn't strike me as a criminal type, and Gus Lafond does. If only I could break down that alibi of his! Well, I have hopes!"

The doctor whistled when he heard what Archer's hopes were based on. "Don't take any chances," he said. "Especially if you think Lafond may be the murderer. We don't want to lose you!"

Archer said he guessed he could take care of himself.

Dr. Partridge continued, "I don't suppose you found any dope hidden in the Deacon's house? No? Then why don't you search Lafond's place?"

"Because I'd have to get a warrant and go through lot of red tape. Besides, if there ever was anything there, you can bet Gus has got rid of it before now. He's smart."

"Can't you give him the third degree?" the doctor inquired hopefully.

"No use, even if I was allowed to, which I'm not. He's too cute, been coached repeatedly by crooked lawyers. No, that's out."

The doctor asked about Leonard Grimm's past, and whether anything new about him had come to light.

"We haven't learned much we didn't already know," Archer returned. "He wasn't in any financial trouble, and while he was mixed up in some legal tangles, we can't see how they could have had any bearing on his death. He had a bad reputation where women were concerned, but we knew that to start with; everybody knew it."

"Hadn't he ever married?"

Archer shook his head. "Not that we know of. After his mother died, he had a succession of housekeepers, but none of them succeeded in marrying him, though some of them tried pretty hard, by all accounts. Then about twelve years ago his sister lost her husband in an accident, and was left with a boy about fifteen and no money. Grimm took them to live with him, and they all seemed satisfied with the arrangement, though I gathered that Mrs. Cummings, that's the sister, and the son both had to work pretty hard. In the summer, the sister got a small legacy from a cousin who'd died, and as she was a bit run-down, the Deacon fixed for her and her son to visit some other relatives in Los Angeles. Maybe he had his own reasons for doing it, but anyway, they went."

"Doesn't seem to be much material there," the doctor agreed. Then he inquired about the Patterson household, and was considerably intrigued by Archer's method of having its members keep track of one another. "I hope they aren't all in it together," he said. "If they are, you're playing right into their hands."

Archer thought there wasn't any danger of that. "But I don't enjoy doing some of the things I have to do," he said soberly. "I hate to act like a spy, taking advantage of their hospitality; yet all the time watching and listening for a word or a clue that may bring a murder home to one of them. I don't like it."

"'A policeman's life is not a happy one,' eh? But if you gave the job up," the doctor pointed out, "someone else would take over, and probably it'd be somebody with fewer scruples and worse manners than you've got! And, after all, you're only after the truth. We can't have people committing murders right and left."

"I know all that. And I don't want to give the job up; I want to finish it. But this case is a lot different from the others I've worked on. These people aren't professional criminals, except maybe Gus Lafond. They're just regular everyday folks, and this business is making lots of trouble and worry for them, I can see."

"All the more reason to find the guilty one and clean up the mess," Dr. Partridge returned. "Then the innocent ones can stop being bothered. Well, I've got work to do." He rose. "Don't get discouraged, Archer. It's only been four days since the man was killed; you've covered a lot of ground, seems to me. You'll get a break before long. And let me know if you learn anything from Madame Lafond, anything relative to the case, that is! And watch your step!"

After the doctor had gone, the telephone rang, and Archer heard the now familiar low tones of Rhoda Buckley's voice. She apologized for troubling the sergeant when he was busy, but would he stop in and see her as soon as he conveniently could? "I have some important news for you," she said. Archer promised to see her that afternoon, though he had no great faith in the importance of her news. "But I suppose she thinks she's helping," he reflected. And she had been right about Ann's visit to the Wayland house.

He went out for a hasty lunch, and on his return found Henry Burke, and a bottle of "White Rose Special," which he put in his pocket. "We'll go out to Highbrook now," he told the trooper, "and, on the way, you can tell me anything else you've found out."

"I didn't find out an awful lot more," Henry admitted, when they were en route. "None of the people besides Lafond have police records. I tried to get more details about the trouble the Deacon had with Martin; but there wasn't anything official, because Martin was never actually arrested. The Deacon did have a pull with some 'higher-up' in Rumford, for that story about his getting that apple contract away from Patterson was true. But nobody knows who the 'higher-up' is, or how the Deacon worked it."

Nobody would, of course.

"What about the Buckleys?" Archer asked. "Did you learn anything more about either of them?"

"Not much. The old man was born in Rumford, but he went to Boston years ago, and made his money there; something to do with wool. Then, when he retired, he took up hens as a hobby, and fixed up the place over to Highbrook; it used to belong to his grandfather, or somebody. A lot of people think he's a little bit off, but one man I talked with—he's a hen fan, too—he said the old man is smart enough, when he wants to be. He said the biggest fool thing Buckley ever did was to marry Mrs. B., but he wouldn't or couldn't give any reasons. Just didn't like her, I guess."

"Couldn't you find out anything about her? How long have they been married?"

"Seven years," Henry said. "They were married by a j.p. in Rumford, but he's dead now. Her name was Rhoda Temple, and her age given as forty—that'd make her forty-seven or -eight now. She belongs to the Rumford Women's Club, and the Phil— Phil—something Literary Society, and a couple other organizations, and is what one woman called 'active' in Rumford society, if you know what that means. I ain't a society man, myself. Her credit's good at all the stores, and the salespeople seemed to like her; I guess she spends a good deal of money. But nobody knew anything about her private life, or where she comes from. Buckley hasn't got any relatives to speak of, not any female ones, so that probably explains it," he concluded.

Archer sighed. If only he could get a few hard facts to put his teeth into. Wherever he turned, he came up against the same jumble of hearsay, rumors, indefinite implications, and personal opinions—all of them without real value. It was pretty discouraging. If he didn't make an arrest before long, the newspapers would begin to complain, and worse than that, State's Attorney Golding would start squawking. But Archer told himself that he was damned if he'd make an arrest just for the sake of making an arrest. He wouldn't do it. But, subconsciously, he was beginning to wish that Deacon Grimm had gotten himself murdered in some other neck of the woods.

Henry Burke voiced a few views of his own, but they were more original than convincing. Henry was inclined to suspect: first, Forrest Martin, whom he hadn't even seen yet; and second, Frank Patterson. He thought that Gus Lafond was too obvious a suspect to be really guilty. Henry read detective stories, occasionally, and was aware of the currently popular device of making the least suspected character guilty in the end.

"If you do that in this case," Archer told him unkindly, "I might as well arrest Mrs. Patterson as soon as we get there!"

Henry hastily abandoned that theory in favor of another one sometimes resorted to by mystery-story writers: the device of the double cross, where a character is so loaded down with suspicion that the reader decides he cannot possibly be guilty; after which, the author makes him so, and the disgusted reader has guessed wrong again.

"If we do that," Archer argued, "it brings us back to Lafond; he's the most suspicious-looking of the lot. And after him, Martin. But go on with your suggestions; these writers seem to have more ideas than I've got, though that isn't saying much. What else do they do?"

Henry frowned in concentration, and recalled some of the time-worn tricks employed by his favorite authors. "Sometimes it turns out it was the investigator who did it," he said; "but that's not fair, and not many writers do it. And, once in a while, the author drags in somebody new at the last minute, or pins the crime onto a character who's been mentioned right along, but hasn't figured prominently. But the best authors don't do that, either, and it always gets my goat when they do."

Archer thought that this last idea was plausible enough, and more than likely to happen in real life, which is less carefully plotted than mystery stories. "That's the way this case'll come out," he predicted gloomily. "The murderer will turn out to be some stranger, a tramp or somebody we haven't heard about yet; or else it'll be somebody we've passed over as harmless,—old Buckley or that hired man, Luke what's-his-name, or the Deacon's sister, out in California."

Henry pointed out that Luke Prindle and Mrs. Cummings had unimpeachable alibis. "Though probably Inspector French or Captain North could find holes in them," he said thoughtfully.

Archer stopped his car at the Buckleys' gate and got out. "Go on along to Pattersons'," he directed, "and think up some more ideas out of stories, if you want to. I always thought they were a lot of bunk, but I'll read 'em, hereafter, if they help me with this affair. Tell Mrs. Patterson I'll be there for supper, if not before."

"Okay," said Henry Burke, and drove away.

Rhoda Buckley opened her door and ushered the sergeant into her living room. Seeing no sign of her husband, he avoided the davenport, and chose a chair some distance from it, thinking to himself that while Mrs. Buckley and Clarabel Lafond were unlike in most ways, they both seemed able to dispose of their husbands when they wanted to talk privately to another man. He supposed he should have felt flattered, but didn't.

Rhoda took a chair near Archer's, and lowered her voice to its usual throaty murmur, "It was so good of you to come in," she said. "I hope I have something really useful this time."

Archer said, "Yes?" and waited.

Rhoda clasped her large hands in her lap. She wore some excellent rings, the sergeant noted; he wondered if she had coaxed them out of Buckley, or acquired them elsewhere. They looked genuine and expensive. She went on, "I see you have found Forrest Martin. I hope that my hint was of assistance, though I'm afraid you may think me a busybody for interfering in something that doesn't immediately concern me. But I felt sure he was hiding in the Wayland house—I'll tell you why, later—and while I don't like to interfere, I feel that one must always give the law one's full assistance. Of course, you would have found him without me," she added hastily, and continued, "I suppose you had to wait for a warrant before arresting him?"

Archer blew his nose, to avoid answering. Rhoda went on, "There's no doubt in my mind but what he killed Leonard; but I realize that you may not have much evidence against him, in spite of what I might call moral certainty of his guilt. That is where I hope I can really help."

Archer indicated that he was ready and waiting to be helped.

"I believe I told you," Rhoda resumed, speaking with conscientious care, "that Mr. Buckley was away on Saturday night, and that I went to bed early, about eight-thirty.

That was entirely correct, but there was something else that I didn't tell you. I intended to, but we got talking of other things, and it slipped my mind. Then, too, I wasn't quite sure—then. But since you've found him— Well, anyway, just before I went to bed, a little before nine, I stopped in the upper hall and looked out the front window there, to see what the weather was like. I often do that. While I was looking out, I saw a figure come out from among the trees by the Wayland house; or, anyway, it appeared right by the trees there, and went along the road in the direction of Leonard's house, and the Pattersons'. Of course, it was dark, and I couldn't see the man's face; but from the height and build of the figure, and the way he walked, I'm sure it was Forrest Martin. I saw him for only a moment, and I turned away from the window without thinking anything more about it, at the time. It was only later, after I heard about Leonard's death, that I realized the significance of what I had seen. Even then, I might have hesitated to tell you about it; but now that you've found the man, I thought it would help you if I told you."

"That's very interesting, Mrs. Buckley," Archer said slowly; and it was, in more ways than one.

Rhoda said, "I feel sorry when I realize that my evidence may help bring about the imprisonment or death of any human being, even a murderer. But then I think of poor Leonard, killed so brutally, and I know that a man like Forrest Martin should be put where he will cease to be a danger to anyone."

Archer was trying to puzzle out why Rhoda hadn't given him this piece of information before. Had she really forgotten it, or hesitated to mention it from sheer kindheartedness? It didn't seem very likely. It seemed more probable that she had deliberately withheld it. If so, what did that mean, and why was she telling him now? "Looks as if she was doing her best to pin it on Martin," the sergeant thought, and had to admit that if she were telling the truth, it looked bad for Forrest. But was she? Either she was making the whole story up, in which case her reason for doing so would bear investigation, or else she really had seen someone. If the latter were the case, she might have seen Martin, or seen someone whom she honestly thought was Martin, or seen someone whom she recognized as not Martin. Whom else could she have seen, about that time? Her own husband was not supposed to have returned that early. Archer had contacted Mr. Buckley's football-fan friend, who had seemed quite certain that it had not been earlier than nine-thirty when he brought Buckley home. But there was no guarantee that he was telling the truth. If Rhoda had seen Gus Lafond, Archer thought she would have said so; she didn't seem to care much for Gus. Frank Patterson didn't fit into this part of the picture. Could it have been Deacon Grimm himself that Rhoda saw? He was as tall as Forrest, if not quite as broad. But if she had seen the Deacon, why not say so? Archer realized that only a stubborn belief in that hunch of his prevented him from accepting Rhoda's story unconditionally. Probably she really had seen Forrest. And yet, above his mental floundering he heard Rhoda saying, "It will be a relief to know that Forrest Martin is under lock and key. I hope I'm not vindictive, but when I think of Leonard, I can't really feel sorry that the man who killed him will pay."

Archer was still arguing with himself. "I don't believe Martin did it!" he thought, and then jumped—he had spoken the words aloud! He hadn't meant to, but they had spoken themselves, as it were. Rhoda's persistent assumption of Forrest's guilt and his own carelessness had trapped him. "You fool!" he told himself.

But no damage appeared to be done. Rhoda leaned forward a little, and something flashed for an instant in her dark eyes. Then it was gone, and she said, nodding, "Of course, you can't afford to make any mistake. But it does seem as if Forrest must have done it. I'm sure he was the man I saw."

"Well," Archer said, rising, "I'm much obliged for your help, anyway. I shall have to use my own judgment about making an arrest. But every bit of evidence helps," he added cryptically.

"Yes," Mrs. Buckley replied, "and you have your own interests to think of, too." (What the devil does she mean by that? the sergeant wondered.)

As he was leaving, he recalled that he wanted to talk with Danny Cheever, and asked where he was likely to be found. "He should be feeding the hens about now," Rhoda said. "If he isn't, you'll find him in the barn somewhere. I think . . ." she stopped abruptly. "I can call him in here," she suggested, evidently deciding not to say what she thought.

"Please don't trouble," Archer said. "I'll find him all right."

Rhoda led him through the house and out the back door. She was more silent than usual, and said "Good afternoon" without indulging in any confidential byplay, for which the sergeant was duly thankful. But, if he had been able to read her mind, he might have felt apprehensive instead.

Danny was discovered in the farther hen house, doling out something that looked like breakfast food for the delectation of Mr. Buckley's prize Leghorns. The sight of the sergeant upset him temporarily (it upset the Leghorns, too); but Archer had a soothing way with him when he wanted to exercise it, and he soon had Danny restored to normal, or as near normal as the boy ever got.

Archer made flattering comments on the excellent appearance of the hens, and found that Danny not only understood his charges, but was enthusiastic concerning them. It developed that his cherished ambition was to possess, sometime, hens of his own to take care of. The sergeant kept him talking, and gradually brought the conversation around to Danny's own affairs and life with Clarabel and Gus. It was plain that the boy adored his sister, but his feelings toward his brother-in-law were not so obvious. While Danny said not a word against Gus, he said nothing in his favor; and Archer caught an undercurrent of dislike or fear that cropped out in an occasional phrase, or tone of voice. But on the subject of Saturday night's alibis, Danny's statement was unchangeable. He remembered listening to the radio because he always listened to Silly Billy every Saturday night. The program was on from seven to eight, and while Danny had missed the very beginning, he had heard the end of the program and most of the one following. Then Clarabel and Gus had gone to bed, and Danny had done the same. Archer gathered that he was not encouraged to sit up and run the radio after Mr. and Mrs. Lafond had seen fit to retire. They slept downstairs in a room off the kitchen, while Danny's room was in the attic. Even though Danny insisted that Gus and Clarabel were in the house all night, Archer was satisfied that either or both of them could have gone out any time after eight-thirty without Danny's knowledge. Their alibis were wholly dependent on each other's words, and therefore certainly not above suspicion. Curiously enough, Archer believed Danny, when the boy said that he himself had not left the house that night; Danny's unsupported word was more convincing than the sworn statements of Gus and Clarabel.

It did occur to the sergeant to wonder if Danny walked in his sleep; or whether it was possible for anyone in his condition to do something and then completely forget about it afterwards, like a person who has had a mental

lapse of some sort. But Dr. Partridge had considered
Danny harmless; and no one had mentioned that he had
lapses of any kind. Still, it was another possibility to keep
in mind, Archer supposed.

He presented the boy with a two-dollar bill, as the basis
of a pullet-buying fund, and left, to the accompaniment
of Danny's incoherent thanks. Then, as it was nearly five
o'clock, and there wasn't time to do anything more before
supper, he walked slowly back to the Pattersons', feeling
that he needed a substantial meal to bolster up his morale
for the evening session with Clarabel. It was not an event
that he was looking forward to with any great amount of
pleasure.

At half-past ten that night, as Archer descended the
rickety back steps of the Lafond house, he felt that his
unpleasant anticipations had been well founded. He had
not learned a thing that was likely to be useful in solving the murder of Leonard Grimm. He had used all the
cunning he possessed; but he had not been clever enough
to find out what Clarabel Lafond knew about the case (if
she knew anything), or to shake her alibi for the night of
the Deacon's death—the alibi that was also her husband's.
It was his hard luck that she had turned out to be one of
those people in whom alcohol does not induce a desire to
talk freely. Either she was not naturally loose-tongued under its influence, or else the orders she had received not to
discuss the Deacon's death had made such an impression
on her that not even the most potent brand could over-
come it. Disgustedly admitting to himself that this was
just another good idea gone wrong, the sergeant prepared
to take his departure. Although Clarabel assured him that
her husband would be in Rumford for hours yet, Archer
was taking no chances; he was not anxious to be found
on the premises by the not particularly genial Gus. And

he had had more than enough of Clarabel's company. In spite of her good looks she was terribly tiresome, and the "White Rose Special" (she had consumed practically the whole of it), had not improved her noticeably; it had only heightened her natural characteristics. Archer felt that there was a limit to what could be expected of him, even in the line of duty, so he left. Clarabel put on her fur coat and went with him to the car. She was not unsteady on her feet or confused in her speech, but the alcohol had made her excited and vaguely boastful. As she stood beside the car, with one spot on the running board, she seemed to be struggling between a desire to show off, and a subconscious fear of saying too much. But her caution weakened; she said, suddenly, "I could tell you a lot of things if I wanted to. They thought I didn't know about 'em, but I did. I ain't a fool."

Archer said he was sure of that.

"I know a thing or two, if I wanted to tell," she repeated, with the irritating assurance of the slightly intoxicated. The whiskey was having a delayed effect.

"I don't doubt you know a lot," Archer agreed soothingly. And added, "About the Deacon?"

"About him and about other people," Clarabel said. Without warning, she changed the subject. "A thousand dollars," she said dreamily. Her eyes shone. "A thousand dollars! If I had that much money I'd get away from this lousy town. I'd get away from Gus and the other men around here, and I'd go to New York, or Florida. Or to Hollywood!" The roseate vision held her spellbound. A thousand dollars, to her, meant unending ease and wealth and luxury—a lifetime of gorgeous indolence, spangled with revelry . . . a paradise of dazzling pleasure . . . all the world had to offer. . . .

Then she came abruptly down to earth. "Did you know Deacon Grimm took dope?" she demanded.

Taken by surprise, Archer hedged.

"He did," Clarabel asserted, "And I know where he got it, too."

Archer held his breath, and said encouragingly, "Yes?"

But alcohol plays mean tricks. Clarabel turned suddenly sulky, and said, "There ain't any reason I should tell you about it. You're a cop, find it out for yourself. But I know something better than that . . ." she paused, undecided.

Archer said, with careful indifference, "My dear girl, I don't give a damn whether you tell me anything or not. If you want to tell me something, go ahead. If you don't, don't. Only make up your mind, I've got to be going." (If that doesn't do it, he thought, nothing will!)

But it didn't. Clarabel hesitated a few minutes longer, and then said, "It can wait. There ain't any hurry about it. Maybe you'll come and see me again before long, and we can get better acquainted?" She looked at him invitingly. There was nothing subtle about Clarabel.

But before the sergeant could reply, she shook her head and frowned. "No," she decided, "I'll wait. I can tell you later, if I feel like it." It was a decision that was to have important consequences, for several people. But Clarabel refused to say another word on the subject, and Archer drove away. Afterwards, he wondered if a little more insistence on his part would have persuaded her to talk, there and then. It might have. But, at the time, it seemed best to wait, and try again later.

Archer was tired and discouraged. Every scheme he tried ended in a fiasco like this. Was it just bad luck, or was he such a hopelessly rotten detective that he simply wasn't capable of any success? He began to think the latter was the case. On the way back to the Pattersons', he threw the nearly empty bottle of "White Rose Special" against a convenient stone wall, where it smashed into a thousand pieces. The crash gave him an obscure satisfaction.

6
Thursday—*Confessional*

Thursday started in badly. To begin with, the weather was again overcast, and the heavy, threatening clouds hung low over a gray and dreary landscape. It wasn't raining; but there was an oppressive kind of mist in the air, and the thermometer hovered around the freezing point.

Archer still felt glum and depressed over the failure of his various lines of investigation. His disposition was ordinarily so even that people somehow assumed, most unreasonably, that he never felt bad-tempered or grouchy. Being only human, he sometimes did; but he simply said as little as possible on these occasions, so that often they passed unnoticed by anyone but himself.

Then Henry Burke woke up indisposed. He had eaten too much chocolate cake and date pie the night before; even his Herculean digestive system rebelled, and he felt sick and grumpy.

Everybody was more or less restless and jumpy. The continued strain of uncertainty and supervision was beginning to tell. Suspicion and unease were in the air, they were bound to have an effect, and it could hardly be a pleasant one. Even Lucy was quieter than usual, and her lips were pressed together in the straight line which meant, with her, that something was wrong.

Frank, Forrest, and Ann worked off some of their irritation by staging a political argument during breakfast. They were fairly good-natured about it to start with, but nothing could aggravate already touchy tempers like a discussion of Mr. Roosevelt's policies. They all talked louder and louder, to make their logic more clear to each other, and were joined by Henry Burke, who was nobly trying to forget his turbulent insides.

Archer, endeavoring to make plans for the day, and trying to figure out a line of action that might get results, couldn't hear himself think. "Oh, for heaven's sake, shut up, all of you!" he exclaimed, with more force than tact. They all complied, and an uncomfortable silence fell, very different from the almost friendly atmosphere that had prevailed the day before. Everyone was on edge, and a little later, when Archer asked him a mild question about that not-quite-established alibi of his, Frank Patterson flared up as he had done once before.

"Damn it all," he shouted, standing in the middle of the kitchen floor, with a towel in one hand and a cake of soap in the other, "damn it all, I've told you fifty times already where I was Saturday night and what I was doing. Maybe I can't prove it, but it's up to you to disprove it! Hell's bells, do you have to think a man's a murderer just because he didn't have a witness tagging after him, to tell where he was every minute of the day and night? God Almighty, I've told you all I'm going to, and I won't answer another goddam question!" Frank threw the soap and towel at the sink, grabbed his coat and cap from the back of a chair, and stamped out, slamming the door behind him. Lucy said nothing, but started clearing the table, her lips still pressed together. Ann stared at her coffee cup. Only Forrest, who had beaten Henry Burke to the last popover, seemed undisturbed.

"Frank's a little bit excitable," he said. "He gets mad easy, but it doesn't mean anything. He knows he didn't kill the Deacon, and it makes him madder than all get-out to have anybody act as if he could have done it. That's just Frank's way."

Lucy said nothing, but Ann nodded. "You can't really blame him," she said. "We all feel that way, only we show it differently."

In spite of the atmosphere of strain and tension that she shared with the others, Ann was looking much better than when Archer had first seen her. He was afraid that the improvement noticeable in her appearance and spirits was due to the presence of Forrest Martin. Archer half hoped that there was some other explanation, for while he honestly didn't believe that Forrest had killed the Deacon, still, he couldn't see him as a suitable subject for Ann's regard. Although Archer would never have admitted it, even to himself, it irked him a little that any young or good-looking woman should be so utterly uninterested in him. As a man, that is. As a policeman, Ann seemed to find him likable enough, since she had gotten over her earlier anger and resentment at his questions. As a policeman, she was ready to accept and appreciate his good points. But as a man, he simply didn't exist, as far as she was concerned. This attitude can sometimes be a sort of challenge in itself, rousing in a man an interest that he might not otherwise feel. Without stopping to analyze his feelings, Archer was vaguely irritated and disappointed by Ann's lack of discrimination. He even caught himself toying with the unworthy thought that if Forrest were out of the way for a bit—in jail, say—Ann might realize that there were other men in the world. Angrily, he thrust that thought away. He was not going to allow himself to be influenced or bothered for one instant by any woman, especially one who was patently interested only in a six-foot lumberjack, with a crooked smile, who was certainly a ne'er-do-well and a rolling stone, and very likely a murderer, to boot. No, by God! If Forrest Martin had killed Deacon Grimm, Archer hoped to bring about his conviction. If there was any doubt about it, however, the sergeant swore that Forrest should have a square deal—all the more so because of that unworthy thought he had entertained for one, fleeting instant.

While this admirable resolution was forming in Archer's mind, the subject of it had put on his cap and mackinaw and gone out after Frank; a few minutes later the sergeant saw them walking together toward the wood lot.

Ann was helping Lucy clear the table. The dishes rattled cheerfully, but the girls were much quieter than usual, for some reason; and Archer, glancing at Lucy's face, wondered what was wrong now. Ann seemed to have gotten over her difficult spell; he hoped to heaven Lucy wasn't going to develop one!

"Blamed women!" Archer thought for the twentieth time, and hoped that the next homicide he was called upon to handle would take place in a coal mine or a slaughterhouse, or some other place inhabited exclusively by males!

Henry Burke retired to the sitting-room couch, with a half-hearted reference to his ailing interior. But Archer was unsympathetic; he said, "You might as well go out and help the others cut wood. The exercise'll be good for you. If you stay in here, you'll just eat some more. Then I want you to get hold of that hired man again, by himself, and see if he knows anything at all. I've talked to him, and I don't think he does, but I want you to try once more. Help him with his chores, and act as chummy as you can."

Henry Burke groaned, but rose to his feet and departed, wearing an expression that would have done credit to an early Christian martyr.

Archer decided to tackle Mr. Lafond once more. He had little expectation of success, but hoped that Gus might not be at his brightest and best after an evening in Rumford, and might accidentally let something slip. He got into his waiting car and slammed the door. Then he remembered that he had left his gloves on the desk in the sitting room. So he went back to the house, not making any particular noise—and stopped, with his hand on the kitchen door-knob.

Lucy and Ann were talking, evidently under the impression that they were alone. Feeling lower than a taxpayer's bank account, Archer listened.

Lucy was saying defensively, "I'm not accusing Forrest. But you must see that it's natural for him to be suspected. I'm just as glad as you are that he hasn't been arrested, but all the same, I won't have the sergeant trying to make out that Frank did it. You know Frank couldn't have done it!"

"Yes," Ann said in a peculiar tone, "I know Frank couldn't have done it. But the sergeant doesn't know anything, for sure. He has to consider everybody and Frank's alibi isn't much better than Forrest's, really. You think it's all right and natural for Forrest to be suspected, because he hasn't any money or influence or anything, and had trouble with the Deacon. But I'm just as sure Forrest didn't do it as you are that Frank didn't!"

"Oh, of course," Lucy said. "I can see that."

"If you'd rather Forrest didn't stay here," Ann went on, "he probably could make some other arrangement, if the sergeant will let him. He wouldn't want to stay and have you thinking he's a murderer. I don't have to stay, either, if you'd rather I didn't. We've always been honest with each other, Lucy, and I hope we still are. If you want me or Forrest to leave, you've only got to say so."

Lucy said violently, "Don't be a fool! Of course I don't want you to go, either of you. What do you take me for?

But I won't— I c–can't stand having Frank s–suspected!"
To Archer's astonishment, she began to cry.

Ann said, "Good Lord, Lucy, don't worry about that. I
don't believe anybody seriously suspects Frank."

"Why did he m–miss that bus?" Lucy demanded. "I don't
see how it could have been an accident. To miss a great big
bus in a little place like Pinkney! And then the car breaking down— Oh, I can see how f–fishy it all looks!"

"Forrest is worse off," Ann pointed out. "He had a motive for hating the Deacon and everything. But he hasn't
been arrested—yet."

"Frank had motives, too, some people would think,"
Lucy returned. "You know he and the Deacon had a row
over that apple business; I don't know whether the sergeant
knows about that or not, but he probably does. Then, one
time after that, Frank thought the Deacon was trying to
make up to me—you know what the Deacon was—and he,
Frank went for him baldheaded, and told him to keep away
from here, and not to let him catch him hanging around
ever. If that came out, and it probably will,—you know
Frank does holler so . . ."

"But Lucy," Ann protested, "Frank isn't a fool. He knew
you wouldn't ever encourage Leonard Grimm, or have him
around for an instant. He knew you disliked him."

"I know that. But Frank is jealous, Ann. And terribly
quick-tempered, though it doesn't last long. But he gets
mad first and stops to think afterwards. And he was so
insistent on going to the Convention, when he's never
cared about going before; I couldn't understand that. And
he can't prove about the car breaking down or anything,
and he gets so mad when the sergeant asks questions! He—
he got terribly angry with me when I asked him some this
morning. I can't help wondering."

Ann laughed suddenly, without much mirth. "Well, I've
got more faith in your husband than you have, Lucy. I can

understand how he just naturally got tired of being asked questions. And I don't believe he's in any danger. For one thing, you must remember he's popular around town, and stands pretty well with the powers that be in Rumford, too. That makes a big difference! It's because Forrest isn't a success, and has always had bad luck, that hardly anybody will speak a good word for him." Her voice became bitter. "Everybody is sure he did it, and wonders why he hasn't been arrested before this. I wonder myself."

"Forrest's bad luck was a good deal his own fault, Ann," Lucy observed.

"That may be, but it's no sign he's a murderer, as people are trying to make out. The papers, and people who ought to know better, are only too anxious to believe in his guilt, because he's pretty much of a failure, financially. As if that was the only thing that counted in this world! If he was well off, like—like some people, nobody'd say a word against him. It isn't fair!"

There was a pause. Then Archer heard a clatter of dishes, and Lucy said, "Well, we've got to eat, whatever happens. I suppose I ought to make another cake; Henry about finished the one I made yesterday. No wonder he was sick!"

Ann's voice had returned to normal. "Another one will go the same way unless you hide it," she warned. "You'll have to charge the state double for Henry's board, unless you can get him to wear a sign saying 'I eat Mrs. Patterson's cooking.' He'd be a good advertisement, as long as he wasn't sick!"

Archer grinned in spite of himself, and under cover of the rattling dishes went silently back to his car. He started the engine with a roar, as if just driving up, and banged the door. Then he went noisily into the house, and secured his gloves. As he drove away, he wondered if he had missed anything at the beginning of that conversation, and what he was to make of the part he had heard. He hated to eavesdrop, but if people wouldn't tell him things of their own accord—!

A cat, obeying one of those impulses which are outside human calculation, dashed wildly across the road in front of him. Brakes squealed, Archer swore, and the cat escaped annihilation by three-sixteenths of a millimeter. The sergeant wasn't superstitious, but he couldn't help seeing that it was a black cat—it would be!

The door of the Lafond house was opened by Mr. Lafond in person. He was unshaven, as usual, and looked like a refugee from a crime wave. At sight of the sergeant, he scowled and said truculently, "I ain't going to answer any more questions. I been to consult my lawyer, and he says I don't have to. I ain't going to say a word to you, or any other cop, unless my lawyer's present. I know my rights!"

This was about what Archer had expected, so he wasn't surprised. "Who is your lawyer?" he inquired, "Pettingill? Or that fellow Corbett, the one who served a term for perjury?"

Gus's scowl deepened. "Mr. Corbett was framed," he retorted. "But, anyhow, he knows enough about the law to make it hot for any lousy cops who try to do anything they ain't allowed to! He knows that because a man's poor ain't no reason he should be persecuted! He'll look after my interests, and . . ."

"All right, all right," Archer said wearily. "I know all about Mr. Corbett's disinterested philanthropy; so will you, when you get his bill. I hope he advised you to stick around here for if you try to beat it we'll have to pull you in, Mr. Corbett or no Mr. Corbett."

"I ain't going to beat it," Gus said, "but I ain't going to talk. Nor Clarabel ain't," he added, and shut the door with a bang. Clarabel had not appeared on the scene at all. Well, that was that.

On arriving at Highbrook Village, Archer stopped at the Telephone Exchange to see if any messages were waiting for him. He had gotten into the habit of doing this each time he drove by, and had come to find something pleasingly restful about the crowded-room with its miniature switchboard and blossoming plants. Rose Norton, presiding over it with calm efficiency, was restful, too. She never said much, but she was a good listener; and her cool detachment from the whole confused tangle of Deacon Grimm's death was somehow soothing, especially when Archer felt as downhearted as he did today. He relaxed in the battered Morris chair, and listened absently to Rose's reiterated "Number, please?" and "Do you get them?"

He had tried to get Rose to discuss the case, but she was characteristically reticent. "Telephone operators," she said, "aren't supposed to give opinions." She did go so far as to say she was sure Lucy was innocent; and, when pressed, admitted that she thought Gus Lafond was the likeliest suspect, because she didn't like him. (Archer thought it was lucky there weren't many women detectives; he was afraid justice would suffer!) But Rose listened to his conflicting theories with flattering attention, and managed, in some unobtrusive way, to make him feel a little less of a failure. She seemed to realize that he was trying hard, at least, and after Ann's and Lucy's unpredictable vagaries, her impersonal calm was a relief.

After ten minutes spent in gloomy speculations and wonderment as to why he hadn't joined the Army instead of the State Police, Archer dragged himself out of the Morris chair and resumed his drive to Rumford. He had reluctantly promised an interview to some Boston newspapermen, and saw no way of getting out of it. If he didn't give them a statement they might concoct something of their own, or swallow whole whatever tale the State's Attorney saw fit to tell them. Archer intended to avoid Golding if possible; he didn't want to answer the latter's questions, and he knew without being told that he would have to make an arrest, or do something, pretty soon. He began to think the fairest course (and by far the easiest!) would be to have all the suspects draw lots. There might be one chance in ten of hitting the right party!

Dinner was over when Archer got back to Highbrook. The interview with the Boston press men had made him still more painfully aware of how little he had actually accomplished. Although he had bluffed nobly, talking about "an arrest is expected hourly" and "the police are following a line which indicates an early solution of the case," he doubted whether he had succeeded in fooling those reporters, damn them! He had got to stop wasting time and do something, that was sure. What did it matter whom he arrested, so long as somebody went to jail? That was all the papers wanted, and the State's Attorney, too. Why be so particular, about getting the right one? What the Hell! But Archer Brett was, unfortunately, conscientious. He knew that he couldn't feel easy or satisfied if justice miscarried through any fault of his. Oh, damn it all!

That morning, to augment his usual, report to Captain Randall, he had made a list of suspects, with a rough case "for" and "against" each one. By studying these salient points, set down in black and white, he hoped to clarify the position of each person in relation to the Deacon's death. Perhaps, by elimination, or by a balance of probabilities he could determine who was the likeliest person to have killed Leonard Grimm. He had tried to include all important facts in his list. The question was, had he got all the facts, and could he interpret them correctly? And the answer was, probably not. He had arranged his suspects in what he considered the order of greatest probability, as follows:

1) Gus Lafond
Against: Shady character with a police record; known to be connected with racketeers in Rumford. Has money without visible means of earning it. Might be the one who supplied Grimm with dope? Must have known his wife was intimate with Grimm. Lives only few minutes' walk from where Grimm was killed, and was at home that night Looks and acts like a man capable of murder, but

For: He has an alibi for the whole period during which Grimm may have been killed. Alibi supplied by wife and brother-in-law, both unreliable. But there it is.

2) Forrest Martin
Against: Had serious trouble with Grimm, who foreclosed on his farm and forced him to leave town. Known to have threatened Grimm in the past. Found concealed near scene of crime three nights later, and Mrs. Buckley says she saw him leaving his yard the night of the crime. But

For: He claims an alibi (uncorroborated) for Saturday night. Can't prove it unless we find man who (he says) gave him a lift from Freyburg to Foxboro. Doesn't know man's name, or anything about him. Pretty thin. But Martin doesn't act like a criminal, made no resistance when apprehended, and doesn't seem worried.

3) Frank Patterson

Against: Had trouble with Grimm over politics and over a contract which Grimm made him lose. Made (implied) threats against Grimm and warned him to keep away from his (Patterson's) wife. Is quick-tempered and inclined to be jealous, without apparent cause. Claims an alibi, but can't prove where he was between 5:30 p.m. and 1:40 a.m. Saturday night. But

 For: His alibi may be confirmed yet, if we find someone who saw him between those times. He isn't a criminal type, is respected and well liked in Highbrook and Rumford; and his motives seem insufficient, in his circumstances.

4) Warner Buckley

Against: Had trouble with Grimm over a boundary line and a pig pen, if you call that a motive. Is eccentric (to put it mildly), and has no alibi for Saturday night after nine-thirty o'clock, as he and his wife sleep apart. Admits to arriving home with a friend at about nine-thirty to nine-forty. But

 For: He is elderly, not very robust, and his motive seems weak. Doesn't seem like a killer unless he turns out to be downright crazy.

5) Daniel Cheever

Against: Is subnormal, therefore hard to judge by normal standards. Lived nearby, and is under the bad influence of the Lafonds. Would be an ideal cat's-paw if Gus (or anyone else) wanted one. But

 For: He's never been known to have any trouble with Grimm. Has never acted violent or bad-tempered, and Dr. P. says he's harm-less. His alibi is interdependent with those of Gus and Clarabel Lafond.

6) Ann Barbour
Against: May have hated Grimm because of his past actions against Martin, or may have hated him if he ever made improper overtures to her. She found the body, was practically on the spot when Grimm was killed; and I think she is concealing something she knows or sus-pects. But

For: Mrs. Patterson gives her an alibi, say-ing they were together from 5:30 until around 10:00, if Mrs. P. is telling the truth? Dr. P. doesn't think a woman killed Grimm, though admits it's possible. But I think Miss B. is holding something back. Does she suspect Martin of the crime?

7) Rhoda Buckley
Against: Motive and opportunity same as her husband's? They both were within five min-utes' walk of where Grimm was killed. Mrs. B. has no alibi at all for Saturday night, as she admits, but

For: Her motive is weak. She appeared to regret Grimm's death, and talked freely, with-out attempting to hide anything, apparently. Still, I thought she was rather in a hurry to pin the crime on Martin. If she saw Martin when she says she did, it clinches the case against him. If she saw somebody else, who was it? If she was making it up, why?

8) Clarabel Lafond

Against: Not much, that I can see. She was evidently Grimm's mistress, and may have quarreled with him. She lives near, and her alibi is unreliable; She knew about the dope, and something else, that she won't tell. But

For: She seems to lose by the Deacon's death, and has no strong motive for killing him that we know of. And I can't see her killing anybody that meant dollars and cents to her.

9) Lucy Patterson

Against: Was on the spot, like Ann Barbour. She may have hated Grimm on her husband's account or her own, but

For: She is given a complete alibi by Ann Barbour. I don't see how she could have done it unless she and Miss B. are both lying. It's possible they did it together, but I doubt it. And Mrs. P. seems afraid her husband will be suspected. So, like Burke, I think she is above suspicion.

10) Luke Prindle

Against: Not a darn thing, thank the Lord. Luke had no motive, no opportunity, and a perfect alibi with eight witnesses to it!

11) Mrs. Cummings and Emery Cummings

Against: They may have had a conceivable motive for wanting the Deacon out of the way, as they appear to inherit his property, but

For: They were in Los Angeles when the crime was committed, their presence being vouched for by four relatives and three other

persons. The possibility that they hired somebody to do the job in their absence is unsupported by any evidence or even gossip, so I am
going to disregard it.

Archer had a hunch (for what that was worth!) that
the killer of Leonard Grimm was to be found among the
twelve people he had listed. Every other person in the
vicinity of Highbrook (or elsewhere), who had ever had
any known dealings or trouble with the Deacon, had been
able to produce a watertight alibi for the time of his death.
These alibis Archer had checked, and he felt fairly safe in
dismissing all suspects except the ones on his list, and
he had as good as crossed off Luke Prindle and the Cum-
mingses—that left nine. If he crossed off Lucy, that left
eight. If he crossed off . . . no, he didn't dare cross off
anyone else, yet. He added a few more remarks:

a) If Martin, Miss Barbour, or either of the
Pattersons did it, the dog wouldn't have
made any fuss; she's used to all of them,
including Martin. But, from what I've seen
of her, she'd have kicked up a row if she
thought any stranger was around. (Including the Deacon?)
b) Who is the "M" referred to in that note?
Probably Munsell. But what was he to be
told about? Several persons have tentative-
ly identified the writing as Grimm's, but
they wouldn't swear to it.
c) Did the fact that Grimm took dope have
anything to do with . . . ?

Archer heard a car stop in the yard. Then came steps on
the piazza and impatient knocking. Lucy opened the door,

and Archer groaned as he heard the newcomer's voice. He knew those oily tones all too well; they belonged to State's Attorney Felix Golding. Lucy, having no choice, ushered Golding into the kitchen, where he looked around with a superior air and inquired if Sergeant Brett were available.

"I'm in here," Archer said ungraciously. "What is it?"

"I want a few words with you, Brett," the State's Attorney said smoothly, but Archer sensed a threat—not so much in the words as in the voice that uttered them. He shrugged, and led the way into the sitting room. Golding closed the door behind them. Then he frowned, fixing his pale marbles of eyes on the sergeant's face.

"I've been hearing things, Brett," he announced. "I don't know whether they're true or not; that's what I've come to find out. Is it a fact that you've found this Forrest Martin?"

"Yes."

"Then why haven't you arrested him?"

Archer wanted to say, "None of your damn business," but restrained himself. He said instead, "Because I haven't enough evidence yet to arrest anyone. Besides, I'm not sure he's guilty."

Golding raised his eyebrows. "Oh. And since when have you been an expert at judging guilt or innocence? That's usually left to the jury. There's more evidence against this fellow than against anybody else, isn't there?"

Archer was silent. Golding went on, "I'm not satisfied with the way you've handled this affair from the start. Running around asking questions, but not getting anywhere! When I found out that you'd actually got your hands on this Martin, but didn't arrest him, I thought it was time I took a hand, in the interests of justice."

Mr. Golding's tone of voice was almost too much for Archer, but he merely said, "I didn't consider there was enough real evidence against Martin to warrant his arrest.

I don't think so now."

Golding gave him an insufferable smile. "Maybe you weren't willing to listen to it. There's a good case against him—motive, opportunity, everything. And if you won't arrest him, I intend to, right away. I can get Sergeant Killick very easily. He'll make the arrest for me if you won't."

Archer said, "Well, I won't, and I'm in charge of this case. Martin may be guilty, but there's no more reason to arrest him, right now, than some of the others. I refuse to do it. So call in Killick if you want to. He's used to doing dirty jobs for you, by all accounts!"

The State's Attorney's smug face reddened angrily, but before he could make a reply the hall door opened, and Ann Barbour came in. Her face was very pale, but determined, as if she had braced herself for some difficult effort. She closed the door behind her, and said, "Thank you, Sergeant Brett, for being honorable, and having the courage of your convictions." Then she turned and addressed the State's Attorney: "I overheard what you said just now. Under the circumstances, there's only one thing for me to do. I have something to tell you and Sergeant Brett. Something I should have told before. I—"

Golding broke in, his tone condescending. "This is very irregular, Miss—er—Miss—"

Ann ignored him, turning to Archer. "Will you please ask the others to come in here for a few minutes, Sergeant? I want them to hear what I have to say." She sat down and gripped the arms of her chair with tense fingers.

Archer found Lucy in the kitchen, cutting out cookies. Something in his expression made her ask quickly, "What's the matter?"

"Where are your husband and Martin, Mrs. Patterson? And Burke?"

"I think they're all down cellar," Lucy replied, "sorting apples. But what . . ."

Archer shouted down the cellar stairs, and presently the three men, with Lucy, followed him into the sitting room. Whatever fears they felt they kept to themselves; but the sight of Archer's sober face, coupled with the presence of the State's Attorney, told them that something serious was up.

Ann sat rigidly in her chair, paying no attention to the lecture on justice and its administration, which Golding was delivering in his best courtroom manner. She interrupted it. "Please sit down, all of you. Forrest, Lucy, Frank, I've got something to tell you."

They complied, perplexed and apprehensive. Frank produced his inevitable pipe and lighted it. Lucy looked doubtfully from the State's Attorney to Ann, to Forrest; she had been expecting something like this. Forrest said, "Ann, what's the matter?" He sat down on the couch near her chair, and said something else in a low voice. Ann shook her head.

Golding had resumed his "civic virtue" pose. "This is very irregular," he protested again. "I don't know whether I should allow it . . ."

Archer said, "I think we must listen to what Miss Barbour has to say, whatever it is."

Ann rose and walked over to the fireplace. She stood facing the room, with her back to the mantel, and clasped her hands in front of her. She looked at them all, moistened her lips, and addressed the sergeant. She said, "I've decided it's time to tell the whole truth; I ought to have done it before. I don't know why I didn't, but I suppose I was afraid. Anyway, it's the only thing to do, for the sake of everybody, and I won't be afraid any more." Forrest was watching her intently. Frank smoked hard and stared at his shoe tips. Lucy looked anxious.

As Ann started to speak again, Forrest said quietly, "Don't you think it would be better to keep still, Ann?"

He turned to Archer, "I don't think you ought to listen to her, Brett. She's—"

The sergeant stopped him. "Let Miss Barbour tell her story, Martin. If you've got anything to say, you can say it later. Go ahead, Miss Barbour."

Ann went ahead. She picked her words carefully, and spoke with deliberation; but Archer could see that behind her self-control, she was keyed-up with determination and excitement of some kind. She said, "What I told you before, Sergeant, was all true. But I left out some things. When I went out to the barn Saturday night—it was about twenty minutes to ten, I think, really—I knew Deacon Grimm would be there. I met him in Patch's that afternoon, just by chance, and he said he had something important to talk to me about, alone. He asked me to meet him in the barn at quarter to ten that night, and said that if I didn't do it, I'd be sorry. I couldn't ask any questions, there in the store, so that night I made the excuse about the car switch, and went out to the barn. He was there, waiting. He told me he'd found out that Forrest was on his way back here. He said he was going to have him arrested, on that old assault charge, and sent to jail; or else put in the Hospital for the Insane under observation, as a dangerous lunatic. Either way, he said, he had influence enough to keep Forrest in plenty of trouble for a long time, so that he would be disgraced and ruined, every way. And he'd do it, too, unless I was willing to buy him off. He—he didn't mean with money. You can imagine what he meant without my telling you. If I would—do what he wanted—he said he'd have any charges against Forrest dropped for good, and would see that he was left alone in future. He promised even to lend Forrest money, or get him a job! He promised all sorts of things, if I'd—if I—" her voice wavered with rage and contempt. Archer, glancing at Forrest, saw that the big man's hands were clenched, and he was watching

Ann closely, his jaw thrust a little forward. The faces of the others expressed amazement and incredulity.

Ann continued, "I refused, of course. I didn't believe he knew Forrest was coming back or anything about him. But I told him that whatever he tried to do, I'd stand by Forrest and help him the best I could, and we'd win in the end. I told him what I thought of his beastly suggestions, and that I was half a mind to tell everybody what he was like. Then I started to walk away. While I'd been talking he hadn't said a word, but as soon as I moved he sprang forward and grabbed me, and well, I struggled and managed to get away from him. He looked just crazy, and his eyes were queer and glittered like an animal's. And all the time he was talking, horrible talk. I jumped back, to run through the passage, but he was right after me. I was too frightened to scream, and it wouldn't have done any good; there wasn't anybody around to hear me. There was a pitchfork leaning against the wall, and I grabbed it instinctively, just for something to— to ward him off with. I took it up by the handle, and held it in both hands in front of me, with the tines pointing out and up, kind of. I thought of course he'd stop when he saw it. But he didn't, he kept right on coming. Maybe he meant to grab the handle and pull it away from me. Or maybe he didn't see it; he was like a wild animal. I held on to the pitchfork and stood still, thinking every second he'd stop. But he didn't, and all of a sudden, he pitched forward, right onto the tines of the fork, and wrenched it out of my hands, and fell against the car. I think he must have stumbled, or caught his foot on something. Anyway, he slumped down in a heap. The whole thing only took a few minutes, not near as long as it's taken me to tell it. I—I don't know what I thought—I was stunned, more or less, but I must have had some idea that I ought to pull out the pitchfork. So I did." She shivered, and Archer saw the knuckles of her clasped hands whiten, as she continued, "But I saw it wasn't any use; he was dead. Then, I suppose it was panic, or the instinct of self-preservation or something—anyway, I was terribly frightened, and I wiped off the handle of the pitchfork, and left it lying there, beside him. Then I went back to the house, and everything else was just as I told you before. And that's what happened." She walked carefully to the nearest chair and sank into it, looking exhausted. "I—I should think I'll get off with manslaughter or something, won't I?"

There was an instant of thunderstruck silence. Then Lucy gasped, "Ann! I don't believe you!"

Frank spoke to his wife in an undertone, "There's a little whiskey in that cupboard behind the cellar door," and Lucy went to get it, too upset to be reproachful.

Forrest had reached over and taken both Ann's hands in his. He said, "That was a swell story, Ann, but you don't expect us to believe it, do you?"

She gave a half-hysterical laugh. "Why else do you think I told it?"

Archer had a very good idea as to why she had told it, but he said nothing. The State's Attorney had seen fit to butt in on the case, let him handle it. And there was no doubt that Mr. Golding intended to; he was looking severe and portentous, as he always did prior to making a pronouncement. Lucy returned with the whiskey, and Ann took a few sips, under protest.

Forrest turned to Archer and Golding, and said, "She made that all up. I hope you don't believe her!"

"Don't worry," Golding said venomously, "I don't. Not for a minute. It was a very pretty story, as you remarked yourself, and Miss—er—Barbour told it very convincingly," he sneered, "but it came a little too pat after she'd heard me tell Brett I was going to arrest you for killing Grimm." He looked at Ann and raised supercilious eyebrows. "Miss

Barbour listened at the keyhole, and *after* she heard that—not before, mind, but *after*—she decided it was time to tell this fairy tale. Well, it was a clever idea, but not quite clever enough. All you've succeeded in doing, Miss Barbour, is to make me more certain that your boy friend killed Leonard Grimm, and that you suspect him. Otherwise, you'd hardly go to such lengths to make me think you did it."

Ann said, "But it's true. I did do it! I . . ."

Forrest put a large hand gently over her mouth. "That's enough, Ann. You've done your damnedest, but you couldn't expect to deceive such an intelligent observer, and—er—psychologist, as our great State's Attorney." He turned to Archer. "You're a gentleman, Sergeant, and a square shooter. I'm asking you to arrest me now, for the murder of Deacon Grimm."

Archer stared at him. "But you said . . ."

"Yes, I know what I said. I thought I could get away with that story of not getting here until Sunday night, but I figure I might as well give you the truth, since our brilliant legal light, here, has already got the goods on me. No, I got here Saturday night. Somewhere around nine. I was walking along the road toward Pattersons' when I met the Deacon. I had a few things to say to him that I'd been keeping for over a year. We met right outside Pattersons' barn, and the door was ajar, so we stepped inside, out of the storm, to talk. We got arguing, and he made me pretty mad, so—"

Ann broke in desperately, "Sergeant! Mr. Golding! That isn't true! He—"

"Shshsh!" Forrest said. "You've told your story, now it's my turn. Anyway, that's about all," he concluded. "Everybody in town'll tell you I've got a hell of a temper when it gets going; I guess I had a brainstorm or something. I remember seeing the pitchfork leaning against the wall, and I must have picked it up without noticing. Then everything went blanks and when I came to, there was Grimm lying there, dead. I've seen dead men often enough to know. But I don't remember any details."

"How about the pitchfork?" Archer remanded. "Did you pull it out?"

"I must have, if it was pulled out. I told you, I can't give any details."

"Did you wipe off the handle?" Archer persisted.

"What? Oh, yes, of course. I think I remember wiping it with my handkerchief and leaving it on the floor. There wasn't anybody around, and I figured nobody'd know I'd been there, or connect me with the Deacon's death at all. I went out through that door behind the woodshed, and got to my place without anybody seeing me, I thought. That's the story, so you might as well arrest me, and get it over with."

Archer hesitated. Golding said impatiently, "Will you arrest this man now, Brett? What in hell are you waiting for?"

Archer said, "I don't—"

"Go ahead," Forrest urged him, with the shadow of a smile. "I can't very well arrest myself, can I?"

"All right," Archer said reluctantly. He was far from convinced, but it appeared he had no choice. He made the formal arrest. "But I'm not satisfied," he began—

"Never mind that," Golding ordered. "Trooper, take this man out to the car. Better put handcuffs on him; we don't want him escaping." He turned to the sergeant, oozing self-satisfaction. "I was right, you see, Brett. It was lucky I happened to come out this afternoon, wasn't it?"

Archer said nothing.

But Ann rose and faced the State's Attorney; her face was quite white. She said, without raising her voice, "I've always heard you were a fool, Mr. Golding, as well as a bully and a grafter; but I didn't think you could be such a congenital idiot as to . . ."

Golding's face turned a mottled red; he glared. "Be careful, Miss Barbour, or I'll have you arrested, too, for trying to obstruct justice!"

Archer broke in before Ann could reply. He sympathized with her, but knew that hard words only made the State's Attorney more difficult to deal with. "Take it easy, Miss Barbour," he said, "Such talk doesn't do any good."

Ann began to cry. "I know it," she choked, "but what can I do, to make him see. . . . Oh! I'd like to . . . Forrest!"

"I'll be all right," the big man assured her. "Don't worry, and stick with Lucy and Frank. Be a good girl, and you can come and see me tomorrow, I expect." He held her hand for an instant, and started to say something else, but didn't. Then he shook hands with the Pattersons, and went out with Henry Burke, who had been a speechless spectator of the entire proceedings. Archer and the State's Attorney followed, the latter already planning the statement he would make next morning to appreciative newspaper men.

Lucy comforted Ann to the best of her ability; and Frank, trying to think of something consoling to say, finished the whiskey while his wife wasn't looking.

Three hours later, when Archer returned to the farm to gather up his own and Henry Burke's belongings, he found the three still in the sitting room: Ann rather red about the eyes and clutching a damp handkerchief, Frank still smoking, and Lucy still endeavoring to find some hopeful aspect of a situation that looked dark enough—to Ann, at any rate.

It embarrassed Archer to see the hitherto cool and collected Miss Barbour in tears. He was sorry for her, but didn't know whether expressions of sympathy would be in order, under the circumstances. He was still unable to

wholly fathom her attitude toward Forrest Martin. He
found the big man rather likable, but couldn't see what
there was about him that inspired such strong feelings on
Ann's part. Well, the whys and wherefores that motivated
women were beyond him, he freely admitted.

Ann lighted a cigarette. She didn't want to cry any more,
and you can't smoke and weep at the same time—at least,
she couldn't. Under the steady fire of Lucy's determined
optimism, she was recovering her composure; she began to
discuss possible ways and means of helping Forrest. "Will
they let me see him tomorrow?" she asked Archer.

The sergeant thought they would. "There wasn't enough
evidence to arrest him," he maintained. "If Martin hadn't
insisted, I wouldn't have done it. But, if I hadn't, Golding
would have got that tame polecat, Killick, to do it. Well,
I'm just a stepchild on the case from now on. I might as
well resign."

But he was persuaded that to do that would be to play
into the State's Attorney's hands. "That's exactly what he
wants you to do," Ann said. "I know Forrest didn't kill
the Deacon. I'm sure he was telling the truth when he
said he didn't get here until Sunday night. If I could only
find that man who brought him part of the way down! I
suppose I could advertise for him, or for anybody who saw
Forrest upr north Saturday night or Sunday."

That seemed a good idea, and could certainly do no
harm. But Ann had no great faith in its success. She said,
"If I can't find some support for Forrest's alibi, or if they
won't let him go for lack of evidence, and I'm sure Golding will never do that, I shall just go to the authorities in
Rumford and swear that I killed the Deacon. I don't see
how they can hold Forrest then."

"They'd claim he helped you, probably," Frank said dis-
couragingly.

"Yes," Archer agreed. "Or else they'd say you were doing it to get him off, the way Golding did this afternoon."

"I'll do it, though," Ann said, and evidently meant it.

Lucy, who had been thinking, added her bit: "If they try to arrest Ann, either for killing the Deacon or as an— an accessory, I shall swear up and down that she was with me every minute between six o'clock and ten, and wasn't gone long enough to even speak to the Deacon, let alone kill him!"

"Thanks, Lucy," Ann said, smiling faintly. "Your intentions are fine. But don't you understand I can't let Forrest stay in jail, and perhaps be tried, for something he didn't do? How can I?"

Lucy was silent, but her lips tightened a little.

Ann said wearily, "I know well enough you think he's guilty, Lucy. I don't blame you; I know it looks bad for him. But . . ."

Lucy interrupted her. "I don't know whether he's guilty or not. I hope not, I'm sure. But I do think it's better for him to be in jail than for you to. And, if you make Golding mad, and get yourself arrested as an accessory or something, how are you going to help Forrest?"

This sensible point of view had not occurred to Ann before. "But I can't do much," she said. "Only hire a cheap lawyer, who won't be any use, and go and see Forrest as often as they'll let me."

"I think that's considerable," Frank told her. "And if you're free, you can see about advertising for that man. And you might be able to find out something, some clue, that would prove somebody else did it."

"Nobody would believe a word I said, if I did," Ann returned bitterly. "You saw that this afternoon."

"But that was too unreasonable," Lucy said.

Archer had planned to return to Rumford that night, but it was so late by the time he was ready to start that he was persuaded to stay until morning. And he wanted to think, to try and figure out what was behind the events of that day. One confession would have been all right, perhaps, but two were all wrong. And which one, if either, did he believe? It was a perfect example of the old detective-story device—two characters, each suspecting the other, and seeking by confession to clear each other. In the stories, both would turn out to be innocent. But in this case? Archer shook his head. Anyway, the device hadn't worked, for Golding was too firmly convinced of Forrest's guilt to be led aside by any red herrings, however tempting. Also, Archer suspected that Golding had acquired some added evidence against Forrest, which he was keeping to himself. The sergeant wasn't satisfied that the State's Attorney had appeared on the scene that day purely by accident. Somebody had been talking to him.

Ann rose and went upstairs to bed; she was tired out. Lucy, who had agreed to desert her husband temporarily, went with her.

Archer lighted a cigarette, to keep Frank's pipe company, and tried to think fairly. He supposed that probably Forrest Martin had killed Deacon Grimm. After all, it had been only his hunch that the man was innocent; and the sergeant realized that he wasn't an infallible judge of character, although he had always thought himself pretty good at sizing people up. Yet Forrest's tale about the rainstorm had sounded pretty thin, as if he were afraid to give any details for fear of not getting them right. And how about Ann's story? At first glance it did look as if she were telling it solely to prevent Forrest's arrest. But if she had made it up, she was a good actress; it had rung true, in spots, anyway. She had certainly seemed anxious to convince them all that she was telling the truth. But she would do that, of course, in an effort to keep Forrest at liberty by confusing the issue. Or had they fixed the whole affair up between them? That was a possibility. Archer didn't trust Ann over-much, although he admired her. He wondered if it would do any good to try everybody with the lie detector. But he had seen too much of that instrument's vagaries to have much faith in it. It was a contrivance that sounded impressive in the newspapers, but was a questionable help in reality.

Frank Patterson had evidently been following a similar train of thought, for he said suddenly, "I'm no detective, but it seems to me that either Ann or Forrest must be lying; it wouldn't surprise me if they both were. I don't believe Ann could have had time for all that interview with the Deacon she told about. If she'd been gone that long, Lucy would have noticed."

Archer could hardly tell Frank that Lucy might have her own reasons for suppressing facts; that she, as well as Ann, could be lying. Besides, he didn't really believe it; there was something eminently truthful about Lucy. He nodded noncommittally.

"I think Ann made it up," Frank went on. "And I think Forrest's story was a fake, too. Brainstorm, your grand-mother! The only way Forrest would ever kill anybody would be by hitting 'em too hard with his fists, maybe. He might possibly do that. But take a pitchfork and shove it into anybody? I've known Forrest since we were kids, off and on, and you can't make me believe he'd do a thing like that."

Archer said, "He confessed to it, remember."

"Yes, but that was only after Ann told her story, and he was afraid Golding might arrest her. Though it was pretty obvious she made it up to protect Forrest."

Archer nodded again. "Do you think she thinks he did it?"

"I don't know. She ought to know Forrest well enough to know he wouldn't do such a thing, But, of course, she could see there's strong evidence against him, and that Golding had his knife into him."

Archer said thoughtfully, "They must think a lot of each other."

Frank gave him a quick look. "Apparently," he said drily. Then he switched the conversation to Gus Lafond. "I don't see why Golding didn't pick on him instead of Forrest," he said. "That alibi of Gus's don't mean a thing. And he's a darn sight more like a killer than Forrest is."

But Archer wasn't prepared to go into that. He remembered that he had not entirely cleared Frank of the suspicion of having had a possible hand in the Deacon's demise. It seemed unlikely, but there was still that unaccounted for period between the time he had left Pinkney and had arrived (very late) at Winchester. Probably he had told the truth about his breakdown and delay, but there was still that element of doubt in his mind, Archer found. It was there with all of them at times, even Lucy. While he talked with them, discussing possibilities, there was always lurking uneasily in the back of his mind the thought, "Perhaps he (or she) did it!" He wasn't certain of anyone's guilt or innocence; a damnable predicament to be in.

Frank rose and laid down his pipe. "Well, *I* don't know. They say, 'Murder will out' so we may learn the truth, if we live long enough. I'm going to bed. I suppose I can't expect you to tell me whom you really suspect, if you think Forrest didn't do it?"

Archer said truthfully, "I'm damned if I know."

He wondered, as he lay in bed, what the authorities would do if Ann persisted in her story that she was responsible for the Deacon's death. They couldn't hold Forrest Martin for it and believe her at the same time, not very consistently. Two confessions, each claiming complete credit for a murder, were awkward, to put it mildly. Archer

was glad that the necessity for making the decision between them had been taken out of his hands. He went to
sleep, still wondering.

It was cold and clear that night, with a dry, frosty chill
in the air. The stars were brilliant, and there was a hint of
Northern Lights on the horizon, but there was no moon.
By half-past two o'clock, the farms that made up Highbrook Ridge lay still and peaceful under the sky. They
were as silent as pictured houses and barns in some ghostly, nocturnal etching. They were as still and frozen as the
frozen ground. Only in the distance a dog barked with
maddening regularity, and from still farther away came the
rhythmic rumbling of a freight train.

The farm that had belonged to Leonard Grimm stood
dark and quiet, like the others. In the barn the cattle
moved uneasily, but the curtained windows of the house
were blank and staring. Suddenly, a shadow detached itself
from the mass of shadows made by trees and shrubbery.
It crossed the yard, and slipped furtively up the steps of
the house. A hand touched the back door lightly, and the
door opened, without noise. A voice spoke in low tones;
another voice replied. There were two people in Leonard
Grimm's house. Two people, who talked together in whispers, by the guarded glow of a flashlight. Two people, who
had met by stealth to seal a bargain. Two people . . . but
only one person left the house alive.

7
Friday—*The Morning After*

The next morning Archer allowed himself the luxury of lying in bed for half an hour after he heard sounds of activity downstairs. He firmly intended to solve the Grimm Case, for his own satisfaction if for no other reason, and he was not in agreement with the State's Attorney's solution. But he didn't feel called upon to exert himself quite as strenuously as he had been doing. Golding had horned in on the case, let him do his own getting up early! Archer decided that if he got into Rumford by ten o'clock it would be early enough.

So he hadn't finished dressing when feet rushed up the stairs, and someone pounded excitedly on his door. "Sergeant Brett! Sergeant Brett!" It was Lucy's voice.

Archer ducked hastily behind his closet door. "What's the matter?" he demanded.

"Can you come down right away? Something's happened."

The sergeant hustled into the rest of his clothes and complied. In the kitchen he found Lucy, Frank, and Ann standing around Danny Cheever, who was slumped, white-faced, on a chair. Frank said, "Danny's seen or heard something wrong somewhere, but we can't find out what. He can't seem to talk much." Indeed, the boy looked on the point of collapse. "He came running in here a minute ago," Frank went on, "gabbling something about 'police-man' and 'doctor', but we can't make out what's wrong." Archer sent Frank after a glass of whiskey, if there was any left. He gave a few sips to Danny, who got a little color back, and tried to speak, but without much success. Realizing his inability to make himself understood, the boy got up and ran to the door, beckoning Archer to follow. The sergeant seized his coat and hurried after him. Frank followed suit, after urging Lucy and Ann to stay where they were until he found out what had happened. They stayed, rather unwillingly.

The two men followed Danny across the road to the Grimm place, and around one side of the house. The Deacon's house had a high piazza in back, and the ground beneath sloped away, so that the piazza floor was ten or twelve feet above the ground, and was reached by a long flight of steep steps. It was toward these steps that Danny led them; they soon saw why.

Crumpled in a heap at the foot of the steps, on the hard brick walk that led up to them, lay Clarabel Lafond. She wore her Hudson seal coat over a long, gayly flowered housecoat. Her bright, waved hair glinted in the sunlight, against the soft, black fur, and moved when the wind stirred it. But Clarabel would not move again. She was quite dead, and cold.

Danny sank to the ground beside her, dazedly repeating his sister's name. Archer looked around for possible footprints, but the bare wood of the steps and piazza, the frozen ground and the brick walk were incapable of retaining any telltale marks. He went gingerly up the steps and tried the back door; it was locked, as he had left it several days before. A quick glance through a window showed no disorder inside the house. Everything was peaceful and quiet, except for the usual morning chorus that came from the Buckleys' hen houses.

Frank had produced his pipe, and was smoking furiously, at the same time trying to question Danny. The boy still crouched by Clarabel, regarding her with horrified bewilderment. Archer asked in a low voice, "Did you get anything out of him?"

Frank nodded. "He says he was on his way to Buckleys', to work. He always comes through this way, and he saw something lying there. I guess the poor kid hadn't any idea what it was. He says Clarabel wasn't around when he left home, but he thought she was still in bed."

"Where's Lafond?"

Danny made an effort, and was understood to say that he didn't know where Gus was. He muttered that his brother-in-law had gone to Rumford the night before. But he was in no condition to answer questions clearly. Archer told Frank to go back to his house and telephone for Dr. Partridge. "Tell him to bring Burke and the ambulance," he ordered, "but don't say anything about this to anybody else. And take Danny along with you—no, wait a minute. After you've called the doctor, go down to Lafond's and see if he's around anywhere. If he is, bring him up, if you have to drag him. I want to stay here for the present. And have you got some cigarettes? Thanks."

But Danny refused to stir; they could have gotten him away only by using force. "Let him stay," Archer said. "But you mustn't touch anything, Danny." Frank departed at a run.

Archer sat down on the top step, lighted a cigarette, and tried to think some rhyme or reason into what had happened. "Well," he reflected grimly, "I wonder what Golding will say when he hears about this! Maybe he won't feel quite so pleased with himself!" But he felt that Archer Brett had small reason to be pleased with himself, either. What a mess he had made of things, or they had made of themselves. The one ray of light that pierced his darkness was that he had been right about Forrest Martin.

It began all over again, the depressing routine that follows violent death—the tiring, disheartening round of questions and answers, checking of alibis, motives, opportunities.

Frank reported that there was no sign of Gus Lafond at his house; he was gone. Danny had left the back door unlocked, and Frank looked hastily through the house, but he was sure of Gus's absence as soon as he saw that the brown Chevrolet was missing. He brought Archer some sandwiches and coffee, and then went back to eat his own breakfast, and to try and answer Lucy's and Ann's questions at the same time.

Not long after he had gone, Warner Buckley appeared on the scene. Because of Danny's absence, he had been seeing to the hens himself, and had noticed that something unusual was going on next door. He teetered back and forth on his long legs and made indeterminate noises, while Archer told him briefly what had happened, and requested that he and Mrs. Buckley stand by to be questioned later on. It was hard to tell whether Mr. Buckley's exclamations of distress were genuine or not; his queer, horsy face was hard to read, but its expression of shocked astonishment seemed real enough. Yet Archer felt, not for the first time, that Mr. Buckley's peculiar face and mannerisms were masks that could hide an unsuspected personality, quite different from the one with which people had become familiar. He felt that he had, perhaps, neglected this psychological Mr. Buckley. Suddenly, the appalling number of things which he seemed to have neglected overwhelmed him; he hoped his incompetence wasn't as evident to everybody as it was to himself. But common sense and long training combined to get the better of this temporary inferiority complex, and Archer resolved once more, to do the best he could, and let it go at that.

Meanwhile, the physical Mr. Buckley had hastened home to tell the news to his, wife. Rhoda left what she was doing and stationed herself in the sun parlor, although even from there she could see little of what was actually going on. But she saw the ambulance arrive, and stayed at the window, watching and wondering. Buckley went back to his precious hens.

Burke, Willoughby, and Dr. Partridge came with the ambulance, and the machinery that had functioned for Leonard Grimm was set in motion once more. After examining Clarabel, Dr. Partridge gave it as his opinion, (subject to modification), that she had been dead about six hours. It was then nine o'clock, and he thought she had died around three o'clock that morning. He hesitated about giving a definite cause for death until after the autopsy, but told Archer privately that it was probably skull fracture; she appeared to have fallen (or been pushed) the full length of the long flight of steps, and had seemingly struck her head on the brick walk at the bottom. There were negligible minor injuries, but the doctor thought that the injury to the brain had probably been almost instantly fatal. Of course, he said with a shrug, he wasn't prepared to swear that the fall had caused her death; she might have been killed first and then thrown down the steps; in fact, he suspected that this was the case, but he wasn't sure. He promised to obtain expert assistance for the autopsy, and to arrive at a definite conclusion as soon as possible. "I want another opinion on this case," he said, shaking his head. "I know my limitations. Well, you won't learn anything more from Mrs. Lafond now, will you?"

"I certainly intend to learn something from her death," Archer said sternly. "Two murders should be easier to solve than one—more chance for blunders. Only so far," he added glumly, "I seem to have made most of the blunders."

"You were right about Martin, though," the doctor consoled him. "He certainly didn't have anything to do with this if he's in jail. I wonder what our dear Golding will say now?"

"He'll probably say that Martin killed the Deacon and I killed the woman, just to prove him wrong," Archer said. "Yes, this seems to let Martin out. But about the others . . ." he shook his head helplessly. But he thought things now looked the blackest against Gus Lafond; the very fact of his having disappeared was enough to damn him. His description and the description of his car had been immediately broadcast, and the sergeant was sure that he would be picked up before getting far. But, in the meantime, he couldn't ignore the fact that one of the others could have done it. They would have to remain under suspicion, technically. And for two crimes now, instead of one.

The photographs were all taken, and Clarabel was lifted gently into the ambulance. Little she had thought, when she posed so willingly for the photographers, that her last pose would be involuntary, and staged in such a setting. But Clarabel had never really learned to think. That was why she was dead.

They found no objects of interest or special note on her body; only a scented handkerchief in one coat pocket, and a five-cent piece in the other. But when Willoughby and Burke lifted her to the stretcher, Archer caught a flash of sunlight reflected from something that lay on the ground where she had lain. Quickly, he picked the something up, and put it his pocket. No one else had noticed it.

At ten-thirty, Archer paused to get his breath and to eat a hasty lunch; he didn't expect to have time for any dinner. Had he done all the things he should have done? He tried to think. He had started the search for Gus Lafond. He had talked with Mrs. Randall over the phone,

and she had promised to get word of this latest catas-
trophe to her husband. He had notified the State's Attorney
of what had happened (also by telephone) and had taken
an unkind delight in hanging up while Mr. Golding, was
still sputtering questions. He had arranged for the inquest
to be held Monday morning, as Mrs. Randall thought the
Captain might not be able to get back before then. Also,
Dr. Partridge had secured the promised assistance of a Dr.
Warfield, an eminent personage whose specialty was head
injuries. As a great favor Dr. Warfield had agreed to help
with the autopsy, but he couldn't get to Rumford until
sometime late Saturday.

Henry Burke had been given the thankless task of hunting up Clarabel's antecedents and past history, at the same
time that he kept in touch with the search for her husband.
Trooper Alfred Haley, temporarily borrowed from highway
duty, was commissioned to patrol Highbrook Ridge, and
to see that nobody left it. This was not as hard as it sounded, and meant only that Haley was to keep his eye on the
Buckleys and Danny Cheever, while the Pattersons and
Ann Barbour were under Archer's observation. And once
more it was the sergeant's job to question them all.

First, he tackled Danny, who had more or less recovered
his faculties, although he was still dazed and grief-strick-
en. Boiled down, Danny's story was simple: The night before, he had returned from work as usual, and eaten his
supper with Clarabel and Gus. After supper, Gus had said
that "business" called him to Rumford, had taken the car
and left. This was not unusual, and neither Danny nor
Clarabel thought anything about it; Gus made a habit of
spending three or four evenings a week in Rumford, on
"business." As Clarabel had no other company, she and
Danny had spent the evening listening to the radio, and
had then gone to bed, about ten o'clock, Danny thought,
for they heard the whole of the "Fisher Family," and that

was on from nine to ten. Danny had slept soundly all night, and had not heard any noises of any kind. He waked up at six as usual, and came downstairs; seeing no signs of Gus and Clarabel, he thought they were sleeping late, as they often did. As Danny ate his breakfast at the Buckleys', he left the house at once, and didn't notice that Gus's car was still missing. If he had, he would have thought nothing of it, for it wasn't uncommon for Mr. Lafond to be gone all night. So he had noticed nothing at all out of the ordinary until, on his way to work, he saw the small, dark heap which had turned out to be his sister. Archer asked if Clarabel had seemed unusually excited the night before, but Danny hadn't noticed. "She was feeling pretty good, though," the boy said. "She let me sit up later than she regularly did, and she give me a quarter, and said maybe she'd be rich sometime." His eyes filled with tears. Archer asked what else Clarabel had said, had she spoken of going to see anyone in particular, or mentioned any names at all? But Danny couldn't recall. He admitted that Gus and Clarabel "fought some," but said that they "got along all right mostly." He didn't know what they fought about, not having been sufficiently interested to pry into their private affairs. Clarabel appropriated most of his modest wage, and in return gave him a roof over his head, one meal a day, a quarter when she was flush, and a few kind words once in a while. But in her brother's eyes she had been a kind of goddess, who could do no wrong. Archer was sure Danny would have died rather than hurt her, unless—there was the catch—unless he was abnormal enough to kill her for some crazy reason, or in a fit or something. As Henry Burke had remarked, these subnormal cases couldn't be relied upon. But looking at Danny's reddened eyes and sorrowful face, Archer couldn't believe that he had harmed his sister. He let Danny go, and sent for Lucy Patterson.

Lucy was excited and a little frightened, although not for herself. For as before, when Deacon Grimm lay dead, she had an alibi; almost the same alibi, in fact, for she and Ann Barbour had been together from the time they went to bed until they got up around seven that morning.

"Were you together all the time?" Archer asked.

Lucy nodded.

"Neither of you left the room for any reason during the night? To—er—to go out back, or anything?"

Lucy shook her head. "We talked until late," she said, "and we were still awake when you and Frank went to bed; we heard you come up. We couldn't seem to get to sleep, so finally we took some pills that the doctor gave me for sleeplessness. They're harmless, but they do make you sleep. We each took one, and then we went to sleep and didn't wake up until nearly seven, when Frank began pumping water in the kitchen. That pump makes an awful noise, and always wakes me up if I'm not awake already."

"Are you sure Miss Barbour took her pill?"

Lucy stared. "Of course she did. I saw her swallow it, and take a drink of water afterwards. And she saw me swallow mine, too," she added, with a faint air of defiance.

"Did you hear any unusual sounds during the night?"

"Not a thing," Lucy said positively.

"And you can't tell me anything at all that might shed any light on Mrs. Lafond's death, or on Deacon Grimm's?"

Lucy couldn't. "I'm sorry, Sergeant, but there isn't a thing."

"All right," Archer said. "I'll talk to Mr. Patterson next."

Lucy lingered. "Sergeant Brett, you won't—you won't suspect Frank, will you, just because he was alone last night? It was just chance that I stayed with Ann, because she wanted company. If I'd known—"

"You mean," Archer said, "that if you'd known there was going to be another murder, you'd have tried to give your husband an alibi instead of Miss Barbour, is that it?"

"No," Lucy returned indignantly, "it isn't. Only ordinarily I would have been able to back Frank up. Oh, dear," she concluded, "it's such a mess!"

Archer agreed that it was.

Frank was as excited as Lucy. "By thunder, Brett," he began, "didn't I tell you Gus Lafond was the man you wanted? Now he's lit out and you may not catch him. I've thought all along he was the man to watch!"

"He won't get far," Archer said confidently. "I think myself he's the man we want; but I've got to question you all, as a matter of routine."

"Go ahead," Frank said resignedly. "But don't expect me to furnish an alibi. I can't, as usual. I was sound asleep in my bed all night, but I don't expect you to believe it. 'Most any other night I'd have my wife's word for it, too; but last night she slept with Ann, so Ann's got the alibi and I'm out in the cold. I don't have much luck with alibis. If there are going to be any more murders around here," he added disgustedly, "we'd all better go to jail with Forrest. Not even the police can find fault with his alibi. Alibis! That's all you fellows think about! Why don't you use your heads?"

Archer ignored these remarks. He asked mildly, "Did you hear anything at all during the night?"

"I did not. I'm a sound sleeper."

"Where was the dog, by the way?"

"She was in our bedroom, with me," Frank said. "But she can't tell you so. Not that you'd believe her if she could. You don't believe anybody, as far as I can make out."

"Don't get sore," Archer told him shortly. "This is no fun for you, I know, but it's no fun for me, either. Ask Miss Barbour to come in now, will you please?"

Archer felt that all these questions didn't mean a thing. And, as for noises in the night, he himself was such a light sleeper that he would surely have heard any sounds in the house, if there had been any. Earlier in the week, he had waked instantly when Ann went downstairs. If anybody had left the house, he would have known it. And yet, could he swear to it? He had been tired, and might have slept more soundly than usual. Sudden suspicion stirred in his mind: those sleeping tablets! Vague recollections of cases he had read about, of drugged coffee and opiates secretly administered, he dismissed as too ridiculous for consideration. If anyone had put sleeping tablets in his milk, he guessed he would have known it. Still. . . .

Ann came in. If she was as excited as the others she did not show it. She confirmed Lucy's statement as to how they had spent the night. Yes, she had seen Lucy take her pill, and had taken one herself. They had been together every minute between about ten o'clock and seven the next morning.

"That lets them both out," Archer thought. "Unless they're lying, of course." But he had not heard any noises in the night, he reminded himself. On the other hand, those sleeping tablets. . . .

Ann said, "I suppose I can't go and see Forrest, now this has happened?"

Archer said that, under the circumstances, he thought she had better wait. "But if I get time while I'm in Rumford, I'll stop in a second and tell him how things are."

"Thanks," Ann said gratefully. "They ought to let him go now, but I don't suppose they will."

Archer wondered if she had considered what the alternative would be if Forrest were released; the possible alternative, that is. Her words did not sound as if she had. He said, "This may make a difference, of course. But it takes longer to get out of jail than to get in, always. Captain Randall will be back before long; perhaps he can straighten things out."

Ann said, "It does look as if Gus Lafond is the man you want now, doesn't it?"

Archer looked at her. "Miss Barbour—"

"Yes?"

Archer changed his mind. "We've certainly got to get hold of Gus," he said. "Well, I guess that's all for now, though I may have to ask you some more questions later. Are you sure you can't tell me anything that will help clear up this mess?"

Ann said steadily, "I've already told you everything I know."

She left the room.

Archer found Trooper Haley waiting for him at the Buckleys' gate. "They're all here, safe and sound," Haley reported. "The old gent and the boy are out 'round the hen houses somewhere, and Mrs. B. is in there." He indicated the sun parlor. "She hasn't offered me any dinner," he added sadly. Archer told him to go and throw himself on Mrs. Patterson's mercy.

"She won't let you starve. And tell her to put it on the bill."

Haley departed at a brisk pace (for him), and Archer rang the Buckleys' doorbell. He saw a figure moving in the sun parlor, and presently the door was opened by Rhoda Buckley. She wore a plain, dark dress, which, like her expression, was soberly suited to the circumstances. Her full, dark eyes seemed to have lost some of their sparkle; but whether there was apprehension in them, or only the gravity which the situation demanded, Archer couldn't determine. She said, "This is a terrible thing, Sergeant Brett. Warner told me about it, the little he knew, that is. We are so sorry for Danny. I wouldn't be surprised if he was better off—er—eventually, but it's very hard for him now, naturally. Do you want to see Warner?"

Archer followed her into the living room, and sat down at her invitation, but not on the davenport. "Not yet, Mrs. Buckley. I want to talk to you first."

"Certainly." Rhoda smoothed the dark dress over her knees. "I suppose you are investigating this—Clarabel's death?"

"Yes. First of all, Mrs. Buckley, I want you to describe what you did last night—from eight o'clock, say, until six this morning. I'm asking everybody hereabouts the same question," he added reassuringly.

Rhoda raised her hands in a gesture of helplessness. "That's the trouble, Sergeant. I wasn't doing anything, but I don't see how I can prove it. In the evening we listened to the radio, and I did some knitting. We went to bed about nine-thirty, but as I think he told you before, Mr. Buckley and I occupy separate rooms. I went to sleep almost at once, and didn't wake up at all during the night, When I came downstairs this morning, about eight, I saw that Danny hadn't come; his breakfast things on the kitchen table hadn't been touched. I told Warner—he was just getting up—and he dressed and went out to see to the hens. Then he saw something was going on over at Leonard's house, and he went over to see what the trouble was."

"I see," Archer said. "You didn't hear or see anything unusual in the night?"

He thought she hesitated for the fraction of a second, but she shook her head. "No, nothing at all."

Archer decided on frankness. "I suppose you know that Forrest Martin was arrested and taken to Rumford yesterday?"

"I—yes, I heard so," Rhoda murmured.

"So he, at any rate, couldn't have had any hand in Mrs. Lafond's death last night. Could he?"

"No, certainly not."

Archer leaned forward. "Mrs. Buckley, why were you so sure it was Martin you saw last Saturday night?"

Her eyes widened slightly. "I didn't say I was sure, Sergeant. The man was built like him and walked like him, but I told you I didn't see his face."

"Yet you were ready to swear it was Martin the other day. Weren't you?"

Rhoda gave a slight shrug. "I could have been mistaken. But I'm still quite sure it was him."

"Then," Archer said, "you believe that Martin killed Deacon Grimm, and that somebody else killed Mrs. Lafond; that we have two separate murderers to catch, in other words."

Rhoda's reply was almost deprecatory. "I hardly expect anyone to be guided by my opinion, Sergeant, but as long as you've asked for it—are you so sure Clarabel was murdered? Couldn't her death have been an accident? As I understand, she was found at the bottom of those back steps; I think it more than probable that she went to Leonard's house after something—perhaps something of her own that she left there—and caught her heel on the step, and fell."

This reasonable suggestion, voiced for the first time, made the sergeant pause. After all, perhaps that was what had happened. It would certainly simplify the case tremendously if it were the true explanation of Clarabel's death. He remembered the long housecoat that she had worn, an easy thing to trip over, especially in the dark. Then he recalled the small object which he had picked up, and also Dr. Partridge's obvious doubt that Clarabel's death had been the result of a fall only.

He admitted, however, that the possibility of an accident had to be considered. "Perhaps we policemen are too ready to see murders everywhere," he said. "But we have to make inquiries, to be on the safe side. Now I'd like to see your husband, if I may."

Rhoda left the room, returning in about five minutes with Warner Buckley. It took some tact on Archer's part to induce Rhoda to leave them. Even after she had gone, he was a little fearful that she might be listening at the door; a dominating personality such as hers doesn't like to be left out of anything. He drew his chair closer to Warner Buckley's, and lowered his voice. But he needn't have worried, for Mr. Buckley had nothing important to divulge. He confirmed his wife's story, or rather, lack of a story. Like her, he had "retired" (Mr. Buckley never went to bed), about half-past nine, and had slept the sleep of the just all night, hearing and seeing nothing untoward. Informed, while dressing, that Danny had failed to put in an appearance, he had gone out himself to tend to the hens. "Before I went," he said, "I called the Lafond house, but nobody answered the phone. Then, when I saw you and Mr. Patterson acting so—ah—peculiarly, I felt constrained, to walk over and see what the trouble was. Ah—my wife believes that Mrs. Lafond met her death by accident. Do you share that belief, may I ask?"

Archer answered his question with another. "Is that your theory, too?"

Mr. Buckley passed a thin hand over his bald head. He gave the sergeant an odd look, and lowered his voice a trifle. "It would not surprise me to learn that Mrs. Lafond was ah—murdered. The—ah—wages of sin, you know."

But that was all he would say, and after a few more questions, which brought out nothing new, Archer left, feeling that he knew slightly less than when he came. Neither Warner Buckley nor his wife had the shadow of an alibi for the night of Clarabel's death; but neither had they any motives for wanting her dead, so far as Archer could see.

But Buckley was a queer bird, all tight. And, Mrs. Buckley was the kind that can't bear to be left out of anything.

"She has to have a finger in every pie," Archer reflected, "even murders!" He had come across that type of woman before, and had seen more virulent cases than Mrs. Buckley, who was a comparatively mild example.

Haley was outside, looking, if not "full-fed," at least more contented. The trooper promised to see that no suspect left Highbrook Ridge. "To tell the truth, Sergeant," he said, "I've put all their cars out of commission, only temporarily, of course. So, if any of 'em leave, they'll have to walk, and I guess they won't get far." He regarded his own long legs complacently.

Archer drove to Rumford. He hated to think what the newspapers were going to say, were already saying, most likely. But he felt a little better when he remembered that State's Attorney Golding would have to share his discomfiture.

It was late when Archer returned to Highbrook Ridge—after eight, and cold. But Lucy had kept some supper warm for him. Haley reported that nothing at all had happened while the sergeant was gone; then he left to continue his intermittent patrol. Archer ate his beef loaf and biscuits, feeling grateful to Lucy for her unfailing thoughtfulness. He told her how disappointed Henry Burke was at having to stay in Rumford, and Lucy managed a smile. The whole situation was beginning to tell on her more than she was ready to acknowledge, but she was determined not to let it get the better of her if she could help it.

Frank and Ann had been playing cribbage, but stopped when the sergeant arrived, and joined him and Lucy in the kitchen, hoping to hear about any new developments.

"Have they got Gus yet?" Frank asked.

Archer shook his head. "But they've got his car," he said. "Found it empty on Pond Street, outside an all-night lunch cart, I can tell you that much, for it'll be in tomorrow's papers. The fellow who runs the cart said he saw the car there when he took over at six this morning; but his assistant, who was on duty all night, hadn't noticed it particularly, and didn't have any idea when it got there. Neither of 'em had seen Gus. The car stayed there until a cop spotted the number this afternoon. But I expect they'll get Gus before long." Archer didn't add that he had requested help from the F.B.I. in locating Mr. Lafond, after informing them of that gentleman's possible connection with cocaine selling. He had great faith in the ability of the Federal men, and didn't doubt that Gus would be arrested within a day or two. But he kept all that to himself; the cocaine angle of the case had not been made public.

Ann asked whether he had seen Forrest.

"Yes," Archer said. "I saw him for a few minutes, and told him about Mrs. Lafond, to explain why you folks couldn't get in to see him today. He told me to tell you he was all right and comfortable, and not to worry about him, but that he'd be darned glad to see you when you could come. I told him I'd try to fix it so you could see him tomorrow, maybe."

Lucy said, "I hope he gets enough to eat . . ."

Ann laughed in spite of herself, and so did Archer. "The Rumford House of Detention," he said, "is noted for its superior food and service. No, honestly, he's not a bit uncomfortable. And I took him some papers and magazines. He isn't worrying."

He didn't tell them that he thought Forrest Martin had seemed for an instant curiously disturbed at the news of Clarabel Lafond's death. It was nothing that Forrest had said, yet Archer somehow had gotten the impression that some aspect of her death troubled him more than his own arrest. But the big man's customary self-control was so quickly resumed, and so impervious that Archer was hardly sure of his own impression.

Frank said, "Forrest never worries much; he leaves that to the other fellow. I don't know as I blame him, at that."

"Well, I do—worry, I mean," Archer asserted. "I'm going to have one hell of a time tomorrow, between the reporters and the State's Attorney. He wasn't in his office when I went there this afternoon, but he'll be on deck tomorrow, with bells on." He expressed his unofficial opinion of Felix Golding in words that raised him several degrees in Ann's estimation.

Frank yawned. "I'm going to bed early," he announced. "I've got half a mind, Brett, to have you lock me in my bedroom, and seal the doors on the outside or something, so that if there are any more murders, I won't be under suspicion."

But Ann, feeling more composed, than she had done the night before, decided that she would be all right by herself, and Lucy had better return to her husband. "I'll take Bella in with me," Ann said, "and bolt my door on the inside. Then if the sergeant wants to lock it on the outside, all right."

"What about Mr. Haley?" Lucy wanted to know. "Is he going to stay out all night? The thermometer's going down fast, won't he be awfully cold?"

Archer explained that he intended to relieve Haley at two o'clock. "Then he can take my room. So if you hear moving around or talking about then, don't worry, it'll be us."

After the dishes were washed and wiped, Frank and Lucy said "Good night" and went upstairs. Ann put out two cats, and was calling Bella, preparatory to going up too, when Archer addressed her:

"Just a minute, Miss Barbour."

Ann sat down, thinking that perhaps the sergeant had some further message for her from Forrest. She waited.

Archer, who had been composing an unsatisfactory report for Captain Randall, swung away from the desk and faced her. He seemed to have some difficulty deciding just what he wanted to say. Finally he asked a question:

"Where is your other earring, Miss Barbour?"

Ann looked surprised and put her hands to her ears. "Why . . ."

"I mean the silver one, that you lost."

"That's right," Ann said, frowning, "I did lose one. But how did you know it? Did you find it? I couldn't find it, though I hunted around." She held out her hand.

Archer looked at her steadily. "When did you lose it, do you remember?"

Ann raised her eyebrows. "I don't know when I lost it. One night when I went to bed, and started to take them off, it was gone."

Archer said, "Are you sure it wasn't this morning that you discovered it was missing?"

Ann stared at him. "No, it wasn't. It was two or three days ago. What are you trying to imply?"

Archer held out his hand. The silver earring glinted on his palm. "I found it," he said soberly. "Do you know where?"

"Of course not! Where?"

"It was under Clarabel Lafond's dead body."

Ann was suddenly rigid, her gray eyes fixed on the sergeant's face. Then she relaxed. "Oh!" she exclaimed breathlessly. "So . . . you think . . . you think I killed Clarabel. Is that it?"

Archer shrugged; he felt far from happy. "I don't know what to think."

Hysterical laughter threatened Ann. She gasped and choked; then she got control of herself and spoke fairly calmly. "Well, I didn't," she said. "I've never been near the Deacon's house, nearer than the road, that is. If you found my earring under Clarabel, *I* don't know how it got there. But I did *not* kill Clarabel, I know that!"

Archer sighed. "I'd like to believe you," he said, "but after the way you've—er—prevaricated about certain things . . ."

Ann's control slipped. "I didn't," she cried passionately.

He said, "We won't argue about that. But you must admit you kept things back, suppressed facts, juggled with the truth—"

Ann drew a long breath. She said more quietly, "I told you that I killed Leonard Grimm; it isn't my fault you wouldn't believe me. Now I tell you that I didn't kill Clarabel Lafond. That's the truth, but I suppose you won't believe that, either."

Archer was silent.

Ann lighted a cigarette. "What are you waiting for?" she inquired at last. "Why don't you call Golding, and tell him you've got another murderer? He'll be overjoyed to hear it's me," she concluded.

Archer lighted a cigarette of his own; he felt he needed it. "Because," he said, "I'm trying to believe you."

"Thanks."

He went on, "If you people would only realize that it pays to tell the truth! But no, you give me half-facts and garbled versions of things, and hold other things back, and make an already hard case hopeless. You all ought to know that it's foolish and dangerous to keep things from the police, and just hurts the person who does it; and also anybody they may be mistakenly trying to protect," he added meaningly. "Everybody I've questioned, with the possible exception of Mrs. Buckley, is keeping something back, I'm pretty certain. Mrs. Lafond was keeping something back, and you know what happened to Mrs. Lafond." Another significant pause. "You had no reason to distrust me," Archer continued, "and anything told me would have been kept confidential, unless it actually bore on Deacon Grimm's death. But none of you would trust me enough to play fair. And now a bad matter is made worse, and two people are dead instead of one."

It was Ann's turn to be silent.

Archer added, "You may not realize that I'm risking my job, by not arresting you."

Ann said nothing.

Archer exhaled slowly. "You think Forrest Martin killed the Deacon, don't you?"

"No!" Ann said.

"Martin said at first that he didn't have anything to do with it; wasn't around here, even. Then you learned that Golding was going to have him arrested, anyway, and you said you did it, to prevent his arrest. I suppose," he added, "you thought that being a woman, and not hard to look at, that you'd have a softer time than a man would, and would get off easy, even if we believed your story and arrested you. Then Martin changed his mind and said he did it after all, either because he really did do it, or to prevent our seriously considering your claim, or for some other reason that I don't pretend to understand. Isn't that about the way of it?"

"No!"

Archer went on, "Between you, you've succeeded in confusing the issue pretty thoroughly. *I* don't know who's telling the truth and who isn't, or whether you're both lying. You can't both be telling the truth, that's sure!"

"At least," Ann said, "you can't accuse Forrest of killing Clarabel. Not even Golding can accuse him of that!"

"No," Archer admitted, "he couldn't have killed her. But you could have. After that story you told, if Golding knew about that earring, he'd be convinced you did it. As it is, he's inclined to suspect Gus Lafond. I'd be sure it was

Gus, too, if it wasn't for that earring. But when we catch
Gus, he may be able to prove an alibi. Then what?"

There was a cold feeling in the pit of Ann's stomach,
but she said evenly, "Sergeant Brett, I hope you don't think
I want you to suppress any evidence on my account. You
could have told about the earring right after you found it.
Why didn't you?"

Archer said glumly, "Because I'm a fool. That's why."

After a rather awkward pause, Ann said, "What motive
am I supposed to have for killing Clarabel?"

"I can't think of one right off. Hang it all!" Archer ex-
ploded, "*I'm* not trying to prove you did it. But there's that
fairy tale you insisted on telling about killing the Deacon,
and there's that damned earring—how *did* it get there?"

"That's simple enough," Ann returned. "Somebody put
it there, just to make you think—what you do think. I
lost it somewhere in the neighborhood, and anybody could
have found it. I'm the only woman around here who wears
earrings; whoever found it would easily recognize it. Do
you think, if I'd really killed Clarabel, that I'd have been
such an idiot as to leave that to incriminate myself?"

"N–no, probably not." Archer leaned toward her. "Miss
Barbour, can't you be absolutely frank with me? If I told
you—I haven't any right to, but if I did—that I thought
Forrest Martin had nothing to do with either murder,
would you tell me everything you know? Or suspect? And
try to persuade Mrs. Patterson to do the same?"

Ann hesitated, then answered the last part of his question: "Lucy is afraid that if Forrest is cleared you'll start
suspecting Frank again." She smiled wryly. "Lucy doesn't
really want Forrest to be guilty, but she'd rather have him
guilty than Frank, naturally."

Archer frowned. "But what reason has she got to worry
about her husband? And she certainly has got something
on her mind."

Ann smiled briefly. "I know one thing that's on her mind. I don't think she'd care if I told you, though she's sort of ashamed to tell you herself. It has to do with Frank missing the bus."

"Well, let's hear it, for heaven's sake!"

"Years ago," Ann began, "before they were married, Frank used to be terribly sweet on a girl who lived in or near Pinkney. I don't think he's seen or thought of her for years—I'm sure he hasn't; but when that business of the missed bus came up, it flashed through Lucy's mind that maybe he'd planned that whole trip just so he could stop off at Pinkney and see that girl. She knows better, but all the same, she couldn't help wondering. You have to be a woman to understand that, but you can take it from me that women are made that way."

Archer nodded. "Do you know the girl's name?"

Ann thought. "I've heard it. Miller or Muller or something like that. No, it's Mullins—Harriet Mullins. But I'm certain Frank never thought of such a thing. Only when Lucy kept asking questions, as if she didn't believe his story, Frank got mad and wouldn't say anything more. And then Lucy thought he surely had something to hide, and she didn't know whether it had to do with killing the Deacon, or going to visit Harriet Mullins. She didn't really believe it was either, but the doubt was there, if you see what I mean. That's what's bothering her, but she won't say anything to you until she's sure you've stopped suspecting Frank. And then it won't be necessary."

Archer said nothing for several minutes. He couldn't honestly say he had stopped suspecting Frank, entirely. He didn't dare stop suspecting anybody, entirely. Except Forrest, whose alibi for the second crime was certainly watertight.

He said rather unjustly, "I wouldn't have suspected Patterson if he and his wife hadn't made misleading statements, and if Patterson had kept his temper. Lord! If only people could be depended on to tell the whole truth! I haven't shown much brilliance over this case, I know, but I might have done better if you'd all helped me, instead of hindering at every turn." He ground his cigarette viciously into the ash tray, conscious of the weakness of this speech.

Ann's conscience gave a twinge. "If we'd told the whole truth in the first place, you wouldn't have believed it," she defended herself.

"But you didn't." Archer felt that the discussion was degenerating into an infantile squabble. I did! You didn't! I did! You didn't! It wasn't getting anywhere. He said wearily, "It's almost a week since you found Deacon Grimm dead. The inquest on Mrs. Lafond will be Monday. After that, I shall have to arrest somebody damned, soon, or Golding will do it himself, as he did before—or would have, if I hadn't. I hope we'll catch Lafond. But if you know or suspect anything, anything at all, you'd better tell me pretty soon. That goes for all of you, so tell the others." He rose and went upstairs, leaving Ann to stare the fire.

Ann slept badly that night, which wasn't surprising, all things considered. She was often wakeful, but by tiring herself out, physically or mentally, she usually managed to get sleep enough, such as it was. But tonight her mind couldn't rest. It went on working, working, trying to find some solution, some key to the endless maze of possibilities that seemed to get more and more complicated. It was exactly like a nightmare, a meaningless jumble that went on and on. Only, with a nightmare, you did wake up eventually. But this! Then she thought of Forrest and relaxed a little. Things might be worse. She wished they would let Forrest go. Surely they must realize now that he, who couldn't have killed Clarabel, hadn't killed the Deacon, in spite of what he had said. Unless they considered the two deaths unconnected, and expected to catch two separate criminals. But that seemed unlikely when they were so plainly related. Well, whatever happened, she would stand by Forrest, as he had already stood by her, deliberately getting himself arrested to save her from possible danger or discomfort. She tried to plan what she would do if the authorities refused to release Forrest. She believed in him, and was sure that he hadn't killed Deacon Grimm any more than he had Clarabel. But how could she prove it? Her effort to clear Forrest and the others by herself confessing to the Deacon's death hadn't been notably successful; it was plain that neither Archer nor the State's Attorney had believed her. Yet now the sergeant was ready to suspect her of killing Clarabel, all because of that wretched earring. Someone who did not love her had found that, and had seen a chance to involve her and to divert suspicion from himself or herself at the same time. Oh dear, why didn't the police catch Gus Lafond? It seemed as if with such a good suspect as Gus, they hardly needed to consider anybody else. But apparently, they did.

The sitting-room clock struck three. Ann had already heard the subdued sounds which indicated that Archer and Trooper Haley were changing places. She turned over in bed; the windows were pale rectangles of light, and the only sound in the room was the asthmatic breathing of Bella.

Ann racked her brains. Tomorrow would be Saturday, and the next day Sunday; the next day, Monday, would see the inquest on Clarabel Lafond. After that, what would happen? What could she do if they arrested her for the murder of Clarabel? To be sure, Lucy had given her an alibi, but Ann had an idea that one person's word (and that person a friend) would not deter Mr. Felix Golding at all if he were convinced of her guilt. He could merely claim that she had failed to swallow her sleeping tablet, after making sure that Lucy had taken hers; that would be very hard to disprove, and would invalidate her alibi. And, this time, Forrest wouldn't be here to come to her rescue.

In the distorted miasma of fear that night and worry created, Ann saw a black gulf of danger opening before her. A chill realization of the imminence of that danger drove her: she must *do* something, she must! Who *had* killed Clarabel, and why? Was Clarabel killed because she knew something, or thought she did? Ann sat suddenly up in bed, holding on to this idea by main strength. Clarabel had known something. She had tried to use that knowledge for her own advantage, instead of taking it to the police. Yes, that sounded reasonable; she was the type that would do anything for money, and she was not intelligent enough to realize the risk she ran. It boiled down to one question; whom did Clarabel try to blackmail?

Ann lay down again, for the room was cold. But she stopped trying to sleep, and wrestled with that idea of blackmail, trying to see how it could be proved, and whom, when taken in conjunction with other things, it seemed to implicate. She eliminated Forrest Martin, and after him, Frank and Lucy Patterson. Deep down, she knew that they might not be incapable of murder. She was enlightened enough to know that almost everybody is capable of murder, given the right circumstances. Ann was satisfied in her own mind that neither Lucy nor Frank *had* killed Clarabel, but it was not that which made her dismiss them as possible suspects. It was the earring, placed under Clarabel's body to bring suspicion on herself. Neither Lucy nor Frank, she was certain, had done that. Driven by some inconceivable need, they might kill; but they would never sink so low as to deliberately throw suspicion on her, or a friend. The finding of the earring proved conclusively to Ann that the Pattersons were innocent in this affair.

Forrest, Lucy, Frank and herself—for she knew she hadn't killed Clarabel. Let's see, that left Gus Lafond, Danny Cheever, and the Buckleys; not taking into account, of course, the possibility that some new and unknown actor had come on the scene. But Ann felt certain that Clarabel's death had some connection with Leonard Grimm's, even if it were not a direct result of it.

Gus, of course, seemed to be the best bet. Indeed, when she reviewed it, the cumulative suspicion against him appeared so great that Ann wondered why *she* was worrying. "Only there doesn't seem to be much real evidence against him," she reflected. "No proof." But it seemed to her that an excellent case could be made against Gus, when they caught him. *If* he didn't have an unbreakable alibi.

The others didn't sound so good as suspects. At first sight, Danny looked possible, but he was known to have been devoted to his sister. He had always been a good boy, in spite of his handicaps, and had never shown any inclination toward violence. But he was not normal, and there was always the possibility that his mind might have become twisted or perverted, either through its own weakness or by the subtle influence of some other person. There was an idea! Could Danny have been used as the instrument of someone else's evil will? Ann wondered, but common sense opposed the idea. "I don't believe Danny would have hurt Clarabel, no matter how crazy he might be. And he isn't really crazy, only terribly nervous and not too bright."

She considered the Buckleys, conscious that where Rhoda was concerned it would be hard for her to maintain an unbiased attitude. She didn't like Rhoda, and never had. Ann had a knack of sizing people up, and doing it correctly, eight times out of ten. She seldom misjudged character, once she had seen enough of someone to form an opinion. But with this skill went a fault, for, once having made up her mind about a person, she never took the least trouble to conceal her opinion, either from the person in question or from anybody else. She was entirely honest and usually right; but this did not tend to endear her to some people, Rhoda Buckley among them. Ann's reasons for disliking Rhoda were hard for her to explain, even to herself. But the dislike was there, and it was mutual.

"That business of the earring would be like Rhoda," Ann thought to herself. "And I suspect, from something the sergeant let fall, that she hasn't got too good an alibi. But what motive she could have, or why Clarabel should blackmail her, I can't imagine. I don't know anything about her private affairs; hardly anybody seems to, and that's odd, too, when you come to think of it, in a place like Highbrook!" She frowned, and wondered whether Sergeant Brett had done any delving into Mrs. Buckley's past. But she realized that she was prejudiced where Rhoda was concerned, and hence not likely to reason fairly.

As for Warner Buckley, he was so queer that almost anything might be imputed to him without straining anybody's credulity. He was erratic to the point of eccentricity, and didn't seem to care how he was regarded. His peculiarities could be a cloak for almost anything, and his actual character, underneath them, was an unknown quantity. He was so flagrantly odd that he stood in little danger of being taken seriously, especially where crime was concerned. When the first reaction to the mention of a man's name is loud and indulgent laughter, it is hard to consider him as a potential criminal, even in these days, when all criminals are judged by their very crimes to be necessarily abnormal. All this passed through Ann's mind, and while it was vague and unsupported by any concrete evidence, she saw no reason why Warner Buckley couldn't be the murderer. "Of course," she reflected, "Danny and Rhoda and Mr. Buckley may all have cast-iron alibis, for all I know. But I rather think they haven't, for the sergeant

still seems to be bearing them in mind, along with Forrest
and Frank and me. And Gus. Whereas if they had good,
solid alibis, he'd leave them alone, I should think."

But what to do—that was the problem. Wait a minute, supposing she pretended to know whatever it was that
Clarabel had known. Supposing she went to each of the
suspects, and hinted at the possession of dangerous knowledge that could be bought, at a price. She remembered
a story by P. G. Wodehouse, where a character profited
greatly by going up to total strangers, tapping them on the
shoulder, and whispering with sinister emphasis, "I know
your secret!" She might try something on that order.

"Yes," she told herself. "It's a fine idea. Then when you
got the right party they'd bump you off, just as they did
Clarabel. Yes, that's a real bright notion!" She reminded herself that she was smarter than Clarabel. No doubt,
but was smartness any protection against a crack over the
head in a dark place, or a knife in the ribs, or a bullet in
any of several vital spots? She might take her conclusions
to the sergeant, but she doubted if he would pay them
much attention. "After what's happened, he doesn't trust
me much, and no wonder! No, I can't say anything until I
have some proof to show him. Proof, proof, proof!"

She pulled the blankets closer around her and tried to
think. Before it began to grow light, she had gotten the
first faint glimmerings of an idea.

8

Saturday—*Hide and Seek*

Archer Brett hadn't been far wrong in his estimate of what the next day would be like. The only satisfactory thing about it was the weather, which continued cold but very clear. The sky was intensely blue, and so was the sergeant. Although not naturally a pessimist, he was beginning to despair of ever solving the murders of Deacon Grimm and Clarabel Lafond. Everything about them was so nebulous; he had never seen a case with so few hard facts for the police to get their teeth into. Confusion and contradiction flourished, and he didn't know what action to take next.

Having spent half the night relieving Trooper Haley, he felt tired and unrefreshed when morning came. There was a pronounced air of constraint over the breakfast table: Frank was very silent, for him; Lucy looked worried; and Ann, who was late in appearing, seemed preoccupied, and looked as if she hadn't slept much. Which she hadn't. But Archer was satisfied that nobody had left the house during the night. He had taken precautions, and could swear to it.

Ann was disappointed when Archer said that he thought it would be wise to wait another day before trying to see Forrest. But she accepted his judgment, and promised, with Frank and Lucy, not to leave Highbrook Ridge that day. Haley, Archer said, would continue his irregular patrol of the neighborhood, but would try not to be a

197

nuisance. When reporters showed up, as they undoubtedly would, Haley would deal with them. He was such a deliberate person that most reporters hadn't the patience to cope with him; he wore them out.

In Rumford, the sergeant bought some papers: they came up to his expectations. Large headlines and pictures of Clarabel decorated the front pages. The tabloids had no text worth mentioning, but what there was didn't flatter the police. The local papers were more discreet, but their general attitude expressed the view that there must be something wrong with the guardians of the law if beautiful girls could be murdered under their noses, so to speak; the implication was that if the victim had been old and unattractive it wouldn't have mattered so much! Great emphasis was placed on Clarabel's youth and beauty; her relationship with Deacon Grimm was unknown to the papers, although they speculated freely as to her connection with his death. Mention was made of Forrest Martin's continued detention as a "material witness" in the Deacon's death, but the newspapers were plainly most interested in the disappearance of Gus Lafond. Without actually accusing Gus of killing his wife, they wanted him found, and implied that the police should have run him to earth before this. As usual, their remarks were of that indefinite nature which it is impossible to pin down in court, but which form the desired impression in the (so-called) minds of the newspaper-reading public. And they would get worse and worse until another arrest was made. Archer sighed.

When he reached his office, he found it besieged by reporters; but he hadn't played four years of semi-professional football for nothing. He gained his private room and locked the door behind him, after stating briefly that he would give the press a statement later in the day, *if* he were not disturbed in the meantime.

Henry Burke looked up from his desk as Archer entered. "I'm glad you've got here," he said. "That bunch has been hanging around since six o'clock; waiting for you, like animals waiting to be fed. I didn't tell 'em anything, but you'll have to, or we won't get out of here alive."

Archer consigned the reporters to a place not recommended as a health resort, and said that they could wait until that location grew much more frigid. He asked if there were any news of Gus Lafond.

"Not a bit," Henry said reluctantly. "After he left his car in front of that lunch cart, he just disappeared. We've had reports about his being seen in a dozen different places, but every one proved to be a false alarm."

Archer was disappointed, although he knew it was unreasonable to expect miracles from the police, even those connected with the Federal government. Competent as they were, they didn't claim to be magicians. "Slow but sure" was their slogan; he must be patient; and remember that his own progress on the case had been far from meteoric! He changed the subject:

"Have you learned anything about Clarabel that's likely to help?"

Henry hadn't. Clarabel's history, like that of hundreds of her kind, started with a shiftless and divided family and arrived, by way of the County Farm and an Orphans' Home, at the roadhouse where she had met Gus Lafond.

"She ran away from the Orphans' Home eight times," Henry said, "and the last time she took Danny with her. I guess the people at the Home, were pretty discouraged by that time, for they left her alone, and Danny, too. They said she was incorrigible, and I guess her morals were always pretty bad; but she never seems to have been mixed up in anything criminal. After she married Gus, she minded her own business and he minded his, and if he was bothered by her—er—professional activities, he didn't seem to show

it much. We haven't been able to contact any of her relatives except Danny. Her father died at the County Farm a
couple years ago, and her mother had already run off with
another man, and nobody knows where she is. They ain't
the kind of people that'd call themselves to our attention
unless there was something in it for them. That's all I've
found out, and I don't see what use it is."

Archer didn't see, either. "We're stuck," he said, "until
we catch Gus. I might as well tell the reporters that, and
stall 'em along until the inquest. At least, Golding can't
lay all the blame on me and the police; if he tries to, I'll
tell the reporters what a boner he pulled by arresting Martin. The papers could work up quite a bit of sympathy for
Martin if it came out that he was falsely accused, or forced
into a confession by a brutal State's Attorney. Golding
wouldn't like that a little bit."

Henry looked at the clock. "Doc Partridge said he'd be
in to see you around eleven. I guess that's him now." There
was an increased clamor in the outer office, and the doctor's raised voice was heard insisting that he didn't know a
thing. Archer unlocked the door and admitted him.

"Dr. Partridge is making me a private visit," he told the
newspapermen. "I've got a bad headache and a pain in the
neck." He relocked the door.

The doctor said, "Whew!" and shook himself. "Nice
people, reporters! Well, I suppose they have to live. Better
to look through keyholes for a tabloid than to be on 'relief.' Have you found Lafond yet?"

He was sympathetic when he heard they hadn't. He
said, "I have got a bit of news for you, Archer, though I
wouldn't tell it to those scavengers outside. It's nothing
startling," he warned, as the two policemen leaned eagerly
forward, "but it does confirm my belief that Mrs. Lafond
was murdered. When I got her to the hospital, I made a
more careful examination than I was able to out there,

and I'm pretty sure of what I suspected then. It wasn't the fall down the steps, nor hitting the brick walk that killed her. I found a terrific bruise on one temple, where she was hit by some solid, but probably not rigid, object; a sand bag, or something similar. That blow rendered her unconscious, and probably caused almost instant death from skull fracture and injury to the brain. I'll want Dr. Warfield's opinion, so you'll have to wait until after the autopsy for the technical details. But that blow wasn't caused by the fall, and it's my opinion she was already dead when she was pushed or thrown down the steps. The murderer thought, no doubt, that in the general damage resulting from the fall, her death would pass as an accident. The knowledge of most people is so slight they wouldn't realize how easily a doctor can discover the truth." He lighted a cigarette. "I'm not telling this officially until the inquest, but I thought you might like to know it right away."

Archer thanked him. "It's something to eliminate the possibility of accident," he said. "By the way, Doctor, was Mrs. Lafond a cocaine user?"

"I've no reason to think so. Tobacco and whiskey only, I should say."

"I can search their place for drugs, now," Archer said. "I haven't a scrap of proof, yet, that Gus had anything to do with cocaine. Deacon Grimm may have got his from some other source entirely."

The doctor doubted it. "When you find a dope user and a possible dope seller as near each other as those two— well, it's reasonable to put them together."

"And the chances are there's nothing in Lafond's house now, even if he does handle it," Archer said. "And if there is any, it'll be so damned well hidden we'll have to tear the house apart to find it."

The telephone rang, and Henry Burke answered it: "Hello? . . . I'll see, but I don't think he's come in yet.

Just a minute." He put his hand over the mouthpiece, and his lips formed the word "Golding."

"Tell him I'm out," Archer whispered. Henry did so, and hung up.

"And I'm going to be out, to him, until the Captain gets here," Archer said, "If Golding comes 'round, you go to the door, Henry, and don't let him in."

The doctor rose. He said, "I've got a kind heart. How would it be if I gave those reporters a nice re-hash of events for tomorrow's edition? 'The Doctor's Viewpoint,' or something like that. I won't tell 'em anything important, but I might keep 'em quiet until you're ready with your statement later. Okay?"

"You ought to have a medal," Archer said. "Will you do us one more favor, and stop in at the Pilgrim Diner, and ask them to send some dinner over to us here? I don't want to be seen yet, in case Golding's got us under observation. Any thing'll do for me; liver and bacon if they've got it."

"And a steak for me," Henry Burke said, with a sigh. "And French fried with onions. And a bottle of beer. But," he added, after the doctor had gone, "I haven't had anything really first-class to eat since you dragged me away from Mrs. Patterson's. How is she?"

"She's all right," Archer assured him. "And if this case is ever cleared up, I'll get you leave, and you can go and board there for a month. Now, let's see those reports."

After the sergeant had gone, Ann Barbour shut herself in the sitting room with some books that she had been commissioned to review, and thought. Regarded in the cold light of morning, the plan she had conceived the night before looked not only illogical but impractical, if not downright impossible. But her apprehensive dread had not departed with the daylight, as she had half expected it

to do; it still lurked in the background of her conscious-
ness, like a gray and formless mist of uncertainty and fear.
It fogged her ability to think clearly, and distorted her
judgment, so that the more she thought, the less sure she
became of the truth of her conclusions. She felt positive,
from the sergeant's attitude toward her, that he was undecided about her innocence. As a matter of course, he
was trying to catch Gus Lafond, and Gus looked like the
most reasonable person to arrest, when he was caught. But
after all, the sergeant had found that earring; he knew
how hard she had tried to convince him and the State's
Attorney that she had killed Leonard Grimm; and he knew
that she had not been frank with him in the past. How
could he help suspecting her? And she was afraid that Gus,
when found, might produce an unbreakable alibi; he had
friends who could easily manufacture such things. If that
happened, and Archer told Golding about the earring, as
he would have to—Ann shivered. She felt that she couldn't
sit still doing nothing, while every minute danger might
be coming nearer, and a net drawing closer that she might
find impossible to break. No, she must *do* something; she
must try to carry out the plan she had made, ridiculous as
it might appear. But how she was going to set about it, she
had only the haziest idea.

She wished she could talk things over with Lucy, but
she didn't dare. Not that she distrusted Lucy, but she knew
subconsciously that her cousin would try to dissuade her
from doing what she planned. Lucy would urge her to
wait; to leave detecting to the detectives, and not to meet
trouble halfway. But then, Lucy didn't know about that
miserable earring. Ann felt that she couldn't bear to have
anyone else suspecting her of having caused Clarabel's
death. And she knew how insidiously suspicion creeps un-
wanted and uninvited into the most determined mind. No,

she couldn't tell anyone about her plan, until it had succeeded—or failed.

After dinner, she said matter-of-factly, "I can't sit
around here any longer, Lucy. I'm going for a walk, just
around the neighborhood." She knew that Lucy wouldn't
offer to accompany her, for Lucy hated walking, unless
there were store windows to be looked into.

"All right," Lucy said, "if you think it's safe. But why
don't you go along with Trooper Haley? He'd probably be
glad of company."

Ann made a face. "I don't care much for Trooper Haley.
I prefer your young admirer, Trooper Burke. Which way
did Haley go, did you notice? I'll go in the opposite direction."

Lucy thought that Haley, after disposing of his last
batch of reporters, had walked down the wood road to
have a smoke with Frank. Owing to the enforced curtail-
ment of his other activities, Frank was cutting more wood
than he had planned to; but he could always find a market
for it.

"I'll go down to the Bridge," Ann decided. "I saw some
black alder berries beside the brook last week, and I'll try
to get some." She put on her coat and leather driving-
gloves. There was a flashlight in her pocket.

"Well, don't fall in," Lucy said. "If you're gone too long,
I'll send Haley after you. Are you going to take Bella?"

Ann had already shut the puzzled Bella in the woodshed, so she hoped she would be forgiven for saying, "I
would, but she doesn't seem to be around. I think perhaps
she went with Frank."

Once away from the house, Ann walked rapidly down
the hill to where the Old Road left the main road. She
hurried to the Lafond house, knowing that at this time of
day, Danny would be at the Buckleys'. The house seemed
deserted, and there were no signs that Gus had returned to

lurk about his erstwhile dwelling place. Ann went through the yard, and climbed the bank to the pathway that Danny habitually used, which paralleled the main road. It led across the fields, and no houses overlooked it until it passed behind the Deacon's buildings. Ann kept a sharp lookout for Trooper Haley or any roving reporters; but the bare meadows were deserted, and the conformation of the ground was such that the path wasn't visible from the road or from the Pattersons' house. And, of course, if she were seen, she was only taking a walk, as anybody had a right to do.

From the back, Leonard Grimm's house looked bleak and inhospitable. The windows looked as if they had never been opened, and weren't meant to be. Three small-paned windows in the shed, which connected the house with the barn, were firmly fixed and immovable. Ann knew that the big barn doors were fastened, and the small one locked, for Luke had the key to it. Also, both barn doors were in plain view of the road and the Buckleys' house. But in the back of the barn was a small square window that was innocent of glass, and looked practicable, although it was uninvitingly draped with cobwebs. It wasn't very big; but Ann, who wasn't very big either, thought that she could get through it. A large empty hogshead was fortunately within dragging distance; Ann maneuvered it into a favorable position, climbed onto it, and managed, after several tries, to scramble through the window. A conveniently placed pile of boxes inside made her descent easy, and she found herself in a musty storeroom. So far, so good. "And it isn't housebreaking," she reflected, "because I didn't have to break anything!"

She went cautiously into the barn proper, where six cows regarded her with no interest whatsoever. The door leading into the connecting shed was easy to find and open, but the door from this shed into the house, when tried, proved to be fastened on the inside, as such doors usually are.

"There," said Discretion. "You can't go any farther, and it's no use trying. Go on home now, while you can, and while the going is good. You're no detective."

Ann was willing to concede that; but she was stubborn, and having gotten this far, she didn't mean to give up if she could help it. For she wanted to search the Deacon's house. She knew that Archer had already searched it, but the idea persisted in her mind that there might be something there; something that would account for Clarabel's visit in the night, and for the presence of her dead body in the morning. Ann believed that only by finding the real murderer could she dispel the suspicion that attached to herself. And some obscure impulse told her that the place to look for a clue to that murderer was in the Deacon's house.

She prowled about the shed, opening every door in sight, but closets and cupboards were all she found. Not very hopefully, she returned to the door that she knew led into the house, and rattled the latch. The door didn't fit very tightly, and Ann discovered that it wasn't bolted, as she had thought, but merely secured on the inside by a large hook and screw eye. Shaking the door would not dislodge the hook, but Ann suddenly remembered a trick she had read or heard about. She hunted through the shed, and finally found what she wanted—a discarded table knife, with a fairly thin blade. It was rusty, but would do the trick, she hoped. She inserted it in the crack between the door and they frame, and gently levered it back and forth. After five minutes of effort, she succeeded in thrusting the edge of the knife against the hook inside, and raising it out of the screw eye. The hook fell back, and Ann unlatched the door and entered Leonard Grimm's kitchen.

She had not been lying when she told Archer that she
had never been inside the Deacon's house. But she had
been inside many similar houses, and was familiar with
their basic plan. This one ran true to form, differing only
in details from a dozen others with which she was acquainted. It had a narrow hall leading from the front door
to the kitchen, with a parlor on one side of it, and a sitting room and dining room on the other, the dining room
in its turn opening into the kitchen. Leaving the shed
door unfastened behind her, Ann crossed the kitchen and
passed between fringed portieres into the hall. With an
uneasy feeling that she couldn't have too many exits, she
unlocked the front door (the key was in the lock) and left
it ajar, in case rapid retreat became necessary. Then she
looked around. The hall was bare, except for a rag rug, and
one of those Victorian monstrosities, a hat stand. A long
flight of uncarpeted stairs led to regions above. The house
was cold, and the drawn curtains made it dim and gloomy,
although the sun was shining outside. A small, unpleasant
shiver went through Ann, in spite of the heavy coat she
wore. But she disregarded it. Of course the house seemed
dank and depressing; it had been shut up for a week: it was
just an unoccupied house. The fact that it had belonged
to dead Leonard Grimm didn't make it any different from
any other empty house. Of course not!

She tackled the parlor first. This dismal survival of
the horse hair era was freezing cold, and looked as if its
ceremonial sanctity hadn't been disturbed for generations.
Dust lay thick over everything, indicating that Sergeant
Brett's search of this room, at least, had been but perfunc-
tory. She closed the door and tried the sitting room opposite, and here the sergeant had been more thorough; while
there was no disorder, the unmarked layer of dust was
light, and under it signs of an earlier search were evident.

But there were no marks that looked really recent, and Ann tried not to make any. Even though she was wearing gloves; she wasn't anxious to leave traces of her presence.

The house was comfortably furnished throughout, and everything was orderly, almost too orderly. Even in the kitchen, there was none of the careless untidiness that sometimes hides a clue. The wood box held only wood; the china closet nothing but china. There were very few personal belongings in evidence, and no books or magazines; only two week-old newspapers lying on the kitchen table. One of them, probably, was the one Leonard Grimm had been reading, before he left his house, for the last time. Hasty inspection of cupboards and drawers revealed nothing suspicious or unusual, beyond the fact that Clarabel had not been an immaculate housekeeper. No, there was nothing at all downstairs that supported in the slightest degree the tenuous theory that Ann had formed.

"I might have known there wouldn't be anything," she said to herself. "If there was anything, either Clarabel took it and hid it somewhere, or else the person who killed Clarabel got it, and destroyed or hid it." Rhoda Buckley's suggestion to Archer—that Clarabel had been merely retrieving some compromising possession of her own—had already occurred to Ann. But that would not explain Clarabel's death, nor the planting of Ann's earring under her body. No, Clarabel had been killed by someone she had met, or who happened on her, in the Deacon's house. But Ann realized the hopelessness of the task she had set herself: a thousand to one there was no clue in the house, and if there were, how was she to recognize it? Like the sergeant, before her, she discovered that clues are seldom labeled for the convenience of the investigator!

She went upstairs, thinking that in the Deacon's bedroom, if anywhere, she might find something. An hour or more had passed; it was getting gloomier and gloomier

inside the house, although it was only about half-past
three. Ann glanced inside the bedrooms, one after the
other. Three were so stuffy and close that, it was plain
they had been shut up by Mrs. Cummings before she left
for California. The other, not so dusty, must have been
Leonard Grimm's. It was a very comfortable chamber, and
the Deacon had evidently used it for a sort of office as
well, for a large roll-top desk stood between two windows.
But to Ann's disgust the desk was locked, drawers and all.
Of course, the sergeant had seen to that. But if he had
searched it, as he undoubtedly had, and found nothing,
probably nothing had been put into it since, for he had
the Deacon's keys. Ann turned to the bureau, but it con-
tained only what might be expected of a bureau: neatly
folded underwear, shirts, ties, socks, and other articles
of male adornment. She looked through everything fairly
thoroughly, but there was nothing resembling a clue.

Next she tried the closet, deep and dark, where the
Deacon's clothes still hung, smelling faintly of mothballs.
Ann felt in all the pockets, but found nothing. She exam-
ined the closet floor, thinking hopefully of secret hiding
places beneath the floor boards, but unearthed only four
pairs of dusty shoes and a derelict mouse trap. Remembering certain ingenious mystery stories, she looked in all
the shoes, but they were empty. "Oh dear," Ann thought,
"what an awful fool I am. Of course the sergeant has been
over all these things." But she had so hoped to find some
clue that had eluded the sergeant, some pointer that might
reveal what Clarabel (or her murderer) had been after.

The house was deadly cold, and still. Shadows were
collecting in the corners of the room, and Ann had to
resist an increasing desire to look over her shoulder. She
returned to the desk, as a last resort. There were a few
books on top of it: several volumes of Town Reports, a
dictionary, and a book on the care and diseases of cattle.

Beside them lay an untidy heap of motion-picture magazines, presumably left there by Clarabel since Deacon
Grimm was well known to have read nothing beyond the
daily papers. Ann looked through all the books, ruffling
the pages, and holding them wrong side up, so that any
loose papers would fall out. Nothing did. She treated the
magazines the same way, without results. But under the
last of those deplorable periodicals appeared something in
strange contrast to their shoddiness—a large, calf-bound
volume, dog-eared and dilapidated but unmistakable, an
old-fashioned Family Bible. Ann opened it. On the flyleaf
was written in faded ink, "Elias Grimm," and a date, 1797.
Ann's hopes rose—here was something at last! A Family
Bible might conceivably hold some such clue as she was
seeking. She carried the big book to the bureau, and began to hunt for the pages of Records, which every Family
Bible possesses. Failing to find them in the middle of the
volume, she was just turning to the back, when she heard
a noise. It seemed to be downstairs. Ann stiffened. It was
imagination, she told herself, or something outside. Or a
noise made by the wind, only there wasn't any wind. Then
she heard it again, and it wasn't her imagination this time;
it was a real noise. It sounded like footsteps, like someone
who wasn't used to doing so trying to walk cautiously. It
was footsteps! Ann felt her heart give a jump, and begin
to thud at twice its normal speed. Her throat grew dry.
Somebody was coming up the stairs.

Archer spent an unsatisfactory hour interviewing various persons who thought they had valuable revelations
to make concerning Gus Lafond. But their information
was all either stale, or so vague as to be worthless. The
search for Gus had spread into all neighboring states, and
his description had been widely circulated. But he hadn't

been found. Archer still hoped he hadn't left the state; the local police systems were moderately efficient, and all bus and railroad terminals were being watched. No cars had been reported stolen since Gus's disappearance; but he might easily have appropriated a car from some friend, who would naturally not disclose the fact to the police. The taverns, pool rooms, and other unsavory places that he was known to have frequented had all been searched, and their proprietors and patrons questioned, but nobody knew where he was. "Gus? Why no, we ain't seen him for weeks. Gus Lafond? No, I haven't any idea where he is if he isn't home. Hey, Dave, seen anything of Gus lately? Naw, I ain't seen him for a month!" And so on. All state and city police were on the lookout, and Archer knew that Gus would be caught eventually; the only real danger lay in the possibility that he might do more damage before he was caught.

While Archer was trying to decide whether he ought personally to join the hunt, a vigorous rattling of the doorknob indicated that somebody was trying to get in. It was followed by a familiar voice, raised in fluent profanity. Henry Burke sprang to open the door, and Captain Randall walked calmly in, carrying a suitcase and a shotgun, which he deposited carefully in a corner.

Archer had never been gladder to see anybody in his life. He knew that the Captain wouldn't waste any time over useless and disheartening recriminations.

He didn't, either. After shaking hands, he plunged into discussion of the case, showing a complete knowledge of all the latest developments.

"I got your reports," he told Archer, "besides reading the, papers. You've done all right. I don't know what more I could have done myself. 'T wasn't your fault that fool Golding butted in. I'll talk to *him!* Now let's hear what's been done since you found the girl. Take it easy."

That was Captain Randall all over, and explained in part why he was so well liked by the men who were under his command. By giving them full credit for what they had done, and overlooking their failures when possible, he made them willing and anxious to do their best, to prove that they were deserving of such square treatment.

Archer told him exactly how things stood, without trying to minimize what he felt to be his own shortcomings; but the Captain brushed those aside. "Main thing is to get Lafond," he said, "and keep good watch on the others. No sense in keeping Martin in jail, now; likely to do more harm than good, as I see it. If he's innocent he'll be working up a case against us for false arrest or something, and if he isn't—well, we'll have more chance to get evidence against him outside than cooped up in jail. I'll see if I can get him out. Let's go see Golding, though the sight of him gives me a pain!"

They were halfway down the stairs when Henry Burke came after them. "The doc just called up," he said in a whisper (there were still newspapermen lurking in the corridors), "That other doc who's going to help with the autopsy came earlier than he expected, and they're starting it now. He said if you call up, or come around to the hospital about six, maybe they can give you all the particulars."

"That's fine," Captain Randall said. "I want you to keep right in touch with the hunt for Lafond, Burke; I've a hunch he'll show up pretty soon. I guess among us we can get this thing cleared up before very long."

Archer felt that Captain Randall deserved a reserved seat in heaven—first row in the balcony, center!

They found Mr. Felix Golding in his office, and alone, for a wonder. Two secretaries (both easy on the eyes), who tried to bar the way to the inner sanctum, were waved politely but firmly aside. "We've got business with your boss," the Captain said shortly.

The State's Attorney half rose from behind his mag-
nificent mahogany desk, and opened his mouth, but the
Captain beat him to the draw, as it were.

"Look here," he snapped, "didn't I tell you not to
interfere with Brett in this Grimm case? What do you mean
by shoving your oar in? What do you mean by arresting
this Martin, with no more evidence against him than you
had? Confession? Hell! Couldn't you see the man was just
making that up because he was afraid you might arrest the
girl? Don't you see that by arresting him you've played
right into the murderer's hands? I'm surprised at you! No,
I'm not—much. First thing we know, some lawyer will get
hold of Martin and try to make trouble for us—for you, I
mean. I should think you'd realize that a lot of people in
this state don't like you, and would be only too pleased to
have any kind of an instrument to use against you. Now,
get busy; I want this man released right away."

The Captain paused for breath, and Golding, recovering himself, said pompously, "This is a serious affair,
Captain Randall. To say nothing of your absolutely in-
excusable attitude to myself, I had excellent reasons for
arresting Forrest Martin. I don't intend to release him on
your orders. In fact, I don't intend to release him at all."

Captain Randall turned to Archer, "Would you just as
soon step outside a minute, Brett? I'll be right with you."

Archer complied.

Captain Randall stepped closer to the mahogany desk.
He rested his hands on its glassy surface and, leaning on
them, brought his face level with Golding's. "I wish you'd
accede to my request, Mr. State's Attorney," he said mildly.

Golding raised his eyebrows. "I don't see why I should."

"Don't you?" the Captain inquired. "Then I'll tell you."
He paused. "You'd better do as I ask you to, because if
you don't, I shall be under the necessity, the very painful
necessity, of informing—er—official circles, and perhaps
the newspapers, too, where you were and what you were

engaged in doing, three weeks ago Sunday night, in a certain private—er—hideaway, which is kept . . .”

Golding sprang to his feet. “That’s a bluff,” he cried. “You don’t know a thing.”

Captain Randall smiled sweetly. “Oh yes I do. I know plenty. I know several people who’ll be tickled to death to testify that they saw you there; in fact, one of them took a picture; these Candid Cameras are wonderful inventions.”

Golding collapsed in his chair. His dark complexion paled. “You wouldn’t do that!”

The Captain shrugged. “I should dislike doing it,” he remarked untruthfully, “but I might feel it was my duty, unless. . . .” He left the sentence in the air.

“All right,” Golding said. He managed a sickly smile. “Of course, I shall be—er—delighted to release anyone of whose innocence you are convinced. And I hope you will—er—realize that your friends were—are mistaken.”

The Captain said shortly, “I’ll say nothing this time. But I advise you to watch your step.”

As he rejoined Archer in the outer office, he thought to himself, “I suppose that’s blackmail, but I don’t give a damn. Got to keep that fellow in his place somehow, or my men couldn’t call their souls their own. That may help teach him to leave catching criminals to the police, whose job it is!” Aloud, he said, “I’ve fixed that. I only hope you’re right about Martin’s innocence.”

Archer said, “He certainly didn’t kill Mrs. Lafond; and I’m positive, myself, that he didn’t kill Grimm, either. And I’m not counting on catching more than one murderer, and darned lucky if I do that,” he added despondently.

“Cheer up,” Captain Randall said. “Of course you’ll catch him.” He looked at his watch, which said a quarter of three. “Come along home with me—my wife doesn’t know I’m back, yet, and we’ll run over things again. Then you can probably carry on. I almost got a deer Wednesday," he finished with a sigh. "A twelve-point buck. I want to get back up there and bag one yet."

The State's Attorney could move rapidly when his own interests were involved. Half an hour after Captain Randall had left Golding's office, Forrest Martin was leaving the Rumford jail, released under a nominal bail, which he had been able to furnish himself. Archer had left word that Forrest, if he wanted, could ride back to Highbrook with him, later in the afternoon. But Forrest, while appreciating the invitation, decided to start at once and to get a lift if he could. He had his own reasons for wanting to reach the Ridge before Sergeant Brett got there.

Ann wrenched herself out of her incipient paralysis. Moved by some instinct, she thrust the flashlight into her pocket and picked up the Bible. Her first thought was to hide in the closet, but she realized that a one-way closet is a poor place to be cornered in. There was no time to pick and choose; it would have to be under the bed. That was better than the closet, for while it might be awkward for the person concealed, it would be equally awkward for anyone attempting an attack. Ann had never taken refuge under a bed before, but she did it as quickly and quietly as she could, clutching the Bible against her breast, and thanking her stars that the bed was an old-fashioned one, fairly high. She rolled over on one side and faced the door. The floor of the room was covered with Brussels carpet, and under the bed it was thick with dust; Ann could smell it. She hoped to heaven she wouldn't sneeze! There came a faint sound from the hall.

The bed was so placed that anyone lying under it could see the lower part of a limited section of the room, including the door into the hall. This door Ann had left shut;

now it was opening, carefully, but rather, as if the opener were taking precautions on principle, and didn't suspect that the room was actually occupied. Ann hoped that it was dark enough beneath the bed so that she wouldn't show. She was thankful that her coat was black, and every other part of her, too, except her face. She suspected, from the amount of dust that seemed to have settled on it, that her face wasn't any too white by this time.

It was almost twilight inside the house now. Watching the door, Ann saw a pair of boots pause on the threshold, while their owner apparently surveyed the room. They were high, laced boots of the commonest kind, with some inches of grayish-brown woolen stockings visible above them. But there was nothing that made their identification possible, in that dim light, and it was hard even to judge their size.

The boots stopped before the desk, while their wearer tried all the locks, as Ann had done, and with no more success. So, whoever it was had no keys. That meant that it wasn't Sergeant Brett, as Ann had half fearfully been hoping. From ensuing sounds, she gathered that the reading matter on top of the desk was receiving careful attention. In spite of her discomfort, Ann felt a thrill. Was the searcher after that Family Bible? That possible repository of family secrets, which was even then pressing uncomfortably against her stomach? If so, what would he do when he found it missing? And what would *she* do if he found *her?* That was more to the point. Ann decided that if she were discovered she would scream at the top of her lungs; it wasn't four o'clock yet, and somebody would be around to hear her—she hoped. She wondered, with a sudden chill, whether Clarabel had screamed. No one had heard *her,* except her murderer. Was this the murderer? Theoretically, Ann hoped so, but actually the idea wasn't reassuring. But

it was proof that she was on the right track. "And a lot
of good it will do me," she thought, "if I end as Clarabel
ended!" She shivered, and tried to breathe still more quietly. The boots walked across the room, and a curtain was
raised at one of the windows away from the road. Ann had
thought of doing this, but was glad now that she hadn't,
as it might have told the intruder that somebody had been
before him. Then the boots disappeared from her line of
vision; she guessed they were going toward the closet, for
an instant later she heard the creak of the door, and faint
rustling as the Deacon's garments were disturbed. Then
the boots reappeared, and the bureau received its share
of attention. It didn't get as careful treatment as Ann
had given it; from the sounds, things were being tumbled
about and put back every which way. Evidently the seeker
had not found what he was after. Ann wondered whether
he had a light, but he would hardly dare to use it, for it
was so dark now that any light could be seen from outside.
But no light appeared, and after prowling about the room
for what seemed hours, the boots finally departed. The
door shut softly behind them, and the stairs creaked once
beneath a descending weight. A door closed downstairs—
the outside door, Ann thought thankfully. She rolled from
beneath the bed, rose, and stretched her cramped muscles. She could not be sure her fellow searcher had left the
house, but she would have to chance it. And she would
take the Bible with her. It might be hard to explain her
illegal expedition to the sergeant; but, he might forgive
her, if her find proved valuable.

Ann removed her shoes, and slipped one in each pocket.
She felt her way to the door and opened it gently. The hall
was dark, and her stockinged feet made no sound on the
stairs. Four faint panels of light marked the position of
the front door; safety was in sight. But when she reached

the door, her gentle push had no effect. She turned the knob—nothing happened. The door had been locked. And in the room to her left she heard footsteps.

When Ann found her retreat cut off, panic gripped her. Her fingers groped frantically for a key in the lock; there wasn't any. She fought the terror back, forcing herself to stand quietly and listen. Had she really heard anything in the sitting room? She strained her ears. Yes, above the pounding of her heart she could hear somebody, something, moving around. An awful doubt came over Ann, a horrible surmise. She had seen only the boots and the woolen stockings above them. Deacon Grimm had worn boots and stockings like those. Suppose it were he who was walking in the house, looking for something, looking, looking. . . . Who had a better right to search his own house than the Deacon? Her eyes, staring into the blackness, pictured Leonard Grimm as she had seen him last; pictured him with that dreadful, twisted grin and the dark ooze of blood on his breast, walking in his own sitting room, walking, walking. Ann wanted to scream; she thought she did scream, but no sound came. By a desperate effort of will she banished the specter her imagination had called up. She told herself not to be an idiot. "It isn't a ghost," she repeated inwardly. "It isn't the Deacon. It's a living person. But it's more dangerous than any ghost. I must keep cool, if I want to get away alive." She thought of the Pattersons' cheerful kitchen, not five minutes away, and wondered if she would ever see it again. She thought of Forrest, of his easy common sense and crooked smile, and the comforting strength of his arms. No ghost could compete with Forrest; Ann breathed easier. Whoever or whatever was in there didn't know of her presence, or it would have attacked her before this. She couldn't hide in the bare little hall—there was no cover—and the thought

of the sepulchral parlor made her shiver. She dared not
retreat upstairs again. The only thing to do was to make
her way out at the back of the house, as she had come in.
But supposing she met the Wearer of the Boots, as Clarabel had met him? Ann set her teeth; supposing she didn't!
Anyway, it was her only hope. She felt her way along the
wall, found the curtains at the end of the hall, and passed
between them into the kitchen. Because she was afraid that
a light might be seen from the sitting room, she elected to
feel her way through the darkness to the shed door—once
there she would be safe. She grazed one end of the stove,
and all but fell over a rocking chair, catching herself just in
time. For minutes she stood frozen, until certain its gentle
motion hadn't been heard. Then she tiptoed on again. Just
as she reached the shed door, she heard a welcome sound
from the front of the house; this time she was sure it was
the front door closing. Whoever it was had gone at last.
Ann went quickly through the shed and into the barn. She
had stopped worrying about leaving traces of her presence;
the principal thing was to get away and get home! She
opened the big barn door a fraction and slipped through,
into the blessed outdoors. She had escaped intact, *and*
she had the Bible. She paused long enough to put on her
shoes and get her breath. Then, hugging the big volume
to her, she hurried toward the road and home. She had almost reached the road, and could see a light in the Pattersons' house, when something moved in the bushes as she
passed. She saw the dark, amorphous shape spring toward
her, out of the mingled shrubbery and shadows. She saw
the upraised arm, and started to run, ducking sideways at
the same time. But it was too late. Something came down
like a thunderbolt, and struck her a glancing blow on the
head. The darkness split in one resounding crash of purple
thunder, streaked with crimson. Then blackness.

When Ann came to, she was lying on the couch in the Pattersons' sitting room, which seemed to be full of people. As far as she could make out, between engulfing waves of nausea, Lucy and Dr. Partridge were sitting beside her; while several other shapes, blurred and uncertain, advanced and retreated in the background. Her head felt as if it had come off second best in a collision with the "Flying Yankee," and her mouth tasted like nothing on earth; but her mind and memory were surprisingly clear. She was instantly aware of what had happened to her, and why. She gasped weakly, "The Bible . . . did he get the Bible?" and tried to sit up. This wasn't allowed, but the doctor gave her a teaspoonful of something out of a glass, and said, "Take it easy now. Don't try to talk."

Ann said, "I can talk perfectly well." And she could, although the trip hammer throbbing in her head went steadily on, and the light, when she opened her eyes, was painfully bright. She was about to shut them again, in a hurry, when Dr. Partridge leaned suddenly forward, and over his shoulder she glimpsed a face she had certainly not expected to see. "Forrest!" she exclaimed. "How did you get here?"

"Walked," Forrest said briefly, "and got a lift, part of the way. How do you feel?" He gently insinuated his large person between the doctor and Lucy, and sitting carefully down on the edge of the couch, took one of Ann's hands and held it firmly.

She closed her eyes and said, "Not too bad. But do tell me what happened, somebody, and how you found me. Lucy, you do it. And by the time you've finished, I think I'll be able to tell my side of it."

Lucy looked questioningly at the doctor, who nodded. "It won't hurt her to talk, if she doesn't get excited." He turned to Ann. "You can thank your guardian angel, young woman, that you've got a good, hard head, and thick hair, and that you side-stepped as much as you did. Thanks to those things you'll be all right again before long. But you had a narrow squeak. If that sandbag, or whatever it was, had struck squarely, as it struck Mrs. Lafond . . ." He shook his head gravely.

Ann made a grimace. Her head was bandaged and her hair felt wet. In addition to the way she felt, she could imagine how she looked. Her narrow escape did not trouble her so much as the knowledge that Forrest, Frank, Archer and several other males were seeing her in this ignominious and unflattering state. She knew it wouldn't make any difference to Forrest, but no woman enjoys being seen at her worst, even by her nearest and dearest. Well, it served her right for being such a fool. But she *had* proved her theory, painful as the proving had turned out to be.

"When you hadn't got back here by half-past four," Lucy began. "I started to worry. Of course, I thought you'd just gone for a walk, as you said you were going to." She looked reproachful. "Then Frank came in, and about five Forrest got here, and wanted to know where you were, of course. He and Frank went and hunted up Haley, but he was down near Lafonds' and hadn't seen anything of you. They looked around, but didn't find you; and then the sergeant and Mr. Burke arrived. None of us had any idea where you'd gone; but I remembered what you'd said about the brook, and thought maybe you *had* fallen in or something. We were just organizing a regular search party when Luke came rushing in, and said he'd found you lying by some bushes over in the Deacon's yard. He—he said you were dead. He'd just finished doing the chores over there, and was on his way back, and he said he almost fell over you. The men went over with him, then, and I called the doctor in Rumford, and he's just got here. I think he flew."

Dr. Partridge laughed. "I did make pretty good time."

"Well," Lucy concluded, "Frank and Forrest fitted a ladder with blankets on it, and brought you home very carefully, and we found you weren't dead. We fixed you up the best we could until the doctor got here. My goodness, Ann, you did look a mess, covered with dust and dirt and cobwebs and scratches—what under the sun have you been up to?"

Ann recognized the relief that lay behind Lucy's crisp words. She took her unengaged hand out from under the quilt and squeezed her cousin's fingers, preparatory to telling her own story.

But Archer had been doing some rapid thinking. He decided that if Ann was able to talk, he wanted to hear what she had to say before anybody else did. He tactfully dismissed them all, except the doctor, and took Lucy's place beside the couch. Forrest released Ann's hand and left rather reluctantly; but he felt that he owed the sergeant too much to make any protests.

As the door closed behind him, Ann thought, "I hope the sergeant isn't going to bawl me out!" But she did Archer an injustice. He looked quite concerned, and asked Dr. Partridge again if it was all right for Ann to tell her story. The doctor said it was, and with pillows propped behind her, and another sip of medicine as a stimulant, she described her visit to the Deacon's house.

"So you see why I asked about the Bible," she concluded ruefully. "I thought I'd been so smart. But whoever was there knew *I* was there, or suspected it, and was only waiting for me to come out. Then he just knocked me over the head and took the Bible and beat it. I don't understand why he didn't stay to make sure I—er—wouldn't do any talking; but perhaps he heard or saw Luke around, and didn't dare linger. But anyway," she defended herself, "it shows I had the right idea. If you can find who's got that Bible, and why they wanted it, you'll know who killed Clarabel."

Archer looked doubtful. He had refrained from cen-
suring Ann for her foolhardiness; she had been punished
enough, without his saying anything. And he would have
felt like a bully, saying hard things to anyone who looked
as washed-out and defenseless as Ann Barbour did then.
He had thought, when the excited Luke led them to where
she lay, that the Highbrook killer had claimed another
victim for sure. He was so glad to find himself mistaken
that he partially forgot his righteous indignation at Ann's
behavior. He said thoughtfully, "But I looked through that
big Bible when I searched the house last Sunday."

Ann sat up, dislodging two pillows. "You—you looked
through it?"

"Of course I did. I went through all those books and
things, and the Bible, too. I thought there might be papers
in it, or the Deacon's will, or something."

Ann asked eagerly, "Did you look at the Records?"

"Records?"

"Yes, the Records of births, marriages, and deaths.
That's what I was after."

As Archer still looked puzzled, she exclaimed, "Don't
you know those old Bibles always had a place for such
things? Usually it's in the middle, between the Old and
New Testaments, but sometimes it's at the end. It wasn't
in the middle of the Deacon's Bible, so I was starting to
look for it in the back part when I heard the footsteps
downstairs. But if you looked all through the Bible you
must have seen it."

Archer looked, sheepish. "I never thought about any
records like that," he confessed. "I—er—I'm not very
familiar with Family Bibles. . . ."

The doctor said with a smile, "It's easy to see you
weren't raised in New England."

"But anyway," Archer went on, disregarding him, "some
pages had been torn out of the back of that Bible. I did

notice that, and I wondered why. But I never thought anything about records."

Ann interrupted, staring at him. "Good heavens, Sergeant, don't you see? That's what Clarabel was killed for!"
Unmindful of her throbbing head, she leaned forward. "I
thought all along it might be something like that. Look!
Clarabel knew about something in the Bible; something
that gave some clue to the Deacon's death, perhaps. Maybe
it was something he'd already told her about. Anyway, she
knew it, and tried to blackmail somebody, and got killed
for it. The murderer found out about the evidence in the
Bible, and was hunting for it this afternoon; that's why he
waited for me, and took it, after he'd knocked me out. He
thought the evidence against him was there. But it wasn't,
because Clarabel had already torn out the vital pages and
hidden them somewhere, to be on the safe side. So the
murderer has got the Bible but not the evidence. Don't
you see?"

Dr. Partridge said, "By George, Archer, I believe she's
hit it."

Archer, said cautiously, "It's possible. But I don't see as
we're much better off, if we don't know where those pages
are, or what's on them."

"But I see," Ann cried. "I've got an idea." She closed
her aching eyes, and continued, "It really is a good idea,
Sergeant, but I don't know as I feel ambitious enough to
explain tonight. But will you and Dr. Partridge do this:
will you make out, from now on, that I'm lots worse than
you thought I was at first? Please do that, and I'll explain
my idea the first thing in the morning. And when you talk
with anybody, anybody *at all,* don't tell how I really am.
If you say anything, you might imply that I'm pretty bad."
Her voice and expression were compellingly earnest. "Will
you do that? It's awfully important."

Seeing no harm in the request, Archer and the doctor promised. So when the other members of the household were allowed to file quietly into the sitting room after supper, they saw a very still and white-faced Ann lying on the couch. Her eyes were closed, and the quilt barely moved when she breathed.

"She's asleep," Dr. Partridge said, in reply to anxious inquiries. "I gave her an opiate, and I think she'd better not be disturbed tonight, as long as she is asleep." He looked solemn. "I don't know but what she ought to have a nurse—sometimes these concussion cases—" He frowned.

Lucy said, "I'll spend the night down here, if you think I ought to; Frank can bring down the cot from Tad's room. Then tomorrow, if you think she needs a nurse . . ."

The doctor hummed and hawed and finally consented to this arrangement. He thought he could guess Ann's plan, and was willing to do what he could to further it. Therefore, without saying anything definite, he managed to convey the impression that Ann's condition might be more serious than had appeared at first. He could see, from their concerned expressions, that Lucy, Frank, and Forrest had no idea he was prevaricating. It seemed rather mean to deceive them; but the doctor, having agreed to Ann's request, was determined to make a thorough job of it.

Later in the evening, Archer hesitantly voiced to Henry Burke and the doctor an idea that had occurred to him. The doctor was quite indignant.

"I tell you she couldn't possibly have given herself that crack over the head!" he said. "I won't swear to a lot of things in this case, but I will swear to that, and so would any other doctor. She was hit with a sandbag or some similar contraption; it was the same kind of weapon and the same kind of blow that killed the Lafond girl, and if Miss

Barbour had got it squarely, it would have killed her, very likely. But the blow glanced off, and while it knocked her out, it didn't cause even a severe concussion. But something hit her—she did not do it herself! And I'm positive Dr. Warfield would back me up."

Archer had already listened to a detailed description of Clarabel's injuries, as revealed by the autopsy. Dr. Warfield's expert opinion had confirmed Dr. Partridge's findings; Clarabel had been struck a violent blow with some implement resembling a sandbag, and the resulting injury to the brain had caused her death. The injuries sustained in the fall down the steps had not been a contributing factor, in his opinion, and had probably been made after death. Dr. Warfield was not overanxious to swear to such a ticklish point, but intimated that he could, if he had to. That was what the official report amounted to, when shorn of its Latin and technical terms. Archer was not going to argue with such erudition.

"All right," he said, "We'll take that for granted, then. And if she told the truth about that, she probably told the truth about the whole business. The Bible was there last Sunday, for I saw it, and it's certainly gone now; I looked around over there, and found everything just as she says she left it. The door was unfastened from the shed to the kitchen, but the front door was locked, and the key was gone. We'll take it she's telling the truth."

Dr. Partridge asked about alibis.

Earlier in the evening, the sergeant had made an effort to place various people at the approximate time of Ann's adventure. It was about a quarter of four, she thought, when she first heard the other person downstairs; and she estimated the probable time of the attack on her at about four-thirty. So Archer had requested alibis for the period between three-thirty and five, at the outside.

"But there weren't any, as usual," he said disgustedly. "I talked with everybody who's the least bit under suspicion, and they were all engaged in the most innocent kind of activities—but every one of 'em was alone, of course! Danny Cheever was alone in the Buckleys' hen houses, looking after those blessed chickens, as usual—*he* says. Mrs. Buckley was in her bedroom, having a nap—*she* says. Buckley was taking a walk through the woods—says his doctor told him to get more fresh air—but he doesn't know whereabouts he was any special time, and he didn't get home until after five. Patterson was plowing; I never knew they plowed at this time of year, but he says he was, and showed me the field, half plowed. But he was all by himself, and the field is right near. Mrs. Patterson was here in the house alone. And Forrest Martin," his voice, changed subtly, "Forrest Martin says he left Rumford on foot about a quarter past three, and got a lift on a truck as far as Highbrook Village. Then he walked the five miles from the Village to the Ridge, and that took him an hour. He says he got here to the house about five, and Mrs. Patterson confirms that. He did get *here* about five, no doubt, but as far as I can see he can't prove what time he got to the Ridge, unless he can find that truck, and even then there's nothing to prevent his having got another lift from the Village here, and keeping still about it." He added drily, "Mr. Martin seems to have hard luck with his alibis; it's too bad—for him—that he didn't wait and ride out with me and Henry. But apparently he didn't want to do that," he added significantly,

"But surely," Dr. Partridge said, "you don't suspect Martin of attacking Miss Barbour, when you were so certain he didn't kill the Deacon, and it's plain he couldn't have killed Mrs. Lafond? Besides, you said, and it's fairly obvious, that he and Miss Barbour are—er—"

"I know," Archer admitted. "I did think so, and it does look so. But damn it, two unconfirmed alibis so much alike are pretty hard to swallow. And I still think there's something funny about a girl like Miss Barbour being so keen on Martin. And now she wants us to pretend she's bad off, to everybody, mind you—and I can't help wondering if she really suspects Martin, or is playing some game we haven't caught onto at all." He scratched a match viciously.

"Besides all that," Henry Burke broke in, "you're forgetting Gus Lafond. I'm not clearing Martin or Patterson, but remember that Gus is still at large and unaccounted for. He's the feller we've been after right along, and the one the Captain seems to think is the one we want."

"I know," Archer said unhappily, "and he does look like the best bet. If only Martin had waited and come out with us, we could have scratched him off the list. But no, he has to rush out here by himself, and be without an alibi while Miss Barbour is getting attacked by somebody that could be him or anybody else in the county. And if I'm mistaken about him, I've put the Captain in wrong . . ." He swore.

"I'll keep my money on Gus," Dr. Partridge said. "He fills the bill better than anybody else. And if he's innocent, where is he all this time?"

Henry Burke had a happy thought. "Perhaps he's been bumped off too," he suggested.

Archer gave him an unkind look. "You would think of that! No, I believe we'll find Gus all right, and find him alive, though how the devil he could get around without anybody spotting him beats me. I thought when they found his car yesterday they'd have him within twenty-four hours. But if he can travel clear out here without any cop seeing him—"

"Don't forget," the doctor said, "that he'd be an expert at keeping under cover. An ex-bootlegger knows all the tricks. But I should think you'd watch his house."

"I am, now," Archer said. "Haley's down there from now on. But hang it, I've only got a few men available. I can't keep the whole countryside under observation. The local constables are no good; they couldn't watch a pig pen!"

"Speaking of pig pens," the doctor said thoughtfully, "you don't suppose Buckley or his wife . . .? After all, they're nearest to the Deacon's house, and either of them could slip over there easily."

"I know it," Archer said. "Anybody could have slipped over there easily. And the Buckleys' alibis are worthless. But their motives, in regard to the Deacon and the woman, too, seem too weak to take seriously. But I'm keeping them in mind."

The doctor collected his belongings. "Well, I must get home. Miss Barbour ought to come along all right, if she doesn't try to do any more detecting."

"She won't if I can help it," Archer said crossly.

Dr. Partridge looked at a hole in his glove. "Just the same," he said, "there may be something in that theory of hers. She's got some plan, and it won't do any harm to listen to it, in the morning."

Archer said, "Oh, I'll listen. I've reached the point where I'll listen to anything! I've made such a mess of this case, I wish to the Lord Captain Randall would take it off my hands, but he won't."

"No, you don't," Dr. Partridge said. "If he did, you'd be sore. Get some sleep how, and don't worry. You'll catch the killer and get the credit yet!" He departed with a wave of his hand.

Archer hoped he was right.

9

Sunday—*Watchful Waiting*

The next morning, when he heard Ann's plan, the sergeant felt rather flabbergasted. At first, he, said he couldn't listen to such a proposition. Then he said it wouldn't work, anyway. Then he said it might work, but was too dangerous. Then he thought it over, and said he supposed it wouldn't do any harm to try it; it could only fail, like everything else he'd tried. He and Henry Burke conferred with Ann in the sitting room while Lucy did the dishes. They had a little trouble in getting rid of Forrest Martin, who seemed disinclined to let Ann out of his sight, even though told repeatedly that she was asleep. But luck aided the sergeant, for one of Frank's cows chose that morning to present her owner prematurely with a calf, and Frank drafted Forrest to help him when the business proved unexpectedly complicated.

So, for an uninterrupted half-hour, Ann explained her idea, and told the two policemen her reasons for thinking that it might succeed.

Archer believed that she honestly didn't know who had attacked her; but he wondered if she had any suspicions. He asked if she thought it was Gus Lafond.

"I don't know," Ann replied firmly. "It could have been; it could have been almost anybody. All I saw was the boots and stockings, and anybody could have worn them. And anybody could have hit me, too, I suppose."

Archer nodded. It took no particular strength or skill, the doctor had said, to wield a sandbag with deadly effect.

"But this is the point," Ann continued, "The murderer—let's call him X—X knows he hit me, and he probably knows, or soon will, that he didn't kill me. But he doesn't know what condition I'm in. He took the Bible because he thought there was something in it that would give him away, if it got into your hands. The first thing he'll do will be to look all through it, and then destroy it. Don't you think he'd look through it first, to make sure it was what he was after?"

They nodded.

"When he finds those pages gone," Ann went on, "he'll see that he isn't any better off than he was before, for he'll realize that either Clarabel or I took them out, and that they're still in existence somewhere, to give him away." She stopped and said thoughtfully, "Seems as if Gus would have managed things differently, though. He wouldn't have had to kill Clarabel to prevent her giving him away, or would he? If he did, wouldn't he have done it at their house, where it would have been likelier to pass as an accident? And, if he isn't guilty, wouldn't he have known Clarabel was blackmailing somebody—and who it was?"

"Perhaps he does," Henry Burke put in, but Archer disagreed.

"If Gus killed her, he'd think staging it up at the Deacon's would bring less suspicion on him," he said. "And I'm sure, from something Mrs. Lafond said to me the last time I saw her, that her husband didn't know about her plans. She expected to get some money, and was going to use it to leave Gus, and to try her luck in some more—er—profitable place than Highbrook. I believe you're right in thinking that Clarabel was blackmailing somebody, and was killed by the—the blackmailee. But as I see it, she'd be just as likely to blackmail her husband as anybody else." And Archer remembered that Clarabel had known about the Deacon's use of dope. If she knew where he got it—as she had hinted—that would be another threat to hold over her husband.

"Well, maybe," Ann said. "But this is my idea: X knows there's evidence that might hang him floating around, somewhere. He knows that he hurt me, but not how bad. I thought we could pretend that I'm badly injured, and spread that rumor so that everybody will hear about it. Pretend that I'm so bad I can't be moved to the hospital. Maybe I'm unconscious, and haven't been able to tell the police all I know yet. But the point is to give out the impression that I know about this evidence against X—or that you think I do—and that he isn't safe while I'm alive to talk. Make everybody believe that you're just waiting for me to tell what I know, and who attacked me. Perhaps you can make X think that I've actually got those pages that were torn from the Bible, and have them hidden somewhere; or, at least, that I know where they are. Oh," she broke off, "I can't make it sound as clear as I want to, but the idea is this: Set a trap, with me and those missing pages as the bait, and you may catch X. You know more about managing such things than I do. I should think you could contrive something that would work."

Henry Burke regarded her with respect. "By Golly," he said, "I think it's a swell idea."

Archer deliberated, and passed by degrees from downright refusal to reluctant acquiescence. But he refused to let Ann act as the actual bait in the trap; that was out of the question, although she was willing to do it. And she must not divulge the plan to anyone outside the police, not even to Lucy. Finally, he would have to get Captain Randall's permission before attempting such an unconventional scheme.

"If the Captain agrees," he said, "and we can dope out the practical details, we'll try it. But you mustn't tell a soul, and you mustn't be angry if the trap is set to catch everybody or anybody, including your friends." He looked at her searchingly. "I believe you're honest in your wish to catch the real criminal, but can you play fair, and not give the show away to your friends? For all I *know* to the contrary, one of them may be the murderer, and they must have the same opportunities as anyone else to fall into this trap, if we set it. I hope you understand that, and will be prepared for—whatever happens."

He waited for an outburst, but Ann said proudly, "I'm not afraid for my friends. I want you to make this—this trial as much for their sakes as for my own, or yours. If you think it's necessary to deceive Forrest and Lucy and Frank, I'll do it. I haven't said a word to any of them this morning yet; when they came in here I pretended to be asleep. Not even Lucy knows what I have in mind. I'll pretend that I feel much worse this morning, and that will be an excuse for not talking to anyone."

"I'll have Dr. Partridge come over, if he can," Archer said. "He can make up some convincing reasons for keeping you quiet, and will be willing to do a little prevaricating, in a good cause."

"How about having him bring a nurse?" Henry Burke suggested.

Ann demurred. "I don't need a nurse. Unless you think it's necessary?"

"It would help with the atmosphere we want to create," Archer said. "I know, I'll have the doctor bring Mrs. Crosse, my housekeeper. She is a good sort, and will do as I say without asking questions. In the proper rigging, she'll look just like a nurse. Now, you better pretend to be asleep until the doctor gets here; then you can come to, a little, but let him handle things."

"All right," Ann said. "I'll act worse than I feel. I feel pretty good, really."

"That's fine," Archer told her, "but try not to show it." Ann lay back on her pillows, and managed to look so pale and lifeless that when Lucy came in she was instantly alarmed, and not only agreed that Dr. Partridge should be sent for, but strongly endorsed the suggestion that he bring a nurse with him. "You shouldn't have let her talk at all," Lucy said, reproachfully. "I'll stay right here until the doctor comes." And she did, so that Archer's conversation with the doctor over the telephone was necessarily guarded. But Dr. Partridge caught his meaning, and promised to come right over.

Ann hated to deceive her cousin, but she kept her eyes and mouth resolutely shut, determined to play her part convincingly. If her plan worked out as she hoped it would, the deception wouldn't be for long.

Archer departed, then, and Henry Burke was left to do some judicious rumor-spreading in Highbrook and vicinity.

When Archer got to Rumford, he drove straight to Captain Randall's house, and caught that gentleman finishing a late breakfast. Mrs. Randall withdrew, and Archer laid his latest facts, suspicions, surmises, and difficulties before his commanding officer. He kept nothing back, and concluded by describing Ann's projected plan.

"Now," he said, with desperate earnestness, "what'll I do? I feel like a baby, coming and bellyaching to you all the time; but I'm willing to admit I'm stumped. I'm so hard up for ideas that I'm ready to try this crazy scheme of Miss Barbour's, unless you order me not to. It might work."

Captain Randall made marks on the tablecloth with his fork—a habit of which his wife had repeatedly tried to break him. He said, "I suppose you tested that earring for prints?"

"Yes," Archer said. "And there weren't any. It had been wiped clean, like the pitchfork handle."

"If Golding knew about that . . ." the Captain shrugged.

Archer saw what he meant. "But the doctor swears," he said, "that Miss Barbour was really struck by somebody. And Mrs. Patterson gave her an alibi for the night Mrs. Lafond was killed. And I didn't hear a sound in the house that night, myself." Again he remembered those sleeping tablets, but the idea that he had been given one was too farfetched to mention. "Anyway," he added, "I don't believe Miss Barbour would have been fool enough to leave her earring there. It looked as if it had been planted deliberately."

"Um," Captain Randall said. "Maybe she's smart enough to figure how your mind would work. But I don't think she did the killing. If she did, what earthly object has she got in wanting to set this trap? No, I think that when you told her about the earring, it frightened her. It would scare anybody to learn that some enemy was trying to get them hanged for a crime they didn't commit. I should say that after Mrs. Lafond was killed, the Barbour girl began to lose faith in your ability to catch the killer."

"Can't blame her much!" Archer interjected.

"She decided she'd got to hunt for him herself, in self-defense," the Captain concluded. He thought for several minutes. Then, "Go ahead and set this trap, as she suggests. I can't see how it can do any harm. Of course, you mustn't let her run any risks. It's easy enough to spread the kind of rumors she has in mind, and if we could get the criminal really flustered. . . ."

They discussed ways and means, and finally arrived at a plan which looked feasible. "You can manage the details," the Captain said. "I'd go out there, too, only . . ." he hesitated. "Well, I'm not going to spoil your case, or have it said you couldn't handle it alone. The newspapers have been blaming you some; if there's any credit going, I want you to have it. You and Burke have done all the drudgery, and all I've done is back you up. Oh, by the way, you said something about a woman in Pinkney that Patterson might have gone to see—did you check up on that?"

"Burke did." Archer made a face. "He found the girl was married three years ago to a man named Peters, and lives in Steele City, Nebraska. That's like all my leads; it fell through." He wondered if he ought to tell Lucy that whatever her husband had been up to in Pinkney, it could have had no connection with—what was her name?—Harriet Mullins.

"Never mind," the Captain said. "You go ahead and carry out this plan, and if it, flops we're no worse off. And as you said, it may work. Think how green Golding will turn if you catch the murderer in *'flagrante delicto!'"*

Archer shook hands violently, and tried to express his appreciation of the Captain's sportsmanship.

"That's all right," Captain Randall said. "Can't have that crook Golding belittling my officers. Good Lord! It's been only a week since Grimm was killed, and it's the meanest kind of a case to handle. That's why I'm keeping out of it; there's nothing unselfish about me! Besides, I still hope to get a deer!"

Archer left, feeling encouraged, and for the next hour was busy spreading the kind of rumors best calculated to make a nervous murderer still more jittery. He talked with policemen and reporters and shady characters, and was satisfied that his statements would spread and spread, like the proverbial ripples made by the stone thrown into a pool.

At headquarters, there were only negative reports on Gus Lafond. Archer hoped that wherever Gus was, he would hear the rumors about Ann. Such things never lose by repetition, and Archer trusted that by the time they reached the murderer's ears they would have grown to alarming proportions. Yet he still couldn't decide whose ears were the right ones.

He drove back to Highbrook Ridge, directly to the Lafond house. While not subscribing unreservedly to the theory of the missing Bible pages, he could see that it was at least a tenable proposition, and if he *could* find them—! Even if he didn't, he might come across some clue to Clarabel's doings, or Gus's dubious professional transactions. But he doubted that; Gus was not the kind to leave any loose ends lying around, even in his own house.

Trooper Haley was sitting disconsolately in the sun on the Lafond piazza. Danny was at the Buckleys'; he worked Sundays as well as week days. Rhoda had offered him a room, temporarily, thinking that he might find his own house too lonely and depressing, without Clarabel. Lucy Patterson, too, would have found a place for him in her already crowded household. But Danny clung to his home; the thought of leaving it upset him so much that Archer didn't insist on it.

Haley was bored. "I wish," he said, "that they sold newspapers around here. That's the trouble with these hick places—no culture!" He added that he hadn't seen a soul but Danny since the start of his present assignment. "If Gus Lafond or anybody else has been around here," he said, "they've learnt how to make themselves invisible, that's all."

Danny had left the door unlocked, but a hasty exploration of the house told Archer nothing new. There didn't seem to be a single scrap of writing in the place, not a notebook, not a letter, not a bill, even! Only a few movie and "true confession" magazines, which had been Clarabel's only mental relaxation, and a dozen newspapers that had escaped being used to kindle the fire. Archer went through them all, page by page, but found nothing.

All the commonplace hiding places were empty, too. Inside the clock, inside the radio behind the pictures, under the rugs—nothing. The flamboyant, pseudo-modernistic furniture apparently held no secrets. The kitchen cupboards yielded only dust, canned goods, and cigarettes by the carton; although one of them, which was locked, ultimately revealed a sizable supply of drinkables, mostly whiskey.

The bureau drawers in the bedroom overflowed with lingerie and cosmetics of a luxurious type; but no Bible pages were concealed, however inappropriately, among them. An equal profusion of silk shirts, silk socks, and silk ties in a chest of drawers proved that Mr. Lafond could array himself like the lilies of the field when he so desired. Several showy but expensive suits shared a closet with Clarabel's finery, but all the pockets were empty. Nowhere was there a line of correspondence or a scrap of writing; not a solitary clue of the kind the sergeant was seeking.

Upstairs, Danny's little room was furnished with only the barest necessities; the rest of the second floor was a mere jumble of dust-covered rubbish.

"I can't stay any longer," Archer told Haley. "But as long as you've got to hang around, I want you to search this place thoroughly. Take your time, and don't tear things apart any more than you have to, but don't miss anything. Don't forget the shed and the outhouse." He described what he wanted Haley to look for particularly, and left the trooper to his search. Haley was a plodder, but thorough.

Dr. Partridge arrived at the Pattersons' not long after Archer had left. He was rapidly becoming acquainted with every bump and turn of the Highbrook-Rumford road. With him was Archer's housekeeper, Mrs. Crosse, in a borrowed uniform. Having learned from Henry Burke what was in prospect, the doctor explained her duties to Mrs.

Crosse, who thought she could play nurse well enough to fill the bill. She was a plump woman of sixty, with white hair and a placid manner. She asked no questions, but established herself in the sitting room with Ann, where her serious demeanor and intimidating uniform did more than anything else to create a sick-room atmosphere of apprehension and doubt.

Lucy welcomed her; while deploring the need of a nurse, she was glad to have Ann in what she thought were more experienced hands than her own. Frank was tempted to ask Mrs. Crosse to take a look at his cow, but decided not to. Forrest, who was inclined to blame Archer and the doctor for Ann's seeming relapse, gave the newcomer a sharp look, but appeared not to doubt her genuineness.

When Ann opened her eyes and smiled wanly, Mrs. Crosse forbade all conversation. But she didn't try to prevent Forrest and Lucy from staying in the room as long as they kept quiet, which they conscientiously did.

When Archer got back, he found a genuine Sabbath calm prevailing. He had instructed Rose Norton not to ring the Pattersons' number for incoming calls; instead, he called her at intervals. He authorized her to answer all questions about Ann, and told her what to say; and if Rose wondered why Sergeant Brett was suddenly so eager for her to become a gossip, she said nothing, but faithfully relayed his reports of Ann's condition to all who made inquiries.

As a propagandist, Henry Burke was a success. By noon, the news of Ann's critical state had spread over Highbrook Township, and most of Clinton County. It became widely known that she was in bad shape, and might not recover; but none the less she was momentarily expected to speak, and to name her assailant. The police, it was understood, believed that Ann held the key to the deaths of Leonard Grimm and Clarabel Lafond—not only through abstract knowledge but by virtue of actual material evidence which was said to be in her possession. They were just waiting for her to talk; then they would act. These rumors had been so thoroughly broadcast that Archer was hopeful the murderer, whoever he was, would hear them, and would be aware that at any minute Ann might give the police the evidence that would identify him. All inquiries, telephoned or personal, received answers tending to deepen this impression. That part of the program, Archer thought, had been well managed without being overdone. He had not entirely discouraged callers, thinking that a visit of inquiry might well serve a would-be murderer as an excuse for looking over the ground in advance. Therefore, callers were allowed to enter the kitchen, and even, in some instances, to glance for a second into the sitting room, where Ann could be seen lying motionless on the couch. Her white face and closed eyes, the bedside table loaded with remedies, and the imposing presence of Mrs. Cross were visual proof that Rumor was not lying. The sergeant hardly expected Gus Lafond to be among the solicitous visitors, but he did hope that by roundabout means the potential dangers of the situation would reach Gus's ears. For he had about decided, in his own mind, that Gus Lafond was the man he would catch—*if* he caught anybody.

Dinner was eaten in subdued silence and, during the afternoon, inquiries prompted by solicitude or curiosity continued. Rhoda Buckley called up and sounded, Rose said, quite anxious. Later, she and her husband came over for a few minutes, to express in suitably lowered tones their hope, that Ann was not as seriously hurt as Rumor said. Even Danny Cheever stopped in to make inquiries that were rather incoherent, but apparently well meant.

Archer was not sure how far he had succeeded in hoodwinking Lucy and Frank Patterson and Forrest Martin. Lucy, he thought, was unaware of the deception that was being practiced. But Frank was a man whose thoughts were not always easy to read; and Forrest, as he had been from the beginning, was a very dark horse indeed. It was impossible to tell what he was really thinking, behind his habitual air of unflurried self-confidence. But, since Archer hadn't noticed any signs to the contrary, he hoped that none of the three suspected the true state of affairs. He honestly didn't think that one of them would turn out to be the criminal, but he realized that his judgment was not infallible—far from it!—and he believed that to be fair and conclusive such a trial must be open to everyone, to give all suspects an equal opportunity of convicting themselves!

The afternoon dragged slowly and uneventfully along. Archer wondered how Ann was feeling; the atmosphere of the house and its occupants was uncomfortably reminiscent of the period before (or after) a funeral; not a cheerful environment under the circumstances. But Ann had actually been asleep a good part of the time. Whatever was going to happen, she intended to prepare for it by getting as much rest as she could. Forrest and Frank played checkers, a pastime that required little conversation, and read the Sunday papers. Lucy talked over the telephone with Tad, who was not wholly reconciled to his exile, but was making the most of his connection with the case, and its attendant fame. But he had not become any more talkative, as several disgusted townspeople had discovered. "They all ask me questions," Tad told his mother, gleefully, "but I don't answer 'em!" Lucy commended his caution, and listened to a résumé of the latest Village happenings, which had been crowded out of her picture by more exciting events. After Tad rang off, she turned to Mrs. Crosse, and embarrassed that lady with polite questions about her nursing experiences. Fortunately, Mrs. Crosse wasn't completely ignorant of the subject, but she did her best to discourage Lucy's interest by implying that their conversation might disturb Ann.

At half-past seven they had "Sunday night supper"—baked beans (warmed up), bread and milk, cheese, cake, and doughnuts. The post-funeral air which had prevailed all the afternoon was still in evidence. While the others ate, Archer and Burke held a whispered consultation with Ann, and afterwards with the doctor and Mrs. Crosse. The sergeant's arrangements for the night were simple, but they required some leading up to, and that was the hardest part of the business to accomplish without rousing suspicion.

Ann was perishing for something to eat, and the aroma of the baked beans (even warmed up) was tantalizing. But she had to be content with a bowl of weak broth, as being more in keeping with her role. She tried to forget her suspense, anxiety, and hunger in further sleep but increasing excitement made it difficult.

Frank and Forrest did the chores and resumed their silent battle at the checker board. Lucy got out her knitting.

Archer paid a flying visit to the Lafond house, to take Haley some supper, and apprise him of the part he was to play later in the evening. Haley had not found any Bible pages, nor any cocaine. His search was more than half completed, and he swore that he hadn't missed anything.

"Well, keep it up," Archer said, but his hopes of discovering anything sank toward zero.

Because the Lafond radio needed new batteries, Danny was staying the evening at the Buckleys'; he didn't want to miss the weekly installments of "Tommy the Dummy" and "Rollicking Romance."

"When he comes back," Archer said, "let him do just as he likes. We want everybody free to come and go when and wherever they want to, tonight." He hurried back to the Pattersons'.

At nine o'clock, Mrs. Crosse duly announced that her patient was asleep for the night, having been given a mild opiate (in other words, a glass of water with a pinch of soda in it.) Mrs. Crosse said that she would take advantage of the fact to get a little change and air. Accordingly, she put on her outer garments and ostentatiously departed with Dr. Partridge, in his car. Frank and Lucy, given vague assurances that all was well, but not entrusted with the truth, went upstairs at their usual time. Forrest Martin, as the afternoon waned, had shown one or two signs of suspecting something queer, although he said nothing. He was tactfully encouraged to go to bed when Frank and Lucy went, but half an hour passed before he tossed aside the sports section of the *Boston Herald* and gave a puzzled glance at the seemingly unconscious Ann. She certainly looked asleep, but Archer was afraid that Forrest might insist on remaining until Mrs. Crosse returned; so he murmured something reassuring about the nurse being back soon, and that he and Burke would be right there. He couldn't tell, from Forrest's expression, whether the big man was taken in or not. But perhaps he was sleepy, for after another sharp look at Ann, he went quietly upstairs. Archer breathed a sigh of relief.

When Henry Burke had ascertained that the Pattersons and Forrest were really in their respective rooms, Ann staged a quick recovery, and vacated the couch. Her place was taken by the substitute which the sergeant and Burke had concocted. This lady consisted principally of pillows, strategically placed beneath the bedclothes, and a hairdresser's dummy, with a wig of the proper color, which Archer had brought from Rumford that morning. (Quite a time he had had getting it, too!) The dummy's head was bandaged to resemble Ann's, and then arranged carefully on the pillow, with its wax face to the wall. Ann stayed to give her understudy its finishing touches, and pronounced it a success; in the not-too-bright light it looked convincingly realistic, even at close quarters.

Then, wrapped in a quilt, Ann was escorted to the seldom used dining room, where the doctor and Mrs. Crosse were waiting. After driving a short distance, they had left the car and doubled back, quietly letting themselves in through a side door in the barn.

All this maneuvering took time, but by ten o'clock the stage was set, and everything ready for any move an unknown murderer might see fit to make. Leaving Burke ensconced behind an overstuffed chair, Archer blew out the sitting-room lamp and went out to his car, which was waiting in the yard with Haley at the wheel. The two men conversed loudly about going to Rumford, banged the car doors, and then Haley drove away, talking in two different voices. After this, Archer cautiously returned to the sitting room and took up his station behind another overstuffed chair, to wait for whatever might happen.

But as time passed, he became more and more convinced that nothing was going to happen; that he was, in fact, making a fool of himself for the umpteenth time. The trap was set, but even if it were correct in principle, the chances were a thousand to one against catching anything in it. He was afraid that it was too obviously a trap; that even a murderer with the jitters would notice that everything was made too easy for him. But perhaps not. Murderers were notoriously single-minded, and this one, with two successful crimes to his credit, might have become careless. Archer fervently hoped so. In the effort to give the hypothetical intruder every encouragement, the back door had been left unfastened, along with doors in the barn and shed. Bella had been a minor problem, but she was finally left in Ann's care in the dining room. Bella liked Ann, and minded her quite well.

The house was silent now, except for the dignified ticking of the clock. A faint rattle of shutters, for the wind was rising, came occasionally from outside. Once or twice a car drove by, its headlights and the noise of its engine growing to a crescendo and then diminishing into the distance. But none of the cars stopped, or even slowed down.

Archer eased his cramped position, and wondered if Henry Burke had gone to sleep. He looked at the luminous dial of his wrist watch, thinking that hours had passed, but it was not quite eleven o'clock. By half-past eleven he was sure he was a fool; and by the time the clock struck twelve, he was wondering why the doctor who brought him into the world hadn't dispatched him then and there, as a hopeless imbecile. Also, uncomfortable doubts as to Ann's honesty, and her real purposes, were again raising their heads in his mind. Ann was hardly in a position to play any games herself, but Forrest and the Pattersons were free to do as they liked. They might be up to all kinds of tricks while he and Henry waited like lambs for a killer who probably had no intention of coming near them; who might, indeed, be warned to keep away. Pictures of Frank and Forrest descending from their respective bedroom windows, or creeping stealthily about on secret and sinister errands, floated before Archer's mental vision. In spite of what Dr. Partridge had said—that Ann's injury could not have been self-inflicted—Archer couldn't forget that she had engineered this present affair from the start. Also, her motives might not be as pure and disinterested as she had made out. Yet, he had foolishly elected to trust her. Archer swore to himself, firmly convinced now that he was being used as a cat's-paw in a game of which he knew nothing, and that he would end up by holding the bag. He was on the point of speaking to Henry Burke, to call the whole thing off, when he heard a faint noise that didn't sound as if it was caused by the wind. It was inside the house. It sounded like a step in the kitchen. It *was* a step, and after an interval it was followed by the ghostly, subdued glow of a flashlight, shining through cloth. The glow approached the sitting room door. Archer shrank down behind his chair and waited. His watch said twenty-three minutes of one.

There was another period of silence—and darkness. But somebody was in the kitchen, standing near the sitting-room door, waiting, listening. . . . The ticking of the clock sounded unnaturally loud. Archer hoped that Henry was awake and ready. After what seemed hours, there came the faint scraping of a shoe on a threshold. Then, in the doorway, the flashlight was switched on again; its rays, dimmed by folds of cloth, played over the room, revealing innocent furniture, and the still figure of a woman, lying under quilts and blankets on the couch. The dummy looked astonishingly lifelike; if Archer hadn't known differently, he would have sworn that Ann herself lay there on one side, with her back to the room.

With infinite caution the unseen power behind the flashlight crossed the room toward the couch. Archer could make out only a vague blackness between himself and the light; a dark shadow, without form or identity. Carefully, silently, he emerged from his hiding place and rose to his feet. The intruder had not yet reached the couch, and Archer crept up close behind him. He hoped that Henry wouldn't spoil things by acting prematurely. They must wait for the visitor to act first.

By stealthy degrees they neared the couch, shadow and shadower, until they stood beside it. The reddish, down-directed light played over dark brown hair, beneath a bandage, and touched the curve of a still check. Then the unknown acted. With the light in his left hand, he took a step forward and raised his right hand. There was something in it, and the movement was swift; but Archer sprang forward and gripped the descending wrist, at the same time attempting to pinion the hand that held the light.

There was a gasp and a grunt, and after that the sergeant couldn't have told exactly what he did. It was like trying to hold a whirlwind, only this whirlwind was armed with a heavy flashlight as well as some other unidentified, but probably lethal weapon. There was a scrambling sound, and Henry Burke joined the fray; but two men are not much more effective against a whirlwind than one. Archer kept his grip on the hand that held the unknown weapon, but the other hand was wrenched loose, and the flashlight came viciously down on the sergeant's forearm. He got his hand on it, but it slipped from his grasp and crashed to the floor. Then there was total darkness, filled with the sounds of conflict.

With no time to waste on idle reflections, Archer was grimly exultant that the trap had worked, after all. But he had not counted on catching a cross between a tornado and a wildcat. He ceased unnecessary speculations in order to concentrate on the business of subduing this unknown antagonist, and on defending himself against its almost maniacal assaults.

Archer and Henry were two to one, both strong men; but in their opponent, whether or not his heart was pure, seemed to have the strength of ten. Nor was he hampered by any of the recognized rules governing a fair fight; he wrestled and kicked and gouged and clawed. Archer heard Henry swearing in gasps. Frantic fingernails tore his own cheek; as he twisted away from them, a knee rose and took him unexpectedly in the groin, doubling him up, and a booted foot cracked against his shin. Involuntarily, his grip loosened for a second, and in that instant the enemy had time and room to raise that right arm again. In the dark, Archer could see nothing, but he felt a sudden, hair-raising movement against his leg, as something lithe and soft moved swiftly amid the tangle of feet. There came a swishing sound, then a grunt, and an outraged squall of pain. The unknown plunged forward off balance, and a heavy, glancing blow fell on Archer's neck and shoulder, missing his temple by an inch. He staggered backward and almost fell, and something struck the floor with a thud. At the same time, a raging and vituperative cat flew snarling out of the melee, and streaked through the door into the kitchen. Where she had sprung from Archer didn't know; probably, finding the doors open, she had stolen in to snooze in a forbidden chair. But the fact that his adversary stepped on her, at a crucial instant, possibly saved the sergeant's life.

Henry Burke, meanwhile, had wrestled the unknown to the floor. There they thrashed about until they rolled against the bottle-covered table by the couch, which went over with a crash. Then they were on their feet again, panting and straining. Recovering his breath, Archer returned to the struggle, striving to secure a hold, or land a blow, that would prove temporarily disabling. But in the dark it was hard to tell friend from foe, and he didn't want to damage Henry. He had already received one workmanlike punch that he was sure came from the trooper's fist! He was thankful that he and Henry had dispensed with their pistols, and trusted to their physical powers alone. A gun snatched from a holster in that free-for-all . . . br-r-r-r-r!

Archer was aware of slamming doors and raised voices—of feet pounding on stairs, and a growing hubbub of excitement and alarm, punctuated by the barking of Bella. He had told his confederates in the dining room to stay there, whatever happened, but he distrusted their obedience. He found breath to shout, "Don't . . . anybody come in here . . . yet! Stay . . . where you are . . . all of you!"

Henry Burke added his bit: "Light a light—in the kitchen!"

But what the members of the household did was of secondary interest to the two policemen. They had their hands full, for the prospect of a light and further odds against him spurred their antagonist to more desperate resistance. But, against this wild savagery, their training and condition told. Slowly they overcame the frantic, clawing thing. Archer succeeded in twisting its hands behind its back, while a lucky blow of Burke's to the stomach gave the trooper his chance: he grabbed the creature's thrashing legs and brought it heavily to the floor. Archer had time to reach for his handcuffs and, with considerable difficulty, he snapped them on. "Get a light," he gasped, "I can . . . manage him. . . . now!" A lamp had appeared in the kitchen; excited voices clamored at the door. Alert for further trouble, Archer hauled their captive to its feet. A match sputtered. Henry Burke applied it to the lamp, and the room sprang into light. It looked as if a hurricane had hit it—a particularly vicious one.

Archer and Burke, still breathing hard, were prepared for almost anything. They needed to be, as their unbelieving eyes stared at the grotesque and manacled figure before them . . . Rhoda Buckley! Rhoda Buckley, her face a scarcely recognizable mask of fury, her gray hair disheveled, while from her lips poured a stream of alternate gibberish and words that were all too intelligible. She wore a man's boots and breeches, and her man's jacket had been ripped and torn in the struggle. On the floor by the couch lay the weapon that had dropped from her hand when she stumbled over the cat: a small canvas bag, knotted at one end and filled with birdshot—a homemade blackjack, as quiet and deadly as an adder.

Archer mopped his face with his handkerchief and turned to Burke. "Get some rope, Henry. Clothesline will do, if you can find some—and have the doc put some iodine on your face. And you folks—" he turned to the thunder-struck audience in the doorway, "please stay in the kitchen for a while, all of you. Except you, Doctor; I'll need your help."

They gathered their miscellaneous apparel around them, and complied. As the door closed, Lucy was heard to murmur a few words about the need for a little something to eat, perhaps?

Archer turned to the telephone.

Half, an hour later they took Rhoda Buckley away, still screaming obscenities.

10

The Truth—Believe It or Not

A week later, just before Thanksgiving, as it happened, Archer Brett, on a Saturday night, drove once more to Highbrook Ridge and into the Pattersons' dooryard. His knock was answered by Frank Patterson, who removed his pipe from his mouth and hailed the sergeant with enthusiasm. "Come right in, Brett. Glad to see you. We thought maybe you'd forgotten us since you got all those newspaper write-ups. How's it feel to be famous and successful?"

Archer followed him into the sitting room; its warmth felt grateful after the biting cold outside, and the logs crackling in the fireplace defied winter and all its hardships. Bella rose lumberingly and came to meet him, actually wagging her tail; and Lucy, who was standing with a plate of sandwiches in one hand and a pitcher of milk in the other, set them both down in order to welcome him properly. Ann, holding a large bowl of popcorn, and Forrest, who was sitting extremely close to her on the couch, both rose to greet him warmly; Forrest gripped his hand in a manner that showed the gratitude he didn't quite know how to express in words. Even the undemonstrative Tad, who should have been in bed, seized Archer by the arm, and wanted to know when he was coming to visit them for a month, "so you can learn me to be a detective!"

Urged to stay, Archer took off his overcoat and sat down in the easy-chair by the fire. As he looked at them all, he was conscious of a feeling of pleasure and internal warmth that surprised him. In this spontaneous friendliness, which he knew would be lasting, he found the reward for his work and worry, and the vindication of his judgment. He had made friends, real friends. He didn't feel even a faint disappointment when he looked at Ann, sitting with Forrest's arm around her; only a sense of satisfaction that he had won her genuine regard and friendship. She happened to be wearing her black dress, but there was no other sign of mournfulness about her now; she looked very different from the weary, watchful woman who had first told him about finding Deacon Grimm. He still thought Martin wasn't good enough for her, but if they were satisfied . . .!

"Well," Archer said, when he finally got the opportunity, "I knew you folks would want to hear all about what happened, but this is the first chance I've had to get over. I tried to come before, for after all, this place was beginning to feel like home to me. . . ."

Lucy told him to consider it home any time he felt like it. "And sometime when you come," she said, "I'll have some nice girl here, so. . . ."

Frank gave an exaggerated groan. "For heaven's sake, Lucy, can't you leave one man alone, to enjoy his liberty? Ain't you satisfied to lead me around by the nose, without trying to put every man you meet in double harness?" Lucy made a face at him, and he turned to Archer. "We're hoping you can tell us the whole story, Brett. All we know is what we read in the papers, and that seemed to leave a lot unexplained."

Archer nodded. "They've got Mrs. Buckley down at the Hospital for the Insane under observation," he said; "but it'll probably be months before those cockeyed alienists make up their minds about her. You know what those birds are like. In my opinion she's sane, but she knows that if she can kid that bunch into calling her crazy, with some fancy tag to it, that she won't have to stand trial for the murders. I think a lot of that crazy raving she did was put on for that very reason, but of course you can't tell those doctors anything—they know it all! Well, I expect I'd better tell you the story from the beginning, including the parts that didn't get into the papers—I'll trust you not to let it go any farther. In the first place, we finally found those Bible pages, Miss Barbour."

Ann leaned eagerly forward. "Then I was right!" she hesitated and glanced at Forrest, who touched her hand and said, "It's Mrs. Martin now, Sergeant, since last Wednesday. I thought she needed a keeper. And she thought I did."

Archer offered his congratulations, and then went on, "Yes, while we were waiting here that Sunday night to nab the killer, Haley was finishing his search of the Lafond place. He was about ready to give up, but he's a sticker, and went over everything again, to make sure he hadn't overlooked anything.

And he found the missing pages; they'd been fastened with adhesive to the under side of the bench that Clarabel used in front of her dressing table. Then a piece of burlap had been tacked over them. She'd done a pretty good job of it, and it was a good place, hidden, yet easy to get at if she wanted to move them. Well, what do you think we found out?"

Nobody knew.

"It was the records of births, deaths, and marriages, as Miss Bar— Mrs. Martin thought. But only one of them was important. And that was the record of the marriage of Leonard Grimm to Rhoda Temple (as she was then) in New York City, twenty-six years ago. And with it was a copy of the marriage certificate. Now do you begin to see light?

"After that," he continued, when the exclamations had subsided, "it was comparatively easy for us to learn more, and to trace the history of the woman we all knew as Rhoda Buckley. Of course, there are gaps in it, but with the help of the New York police we managed to piece out enough facts to make subsequent events pretty clear. Those alienists are right about one thing—Rhoda's got bad blood. We found out her mother was a mulatto who'd been a dancer—and other things—and was an all 'round bad lot. Nobody knows who her father was; he might have been 'most anybody, apparently. Anyway, Rhoda was born in New York, and when she got old enough went on the stage—vaudeville, mostly, and followed her mother's old trade on the side. I guess she was an almighty good-looker in those days, and it was then that Leonard Grimm met her and fell for her. We learned that when he was younger he went to New York periodically on "pleasure trips." Well, he must have fallen damned hard to actually marry Rhoda, for she had a bad reputation even then, and had already been mixed up in a stabbing case, as well as in other unsavory messes. But she was probably smarter than he was, and put it over on him. But he evidently came to pretty quick after they were married, for he left her almost immediately. She won't open her mouth about her life and affairs, and the Deacon can't, worse luck, so I don't see how we'll ever find out just what did happen. But Rhoda never got a divorce. The Deacon had taken good care not to tell her where he came from, and desertion wasn't grounds for divorce in New York then, anyway. Probably she always had other uses for her money, and she wasn't one who'd let the fact of her marriage cramp her style where other men were concerned. And Grimm never bothered to get a divorce, either. He could get plenty of women without marrying them; he didn't especially want a wife, and he figured that as long as his marriage to Rhoda held good he had a valid excuse for not tying himself to any other woman. But he kept the copy of his marriage certificate, and, as a matter of record, entered the fact among the vital statistics in his Family Bible—as a bad joke, I guess. But after that he ignored the incident, probably figuring that if he ever wanted to get a divorce, he could. We think that that memorandum in his wallet, 'Ask M. about—?' may have referred to his marriage or a projected divorce, although Munsell, the lawyer, says he never mentioned it to him. Perhaps he didn't get a chance to.

"Well, for a long time after that there was no trace of Rhoda; likely she was drifting around from one city to another, in the semi-theatrical underworld, where such women make their living. As she grew older and lost some of her looks, the living presumably got harder and harder to make. Anyway, the next fact we learned was that she was playing in a burlesque show in Boston, when it was closed up. Then she disappeared for another year or two, but eventually, about eight years ago, she turned up in Rumford, and somehow happened to meet old Buckley. God knows how she scraped acquaintance with him (he won't tell us; Buckley, I mean!) but she did, and he looked like the answer to her prayers, and the means of getting what she wanted more than anything else on earth: plenty of money and a nice, respectable position in society. I don't know why it is, but women like that, when they reach a certain point, want above all things to be thought respectable, and to parade their respectability; I expect the psychologists have a word for it. Rhoda was clever, and a skillful actress. And she was still good-looking, for her age. She handed Buckley some plausible, hard-luck story, and he swallowed it. He'd never had much to do with women, and didn't have any close relatives or friends to keep an eye on him, so he was taken in, as better men have been before him. Rhoda married him and his money, and was all set for life—she thought. Then, lo and behold, he fixed up this place in the country, so that he could raise his blessed chickens; and Rhoda found out what's meant by the long arm of coincidence—for there was Leonard Grimm, living right next door!"

Archer paused to eat a sandwich.

"We have to guess what happened after that," he resumed. "But Rhoda must have felt she was sitting on a volcano. Any time the Deacon wanted, he could show that marriage certificate—and where would her nice, secure, respectable life be then? A prostitute and a bigamist, and a partly colored one, at that! Can't you imagine how that would set with the Rumford Women's Club, and the other swanky societies that Buckley's money had got her into? And Buckley would have kicked her out quicker than scat if he'd known; he's a highly moral old duffer.

"But apparently the Deacon didn't say anything, for some reason. I've an idea, from what I've heard of him, that he enjoyed the situation, and got a big kick out of having her in his power. For if the facts of their relationship came out, it would ruin her; but it wouldn't particularly hurt him. He was a malicious devil, and liked to keep her in suspense. We did learn from Buckley that she tried to get him to give up the place here and move away—she didn't tell him why, naturally!—but old Buckley was stubborn as Hell on the subject of his farm and his hens; he *wouldn't* move away from here. So there she was. Again, we don't know what happened to brings things to a head. Either she got to the breaking point and couldn't stand the suspense any longer, or else Grimm needed some extra cash or something, and put the pressure on her. Maybe he told her he'd decided to divorce her, and not to do it quietly. We can't know that, but she killed him, anyway, and figured that nobody would ever suspect her connection with him at all."

Frank broke in. "But why in thunderation did she kill him in my barn?"

Archer shrugged. "That's one of the things we don't know. But we think she made some excuse and arranged to meet him there. She wouldn't dare have him come to her house because of Buckley; and she wouldn't go to his place for fear Clarabel would find out. But everybody knew Patterson was away, and his barn was handy, and kind of neutral territory, as you might say. Maybe Rhoda suggested going there if she was planning the Deacon's death. Or, more likely, she didn't intend to kill him at first, but did it during a quarrel; that would account for her using the pitchfork instead of coming prepared with a weapon. Either way, she'd have no trouble doing it; she's a big, husky woman, and plenty strong, as Burke and I found out! Then, after she'd done it, she wiped off the pitchfork handle, and went home to bed, thinking that Grimm's body wouldn't be found until morning, when the hired man came. And there was nothing to connect her with the business—no motive or weapon or anything. I didn't suspect her, even when she had no alibi, and acted so anxious to pin the crime on Martin. It was she, by the way, who sent word to Golding that I wouldn't arrest Martin, and egged him on to make the arrest himself. I suppose she wanted somebody arrested for the crime, though I don't know why she picked Martin, especially."

Ann and Forrest exchanged looks. "I do," Forrest said drily. "Several years ago, Rhoda indicated to me that she liked male company, and that mine wouldn't be—er—distasteful to her. I let her understand pretty clearly there was nothing doing. She didn't like me after that. Not a bit."

"I see," Archer said. "Well, I suppose I ought to have suspected her, but she was so damned plausible!"

"She certainly was," Lucy agreed. "You know, I always liked Rhoda. And she was a good neighbor. But once or

twice I've seen her look—well, I wasn't exactly afraid of
her, but . . ."

"She was clever," Ann said. "She knew how to take most
people in. And Lucy always insists on believing the best
of everybody."

"Yes," Archer said, before Lucy could defend her philos-
ophy, "she was clever. But she couldn't know that Grimm
had kept that record of their marriage, and had perhaps
told Clarabel about it, in a moment of carelessness, or—
er—affection. I'm not sure how much Clarabel knew, but
she knew enough so that when the Deacon was killed she
saw her chance. Knowing what she knew, she naturally guessed that Rhoda had killed him to protect herself.
Clarabel hated Rhoda, who'd always acted superior and
patronizing toward her, and she wanted money. She wasn't
going to give her knowledge to the police when she could
make herself some money and pay Rhoda back at the same
time. She was greedy and dumb; and she didn't realize, any
more than I did, what the real Rhoda was like, behind that
smooth, insinuating manner. Clarabel tried to blackmail
Rhoda, and Rhoda killed her, just as she would have killed
a bluebottle that bothered her. Clarabel had a key to the
Deacon's house, and Rhoda agreed to meet her there at a
certain time in the night, and pay her a sum of money—a
thousand dollars, I suspect, from what Clarabel hinted.
But Rhoda came prepared with that homemade life pre-
server of hers—we found some canvas bags and birdshot
just like it in Buckley's workroom—and instead of getting the thousand dollars, Clarabel got that. Then Rhoda
dumped Clarabel's body down the steps, and put the silver
earring, that she'd picked up somewhere, under it. Then
she took Clarabel's key and went home; we found the key
in her breeches pocket. It was that key that enabled her to
get into the Deacon's house on the Saturday, when Miss—
Mrs. Martin was there."

Mrs. Martin interrupted. "I think, after all we've been through, Sergeant, that you'd better call me 'Ann'," she said. "That'll save trouble."

Archer thanked her. "When you suggested that trap," he said, "Did you suspect we'd catch—who we did?"

Ann considered. "I don't know, really. I didn't like Rhoda, and she was the only one who hated me enough to put my earring there. But I had no proof. I didn't see the other person in the house, or see the person when I was struck. It might have been Gus, or anybody. I think perhaps I did suspect Rhoda more than anybody else; but I knew it wouldn't do any good to tell you so, without proof."

"Planting that earring," Archer said, "was a mistake. Like most murderers, she couldn't leave well, enough alone, and she tried to involve—er—Ann in the second crime just as she'd tried to involve you, Martin, in the first one. But she couldn't find or destroy the evidence she was after, even when she got the Bible, because Clarabel had already taken it out and hidden it. Then Ann, in self-defense, helped us to the solution: she suggested the trap, and we caught Rhoda right in the act of attempting yet another murder. Rhoda won't say anything rational; that's part of her game. But we wouldn't have any trouble convicting her of Clarabel's murder if she hadn't taken shelter behind this insanity pose."

Ann said, "I believe she really is crazy; she certainly sounded so, that night." She shuddered.

"Well, perhaps. I wouldn't know." Archer took a drink of milk. "But that's for the lawyers and psychiatrists to fight out. The way things are done, she'll stay at the Hospital for a year or so—it's nice and comfortable there, good grub and swell service—and then she'll be let out as cured, or on parole or something. By that time, people will have forgotten all about this case, and ten to one nothing more will be said about the murders. Or else she'll just be put in some fancy sanitarium, at Buckley's expense. Or maybe the Deacon's money will keep her; the lawyers are going to have a swell time figuring out how much of his property she's entitled to, if any. Well, maybe she is crazy; I'm no alienist, thank the Lord!"

"It'll be a vacation for Warner Buckley, anyway," Forrest remarked. "I heard today that he's put Rhoda's affairs, with plenty of cash, into Ross and Marble's hands, and he's going to Florida, and taking Danny Cheever with him. He's going to buy prize hens and take sun baths and play golf and have a hell of a time. And he's hired me to look after his place. He's planning to branch out next season, and raise potatoes and apples and maybe, sheep. It won't be my fault if he doesn't have the best farm in Clinton County, after Frank's, of course! But Ann and I are going to stay here for the present. She doesn't like the idea of living where Rhoda Buckley lived."

"I'm so glad Mr. Buckley is taking Danny with him," Lucy said. "The poor kid may have a chance, now that he's out from under Gus Lafond's influence. And here we've completely forgotten Gus! Did you find him, Sergeant? Where was he, all the time they were hunting for him?"

"Gus," Archer said, "was lying low, in a friend's room, in a Rumford rooming house, a very disreputable one. He and the friend had done business together the night before, and they celebrated its conclusion by getting pretty well soused. By the time they'd sobered up next day, the friend had seen a newspaper with the report of Clarabel's death in it, and Gus decided the safest thing for him to do was to lie low and say nothing. But we found him." He hesitated. "I hadn't ought to tell you this, so forget it right away, but the fact is Gus has been distributing cocaine, and Leonard Grimm was one of his customers. We kept that out of the papers, too. Haley came across a cache of the stuff while he was hunting through Gus's place for those papers; Gus hadn't dared go home and move it for fear of being nabbed for killing his wife. So now he's being investigated by the G-men. There's no doubt he sold dope to others besides the Deacon, and if it can be pinned on him, he won't trouble anybody around here for a while. And speaking of selling things reminds me: we had word from that salesman fellow, Martin—the one who picked you up that Saturday night the Deacon was killed. When he read about the case in the papers, he remembered you, and sent us a statement that confirmed your story. And we've got some confirmation on your alibi, too," he added, turning to Frank. "A man and his wife remembered your hailing them while you were stalled, and another man is pretty sure he passed you, going away from Pinkney, around half-past six o'clock. He noticed your number because he's in the habit of looking at numbers. And he noticed too, that your engine was cutting up some. They might have come forward before, but people are always slower than cold molasses when it comes to anything like that. They only consult their own convenience, and never think of what it may mean to somebody else. Well, better late than never."

This information was all very satisfactory. So was the news that Captain Randall was considering running against Golding for the office of State's Attorney, when election time came around. "The Captain beat it back to Canada," Archer said with a grin, "and finally got a deer, and he's prouder than a newly elected Congressman. But he says that as Commandant he doesn't get enough vacations; he says the State's Attorney doesn't have to do any work, and if he can land that job, he can go hunting all he likes!"

"If he gets it," Forrest suggested, "you'd stand a good chance of stepping into his shoes as Commandant, seems to me."

"Well, that's all in the future," Archer said. He stood up, declining more milk and popcorn. "I'm full to the ears already. And I must be getting along. I wish you all luck, and Burke and I will be seeing you sometimes when we get the chance. Henry's going to spend his next leave here, eating himself into a coma! And next summer, Tad, you shall have those lessons in sleuthing—not that I'm very hot as a teacher!"

Good-bys were said and promises exchanged. Ann, with a coat thrown over her shoulders, followed Archer onto the piazza. "Sergeant . . ."

"Yes, Miss Bar— Ann?"

She hesitated. "I'm sorry, Sergeant, that I had to deceive you, and make things harder for you. It wasn't that I wanted to make things more difficult. Only I had to. . . ."

Archer laughed. "That's all right," he declared. "If you caused any complications, you made up for them, later. I admit you made me kind of—er—exasperated once or twice; but I understand how you felt, and it's natural for a good woman to be loyal to her man. I wouldn't think much of one that wasn't, myself." He paused. "And will you allow me to say that I think Martin is damned lucky?"

"Thank you," Ann said. "If—well, if you were interested, I'd tell *you* something: there's a grand girl, much prettier than I am, and just as loyal, down at the Telephone Exchange. She doesn't talk as much as I do, and she's a fine cook. And just think how bored she gets, sitting at that switchboard all alone of an evening."

"Do you think she's sitting there all alone right now?"

"I'm sure of it. Anyway, I could call her, and tell her to sit awhile longer. Shall I?"

He smiled and nodded. "If you like."

"That's fine." Ann shook hands again. "I must go in, or Forrest will be out after me. Good luck, Sergeant, and thanks for—everything." She ran into the house.

Archer, still smiling, turned his car and drove toward Highbrook Village.

Something told him that Deacon Grimm's death was doing him one more good turn—the best one of all.

Lucy and Frank had gone to bed, the sleepy Tad preceding them. Ann and Forrest lingered in the warm sitting room, in the big easy-chair before the fireplace. After some intermittent (and immaterial) talk, Ann referred to Archer Brett, and how sensibly he had handled things. "I don't believe," she said, "that he ever really suspected you. But of course, when Golding acted the way he did, and you insisted on being arrested, he couldn't help himself. I suppose I was a fool to say I killed the Deacon, and be so— so dramatic, but I thought it seemed the best thing, the only thing, to do. And then they wouldn't listen to me. But . . ."

"Honey," Forrest said, "I know you meant to do the best thing for everybody. Whatever you did is all right with me. But you didn't really think I killed the Deacon, did you?"

"Of course not. You know I didn't. You've got a temper, when it gets started, and you might hit a man, if you had provocation. But you'd never kill a man that way. Besides. . . ."

"Besides what, Honey?"

"Besides—I killed him." Her voice was so low he could hardly hear the words. "I did it—just the way I told the Sergeant, and all of you." She gripped his hand in both hers. "Forrest, I killed a man! I couldn't—I couldn't believe it, when I saw him lying there. I ought to have told the whole truth right off that night, but I—I didn't have the courage. I thought nobody would believe how it happened, and I hadn't had time to see how it might affect other people. Then you came back, and I got paid for

being such a coward, for everybody thought you did it! It
was awful, everybody suspecting everybody else—I knew
then I had to tell the truth. But when I did, they wouldn't
believe me! I— I—"

His arms tightened around her. "I knew you did it," he
said quietly. "That's why I told the sergeant I did it, and
made him arrest me. He didn't know who to believe, poor
devil!"

Ann gasped. "You knew? How?"

"Because I knew I didn't. I didn't think Mrs. Buckley
did it, though she had reason to and easily could have.
Besides, sweetheart, I knew you were telling the truth that
afternoon, even when Brett and everybody else thought
you were making up a yarn to protect me. They thought
you were lying, but I guess I just naturally understand you
better than anybody else."

"Oh Forrest, you do, you do!"

After an interlude she raised her head from his shoulder. "You know it really was an accident, it happened exactly the way I said. I did tell the truth; I hadn't any idea
of hurting him. When I picked up the pitchfork, I didn't
think he'd try to—to touch me again. I was never afraid
of a man before in my life, Forrest, but I was afraid of the
Deacon, then. His eyes. . . ." She shivered. "I suppose it
may have been the dope, partly. Darling, had I ought to
tell the authorities all about it again? Explain to them that
I killed him, and that Rhoda didn't?"

Forrest Martin smoothed her hair. "Of course not,
Ann. She killed the Lafond girl, all right, and she tried
hard enough to kill you. She's a bad egg, Rhoda Buckley,
or whatever her real name is. She's caused plenty of trouble to plenty of people, all her life, and she deserves all
she may get; it won't be very tough punishment, according
to Brett. You didn't kill Leonard Grimm on purpose, Honey, and you did it in self-defense, and you told the truth

about it—it wasn't your fault that they wouldn't believe you. It doesn't matter a tinker's hoot to me, and nobody else ever needs to know. So let's forget it, shall we?"

He kissed her; then, leaning over, blew out the light.

About the Author

Dorothy Foster Brown (1901-2011) was an artist from Worcester, Massachusetts, with training at the School of the Worcester Art Museum. She specialized in Art Deco-style illustrations and paintings. She was a published poet and a well-respected button collector. She wrote *Button Parade* (1942, 1968) and *The Big Book of Buttons* (1981). *Grimm Death* (1946) was her only mystery.

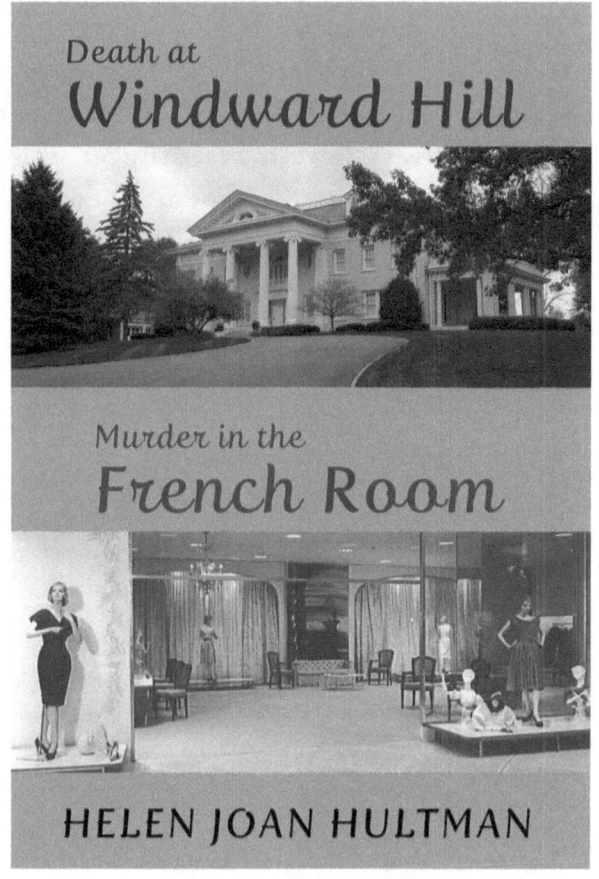

Also Available

CoachwhipBooks.com (print)
Coachwhip.com (epub)

SALLY WOOD

MURDER OF A NOVELIST

DEATH IN LORD BYRON'S ROOM

THE
RUMBLE
MURDERS

Henry Ware Eliot, Jr.

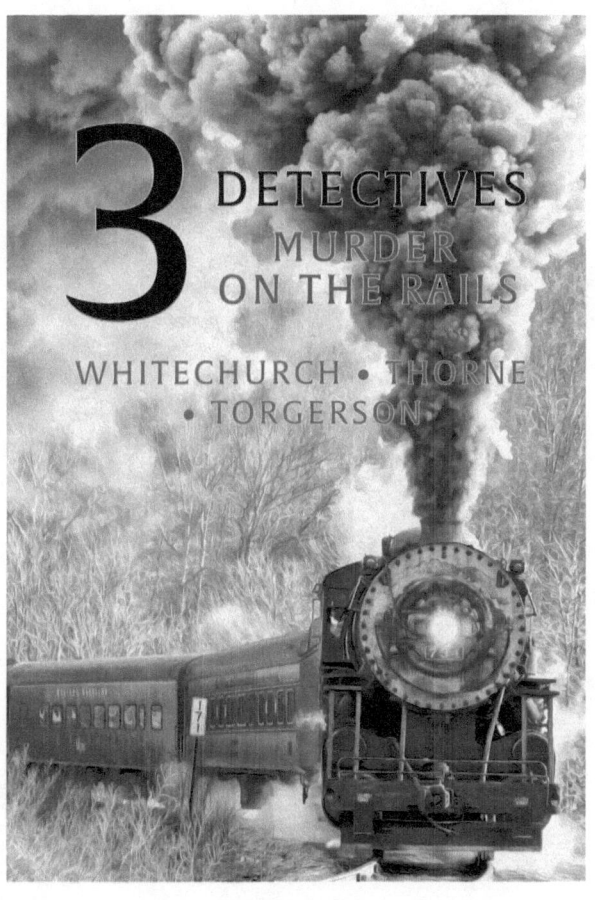

VIRGINIA RATH

THE ANGER
OF THE BELLS